And then there were Crumbs

And then there were Crumbs

Eve Calder

St. Martin's Paperbacks

First published in the United States by St. Martin's Paperbacks, an imprint of St. Martin's Publishing Group.

AND THEN THERE WERE CRUMBS

For information, address St. Martin's Publishing Group, 120 Broadway, New York, NY 10271.

www.stmartins.com

ISBN: 978-1-250-31299-0

Printed in the United States of America

St. Martin's Paperbacks edition / August 2019

10 9 8 7 6 5 4 3 2 1

To BLD, for everything.

Chapter 1

As Kate McGuire turned onto Coral Cay's main drag, named—ironically—Main Street, she checked her watch for the third time in ten minutes. Her interview was in half an hour. And her creaky old Toyota was making some brand-new noises she didn't like.

Never taking her eyes off the road, she groped for the bakery box on the passenger's seat with her right hand and flipped it open.

A tiny, perfect sand dollar cookie. She'd bought a dozen before she left the hotel that morning. After two back-to-back job interviews—and no job—there was only one lone survivor left in the box. She popped it into her mouth.

She tasted butter, sugar, and cinnamon. Bliss.

As Kate slowed, the red SUV behind her hit the horn.

The next interview was a long shot. Prep cook. A trained pastry chef, the position was definitely not her first choice. But she'd been in town for over a week. Countless interviews, phone calls, and drop-in visits had

yielded not so much as a nibble. So when a CIA class-
mate called back and told her about a fish place on the
mainland looking for a prep chef, Kate booked an interview pronto.

Luckily, with island breezes and the windows cranked
down she could give the engine a break and skip the AC.

Kate checked the rearview mirror. That's when she saw
it. Or what could have been it. Three cars back. The silver
car.

She'd glimpsed it a couple of times over the last few
days. Always with a lone guy driving. Sometimes he
wore a ball cap, other times a Panama hat. Or a fishing
hat. And sunglasses. Always sunglasses.

Don't be an idiot, she chided herself. *It's probably
not even the same guy. This is South Florida. Everyone
wears hats and sunglasses. And odds are, some local
rental place has a fleet of cookie-cutter cars.*

Suddenly the Toyota gave an ugly shudder, shimmied,
and lurched to a stop. Steam poured out from under the
hood. Or was it smoke?

"No!" Kate groaned, popping the hood release and
scrambling out of the car. She flicked the hood up with
two fingers and jumped back. Steam and acrid black
smoke poured out. Along with the stench of burning
rubber.

Dead. Definitely dead. Just like her career prospects.

The SUV leaned on the horn again. Three long, loud
blasts.

"Damn!" she swore under her breath. One slim
chance at a paycheck, and it was gone. Along with her
wheels. What was she thinking, coming here from New
York without a job? Or even a lead on a job?

Kate knew she should move her car off the road. But
there weren't any empty parking spots nearby. And how

exactly should she approach something that was spewing smoke like a volcano? What if it exploded?

Too bad her little nephew Billy wasn't here. He lived for explosions.

"Wow, I haven't seen one like this in a while."

Kate looked up and saw a big, burly man in a yellow and orange Hawaiian shirt, tan board shorts, and gray suede work gloves ambling up to the car. A lime-green tow truck was double-parked behind her.

"It's my latest creation—auto flambé," Kate said grimly.

"Not flambé yet. More of a *fumée,* really."

She gave the guy a second glance. She hadn't met many auto mechanics well versed in French culinary speak. But then, after eight years in the city with no car, she hadn't met many auto mechanics.

Hawaiian Shirt had already turned his attention to the engine.

"Hey, before you get started, I don't have any cash to pay you just now," Kate said, addressing the back of his close-cropped brown head as he sidestepped the smoke plume. "I'm out of work and low on funds. I was on my way to a job interview when this happened."

"So you want to just leave her here?" the mountain said, turning to give her a half smile. She could see her own stressed face glaring back in the reflection of his wraparound sunglasses.

Seemingly out of nowhere, he produced a blue rag and used it to twist and turn a few things in the engine. The noxious cloud slowed to a stop. He stepped back and carefully dropped the hood.

The SUV laid on the horn. Joined by an off-key chorus of backed-up traffic.

Hawaiian Shirt stepped into the middle of the street,

pushed his sunglasses onto the top of his forehead, and made eye contact with the SUV driver. "Around," he said, flicking his wrist.

The cacophony stopped.

"Look, free diagnosis," he said, walking over to Kate. "This car is suffering from an acute case of neglect. Not fatal, but it's going to need some serious TLC before you can drive it again. It's been in storage for a long time."

"How did you know that?"

He stared at her.

"I live in Manhattan," Kate offered. "I was storing it at my sister's place in New Jersey. She promised that Deacon Dave was starting it at least once a week. And I was paying her for car washes and oil changes a couple of times a year."

"Deacon Dave?"

"Her husband."

"Far be it from me to impugn the word of a church elder, but no one's touched this engine since the London Olympics. Aside from a couple cans of oil someone dumped in recently."

"I took it to their garage before I hit the turnpike. The guy gassed it up and added some oil."

Hawaiian Shirt shook his head sadly.

A line of cars slowly and carefully snaked around her hobbled sedan. But nary a beep or a honk. Kate was amazed.

As the silver car passed, the driver turned away. Kate noted his tan ball cap. And a sticker in the back window with a neon-orange palm tree—Sunshine Rental Car.

"So what's the job interview?" the mountain asked, hands on hips.

"Chef. Prep chef. At a place called Fish-a-Palooza. On the mainland."

"Yeah, I went there once," he said.

"So you know it?"

"Enough to know that nobody ever goes there twice. They cater mainly to the tourists. Anybody else knows better. Frozen fish. You're a chef?"

"Pastry chef. Trained at the CIA. Not the spy agency, the other one."

"Yeah, Culinary Institute of America. Got it. So what's a New York pastry chef doing down here trying to get a job with a second-rate seafood joint?"

"Long story," Kate said, exhaling deeply. "The short version is the restaurant I worked for closed. My apartment building went condo. And I called off my wedding."

"Perfect storm," he said matter-of-factly.

"Pretty much. I'm Kate McGuire, by the way," she said, extending her hand.

"Gabriel Louden—Gabe," he said, shaking it cordially. "Why Coral Cay?"

"We were going to spend our honeymoon here. I figured I could get a job and start over. I sold pretty much everything I owned. Liquidated my savings and my retirement account, and . . . well, here I am."

"Yeah, we get a lot of that. People want to get a fresh start, they either roll west or south. This is as far south as you can go without hitting water."

"Well, that's kind of reassuring. I'll be in good company."

"Between the heat and the mosquitos, most of 'em don't make it through the first summer," he said, rubbing the back of his neck. "Turns out Dante was right."

"About Coral Cay?"

"About hell. Dante claims the better zip codes in the netherworld are bathed in flaming heat. Which pretty accurately describes late summer. Locals contend it's hotter than hell and twice as humid."

"There's the slogan for the next travel poster," Kate said.

"Then there's hurricane season. Officially it starts in June. But between you and me, August and September are the worst of it."

"Did Hurricane Irma do much damage here?"

"Oh, we were lucky with that one. Barely a glancing blow. A few loose roofing tiles and some of us lost power for a day or two. But that was it. Really lucky. So what's your backup?"

"My what?" she asked.

"Your backup plan. In case this doesn't work out. Back to Manhattan? Miami? Disney World? Everybody's got a Plan B."

"After today? Plane ticket to New Jersey. To live with my sister, Deacon Dave, and the twins."

"The twins?"

"One plays the violin twelve hours a day. Badly. The other likes to make things explode. And right now, he's my favorite."

He smiled. "So, no Plan B."

"Ten days in a hotel, I've had a great vacation but no job offer. I've still got some savings. But without an income, I can't get a place to live. And my stuff, what's left of it, is stashed in a storage unit on the mainland, outside Hibiscus Springs. I even toyed with the idea of living there temporarily, but I'm pretty sure it doesn't have plumbing. Besides, at this point, I'd have to hitchhike," Kate said, nodding at her car.

"Well, in my humble opinion, you dodged a bullet with Fish-a-Palooza. And don't let me scare you—Coral Cay really is a great place to settle. Hey, I know one job opening right here in town," he said, suddenly snapping his fingers. "Should be right up your alley. A bakery. The pay's probably crap. The boss is a cranky old goat. And a real tightwad. But he's good at what he does—great breads. Oh man, his sourdough melts in your mouth. Upside is he spends a fair amount of time on the beach with a bottle of rum and a metal detector, so he probably won't micro-manage. I think you'd be a shoo-in."

"Because of my credentials?"

"Because you're the only person I've met desperate enough to apply. But you never know. 'The path to paradise begins in hell.'"

"Wow, you should write his help-wanted ad."

"Dante truly understood life. Word is Sam Hepplewhite—that's the baker—old Sam's getting ready to sell the place. The Cookie House. And you didn't hear that from me. So the job's temporary, at best. But it would give you time to get something better. And anything beats Fish-a-Palooza. Besides, underneath it all, Sam really is a good guy. And he needs the help. If you can find a local room for rent, you're good to go."

"If I say yes, will you help me push this thing off a cliff? Preferably a really steep one?"

He lowered his sunglasses into place and patted the hood. "She's not so bad. Just acting out after years of neglect. Go talk to Sam. The bakery's just up the street. See what happens. In the meantime, I'll tow Gwendolyn here to the shop. We can park her out back until you decide what you want to do. Sound fair?"

Kate shook her head. "I don't have enough cash on me to pay for towing. Or for storage. And my credit card's maxed out at the moment. I don't suppose you'd take an out-of-state check?"

"Don't worry about it now. Got a vacant lot behind the garage. Plenty of space."

He reached into his back pocket and pulled out a wallet, which he peeled open to produce a business card. Embossed with "Gabe's Garage," plus a business address and phone number, it featured a smiling cartoon car.

"I'll pay you back," Kate vowed. "Every cent."

"Never doubted it. Besides, 'He who sees a need and waits to be asked for help is as unkind as if he had refused it.'"

"Dante?"

"Yup. And if a loaf or two of that sourdough dropped from the sky, I definitely wouldn't refuse it."

Chapter 2

Walking down Main Street, Kate sensed she was experiencing the real Coral Cay for the first time. In the week she'd been here, she'd spent every minute at the beach and resort areas. That, she had thought, was where they were going to need a professionally trained pastry chef. And where her skills would bring top dollar.

Now she was seeing downtown. On foot. But the atmosphere was somehow comfortable and comforting. A cool breeze off the ocean carried the scent of salt water, mingled with something tropical.

The Old Florida–style town center could have been built in the late 1800s or yesterday. Immaculately maintained shops were a rainbow of pastel colors. Bright flowers tumbled out of window boxes and stone planters up and down the street. And the wide sidewalks were spotless—like they'd been regularly scrubbed.

The odd note: dog bowls, filled with water, outside many of the shop doors. Each bowl was different.

Some were china or stoneware. Others stainless steel or brightly colored plastic. And one, outside Seize the Clay pottery studio, looked handmade.

Kate was surprised at the number of tourists she saw here, too. Sporting deep tans, new cruise wear, and top-of-the-line sunglasses, they were easy to spot. But with a post office, grocer, bookstore, and shops for other necessities, Coral Cay was clearly a working small town. She got the impression that if the tourists disappeared tomorrow—or later in the season, when the worst of the summer heat hit, according to Gabe—the locals would carry on just fine.

Looking into a shop window, Kate glimpsed a figure in the reflected glass that wasn't her own. One with a ball cap and sunglasses.

She turned and saw him. Across the street. Studying a store window, with a mint-green shopping bag dangling off one hand. Same guy from the car? She couldn't tell.

This is nuts, she thought. *I'm not carrying a wad of cash or credit cards. And I don't know a soul in town. Who'd be following me?*

When she looked down, a large oatmeal-colored dog blocked her path.

It looked sort of like a poodle. A big poodle. But instead of the fussy pompoms, it had a smooth, natural clip.

The dog stared up at her, almost expectantly. Like it recognized her.

A blue collar but no leash, Kate noticed. A boy? She looked around for an owner. No one seemed to be missing him. Or paying any attention to him at all.

Sitting back on his haunches, his black button eyes studied her face. Worried?

"Uh, hello?" she said.

He politely offered up a paw—the way a new acquaintance would proffer a hand.

Hesitating, she reached out and gave it a gentle shake. His fur was impossibly soft. Like a child's plush toy. She patted the back of his head. Silky. Clean.

He eagerly sniffed her hand. And her knees.

That's when she noticed two silver tags on his collar and reached for them. The one on top read: "Oliver, Coral Cay, FL"

"Well, hello, Oliver," she said, slipping her hand around to give his ear a scratch.

No street address. But in a small town, that probably wasn't necessary.

Was he the reason for the water bowls?

She stood and glanced over her shoulder. The stranger had vanished. But as she strolled down the street, Oliver stayed with her, matching her steps.

That's when she spotted it at the end of the block— the Cookie House. A delicate sunset pink bearing a large sign that affirmed its name. The building looked like an old Victorian home—complete with scuffed white gingerbread trim—that had seen better days.

The pink paint was worn in places, exposing a muddy green underneath. The plantation shutters were peeling. And the bakery's second-floor window boxes were empty, save for one dead bush.

The old worry knot hardened again in her gut. Kate pulled out her cell phone. If she was lucky, she could reschedule Fish-a-Palooza. Maybe there was a bus service she could use. Or, worse to worst, she'd grab a Lyft. If she landed the job, it would be worth it.

Nothing. She checked the screen. No bars.

"Can't go back, have to go forward," she sighed.

Oliver looked up at her, puzzled.

OK, so the Cookie House wasn't a tony French restaurant, like her last gig. But it wasn't a dark storage unit or Jeanine's rec room, either.

She turned. Ball Cap Man was back, standing in front of another shop, chatting with someone she pegged as a local.

The poor guy is probably killing time waiting for his wife.

Just off the porch, Kate stretched her phone skyward trying to catch a signal. Nada.

As she climbed the steps, the poodle raced ahead. He hopped onto one of the two white benches flanking the bakery's front door, turned around a few times, and stretched out.

Relaxed, with one paw crossed casually over the other, he cocked his head and looked at her.

"OK, Oliver, wish me luck," Kate said.

She could have sworn he smiled.

While the outside of the bakery was neglected, the inside was just the opposite. Every surface—from the glass cases to the wide-plank floors to the stainless-steel counters—gleamed. It looked like most of the first floor was devoted to the kitchen, hidden behind a pair of swinging doors. The shop smelled of freshly baked bread, butter, and yeast.

Kate stood at the back and waited her turn. With a one-man operation, customers would take precedence over job interviews, she reasoned. Besides, this would give her time to scope out the place. Not that she was procrastinating.

A well-bronzed man with a beer gut encased in a lemon-yellow golf shirt stood in front of the bakery counter. "How are the cheddar biscuits today?"

Kate pegged his Brooklyn accent and felt a stab of homesickness.

"If they weren't good, I wouldn't bake 'em," the proprietor said. "How many you want?"

"Yes, but are they fresh?" asked his wife, who'd paired her Lilly Pulitzer sundress with sky-high pink espadrilles and a matching straw hat the size of a truck tire. "And are your ingredients locally sourced?"

"Made 'em this morning," the baker replied. "Ingredients came outta my storeroom. You want any or not?"

"We'll take a half dozen," the husband said decisively.

As the tourist couple exited, a middle-aged blonde stepped up to the counter. Clad in a white T-shirt and well-worn jeans, her hair was pulled into a high, messy ponytail and topped off with a faded Marlins cap. "Hey, Sam," she said with a smile. "Need a loaf of that sourdough and two of the whole wheat."

"You want 'em sliced, Sadie?"

"Just the whole wheat. Kids are out of school for the summer. They're eating me out of house and home."

"Yup, they'll do that."

Kate scoped out the bakery case. Focaccia. Corn bread. Several kinds of biscuits—including one with sour cream and chives. And about five different kinds of bread, including whole-wheat pita and golden-brown naan.

But no pastry. No cakes, cupcakes, or cookies. No pies or delicate tartlets. No bear claws topped with crunchy sugar. Or Danishes with sweet, moist filling. Not so much as a doughnut.

What kind of bakery sold out of sweets? They must have more in the back, she reasoned.

The front door burst open, and a pack of kids ran in shrieking. "Cool it, you little gremlins! Inside voices!" a woman behind them hissed over the din.

As she waddled through the door, Kate saw that she was heavily pregnant. "Bobby! Don't touch the glass! And stop jumping! Becky, quit poking your big brother!"

Kate stepped aside to give her more room.

The woman smiled sheepishly. "I had to get off the beach and out of the sun for a little while. I promised them cookies."

"Sounds like a smart move," Kate said.

"OK, you little ruffians, get over here and pipe down—or we're leaving. Jennie! Get your hands off the glass! Becky, if you don't stop poking Bobby, you're going outside. Empty handed. Is that what you want?"

Becky looked startled, shook her head, and dropped her hands to her sides. Next to her, the youngest sibling, who looked about two, pulled his thumb out of his mouth and assumed the same position—with a proud grin on his face.

"The magic of cookies," Kate whispered to the mom.

"Amen to that," the brunette replied, rubbing her back, as the four kids gathered around her.

"Are you getting cookies, too?" Jennie asked Kate.

"Not exactly. I make cookies. I'm here about a job."

"You make cookies?" Bobby asked. "For real?"

"Cookies, cupcakes, all kinds of good stuff." To their mom she explained, "I'm a pastry chef."

"Oh God, that would be so dangerous. Right now, I could eat my weight in eclairs. All two tons of it."

Suddenly all four kids clustered around Kate.

"What kind of cookies are you gonna make?" Becky asked.

Kate started to laugh. "I can't make any now—I haven't got the job yet. But how about if I tell you what kind of cookies you like best?"

"Cookies!" the littlest boy said, throwing both hands up into the air like a referee signaling a touchdown.

"Yes, Charlie, cookies," his mom said, ruffling his sandy-blond hair. "Can you really do that?" she asked Kate. "Guess their favorite cookies?"

"After four years as a Girl Scout and eight years as a pastry chef, you'd be surprised," she said, her amber eyes twinkling.

"OK, what kind do I like?" Bobby asked.

Kate took a minute and sized him up. "Oatmeal. No raisins."

Bobby's eyes widened. "How did you know?"

She smiled mysteriously.

"What's mine? What's mine?" squealed Becky, bouncing up and down. "What do I like?"

"Peanut butter. Preferably with chocolate chips."

"Oh yeah!" Becky said, twirling toward the counter.

"Betcha don't know mine," her older sister dared.

"Ah, a challenge," Kate said, refocusing. "Let me see. I'm thinking . . . lemon coolers!"

"Whoa!" the little girl said. "Are you a witch?"

Kate shrugged and squatted down to eye level with Charlie. "And I bet you like animal crackers." She lowered her voice so that only he could hear. "And the chocolate ones are your very favorites."

He beamed and nodded vigorously.

"That is amazing," their mom said. "You're a cookie whisperer!"

"Hey, tell me what kind of cookies I like," implored a voice behind her. Kate turned to see a young guy in purple board shorts and blue flip-flops.

"Shortbread," Kate said without hesitating.

"Damn! That's awesome!"

"I bet you can't tell what kind of cookies I like," said the blonde next to him. Dressed in a yellow beach romper, she crossed her arms and fixed Kate with a defiant squint.

Kate took a deep breath and gave the woman a once-over.

"Well, you tell people you don't eat dessert," Kate started. "But the truth is you'd sell your grandmother for a dozen of those chewy lace cookies with the chocolate drizzle. And you dunk them in milk."

The woman's mouth dropped open, and she turned beet red.

"For what it's worth, I love those things, too," Kate added.

"Awwww, sis, she nailed you," Board Shorts said, snapping his fingers. "Hey, Sam, you gotta see this. This woman is great! She's a cookie whisperer."

"I don't sell cookies, Justin," the baker said matter-of-factly. "Bread and rolls. No fancy stuff."

"No cookies?" the three older kids repeated in unison as Charlie's face crumbled.

"You want sweets, we got an ice-cream shop at the other end of Main Street," the baker said. "They sell a fair amount of candy, too."

"But this place is called the Cookie House," the mom said, her voice stressing up half an octave. "How can you name it that and not sell cookies?"

The baker shrugged.

Kate leaned over, speaking quietly. "Those sour-cream biscuits just came out of the oven. I can tell by the way they're radiating heat. And it looks like a good batch. See the way they're all evenly golden brown? There's an empty bench outside on the porch. You guys could sit in the shade for a while and have a picnic."

The mom clapped her hands. "OK, kids, first a snack. Then we get ice cream!"

"Ice cream! Ice cream!" the kids sang, bouncing up and down.

"I'll take a dozen of the sour-cream biscuits. And you three wild things—outside! Find a place to sit on the porch. And look after your little brother."

"Yes, Mooommm," Jennie said, grabbing one of Charlie's hands as Bobby held the door open.

"I wish I had half that energy," the mom said, watching them dance, skip, and hop out to the porch. "Good luck with the job interview," she said, dropping her voice. "Ichabod Scrooge over there could really use you."

"Man, that is some party trick—I would love to know how you do that," Justin said, collecting two loaves of sourdough and heading for the door.

His sister strode ahead, ignoring them both.

"Can I help you?" the baker said to Kate.

"I'm Kate McGuire—I'm actually here about the job." She pointed to the "help wanted" sign in the window. *This is it. Go big or go home. Literally.*

She took a deep breath and started her spiel. "I'm a graduate of the Culinary Institute of America with a degree in baking and pastry arts. I've been a professional pastry chef in Manhattan for the last eight years, and I have an extensive list of excellent references."

With that, she proffered a slick black folder containing her résumé and two pages of references on creamy white vellum.

"Not right for the job," he said abruptly, slapping the folder onto the counter.

"Excuse me?"

"Don't sell pastry or any of that frilly stuff. Need someone to tend the counter. And pitch in hauling supplies to and from the storeroom. Fancy degree won't help with that."

Kate walked over to the window, pulled down the "help wanted" sign, and examined it.

She glanced outside. A guy was sitting on a bench across the street. The upper half of his body was totally obscured by the newspaper he was reading. But there was a familiar green shopping bag parked at his feet.

"So how long have you been looking for help?" she said quietly, turning toward the baker.

He shrugged.

"This sign is faded, so I'm guessing it's been a while. It's the tail end of tourist season, and it's also the start of summer break. But you haven't gotten so much as a nibble. In spite of the fact that you bake a first-class sourdough. You've been blunt, so I'll return the favor. I don't want this job long-term. I'm moving to Coral Cay and looking for a permanent spot as a pastry chef. But I need something to tide me over in the meantime. As you know, baking is hard work. I've spent the last eight years on my feet all day every day, in a hot kitchen, pounding dough and hauling supplies."

Kate mentally crossed her fingers behind her back for that last part. At the restaurant, the busboys, dishwashers, and delivery guys did all the heavy lifting.

Hepplewhite shrugged again. But she noticed he hadn't said no. At least, not outright.

"So how much does the job pay?" Kate asked.

"Minimum wage. Seven twenty-five an hour."

"That's the national minimum wage," she said. "Florida minimum wage is eight ten an hour."

"Last time I checked, Florida was still part of the country. Pay is seven twenty-five an hour."

Inwardly, she rolled her eyes. This guy was tighter than Deacon Dave. She'd never worked so hard to land a job she didn't want. Out of the corner of her eye, she spotted a narrow hallway. She remembered the second-story window boxes. And the dead bush.

"What's upstairs?"

"Storeroom. Like I said, no work for a girl."

"Do you use all the upstairs rooms for the baking supplies?"

"Just the one. On the back side of the house."

"What about the rooms on the front side?"

"Just two rooms. One in the back for baking supplies. Other one's for extra cleaning supplies and some old junk. Why?"

"I'll make you a deal," Kate said. "I'll take your seven twenty-five an hour if you let me camp out in the front storeroom. Just for a couple of days. Until I can rent a place in town."

The baker shook his head. "Already said, this work isn't for you. Besides, this area's commercial. No one's s'posed to live here. Probably a health code violation, too."

Suddenly Kate remembered something—something Gabe had mentioned. *What could it hurt?*

"Here's my offer: If you don't like my work, you can fire me. And it won't cost you a dime. I'll walk away without a paycheck. But wouldn't it be nice to have someone to tend the shop, when you want to get away for a while?" *With a metal detector and a bottle of rum?*

"And I've shown I'm very good with customers," she added.

Hands flat on the counter, the baker narrowed his eyes, clenching and unclenching his jaw. For the first time, he seemed to be genuinely considering the idea.

"I do the baking," he said finally. "You just mind the counter and fetch supplies now and then. And cut all that cookie-talk nonsense. I don't sell that junk. And I'm not gonna start now."

"Fair enough. I'll have my stuff sent over from the hotel, and I can start this afternoon. Um, what should I call you?"

"Name's Sam Hepplewhite. Mr. Hepplewhite to

you. And if anyone asks, tell 'em you're still staying at that hotel. Don't want the Board of Health getting their panties in a twist. Don't expect you'll last the week, anyway."

Chapter 3

Promptly at six o'clock, Sam walked to the front door, turned the "open" sign to "closed," and flipped the dead bolt. "Done for today. I'll be back tomorrow morning."

Kate was ready for a break. Maybe a walk on the beach. For the last three hours, she'd waited on customers while Sam disappeared into the kitchen for long stretches.

At the now-defunct Soleil, she had been an accomplished—and appreciated—pastry chef. Today the closest she got to baking was running the bread slicer.

But the people were fun. It was an interesting, eclectic mix of tourists and locals. And she was amazed at how much they shared in just a few minutes of conversation. The tourists were on vacation with a relaxed attitude about everything, she reasoned. And the denizens of small-town Coral Cay seemed accustomed to everyone knowing their business.

Spritely octogenarian Sunny Eisenberg invited Kate

to drop in for yoga classes at her studio, just off the square.

"The secret to youth is flexibility," she confided to Kate. "And it all starts with your spine. Doesn't matter how old you get. If your spine is supple, you'll stay young." With that, Sunny stretched over backward and just kept going, executing an impressive backbend.

"H-harrumph!" Kate heard from the direction of the kitchen.

Sunny straightened up, laughing, and brushed her short champagne-colored hair into place with one hand. "Don't mind that old sourpuss. I've been trying to get him to sample a class for years. But he's too set in his ways. He's afraid if he ever loosened up, he'd fall apart." She lowered her voice, stage-whispering to Kate, "And he just might, at that!"

Later a woman popped into the shop bearing a newspaper-wrapped bundle of sunshine-yellow blooms. Barely five-two with glossy black hair, she pulsed with energy, like a hummingbird mid-flight.

"These are for Sam," she said, handing off the flowers to Kate. "Lemon lilies. From my garden. I'm Maxi Más-Buchanan. I run Flowers Maximus next door."

"Your yard is incredible," Kate said. "It looks like something out of a magazine."

"It's a work in progress," Maxi replied in a voice Kate found musical. "Emphasis on work. You like plants?"

"I love them—especially flowers. But living in New York with no patio, I haven't really had a chance to try my hand at growing anything."

"Then you're definitely in the right place," Maxi said, smiling. "The flowers in this town—spectacular!" she said, punctuating the statement by spreading both hands wide.

Suddenly Hepplewhite bustled in from the kitchen. "Those kids of yours out of school?"

Kate was dumbfounded. It was the first time she'd seen the baker actually initiate a conversation.

"All three of the little terrors," Maxi replied with a grin. "I told Peter if he's not home for dinner by six, I'll drive them to his office and drop them off. Then I'm checking into a hotel."

As Maxi and Hepplewhite debated the relative merits of corn bread versus brioche rolls with roasted chicken, Kate headed to the kitchen with the flowers. She stripped off the newspaper, grabbed a clean pitcher off the counter, filled it, and settled them gently in the water.

Returning to the shop, she placed the pitcher carefully on top of the counter, admiring the vibrant yellow blossoms.

"Is there a secret to it?" Kate asked. "Growing such beautiful flowers?"

"If you love them, the plants can feel it," Maxi said with a smile. "And when you have to be up early, treating yourself to a few cups of strong Cuban coffee doesn't hurt, either. When Sam gives you a break, c'mon over and I'll pour you a cup. And don't let this old rascal work you too hard," she said with a wink.

Kate had noticed that when Hepplewhite filled Maxi's order "a dozen" brioche rolls actually numbered fourteen. And he slipped a loaf of challah into the bag without charging her. "Her husband likes it," the baker had said later, with a shrug.

Now checking his watch as he motored for the back door, Hepplewhite called over his shoulder, "Not much left in the cases. But you can wrap it and bring it to the pantry in the back."

I wanted this job, Kate reminded herself lightly. *I begged for this job. And I am a total moron.*

"Um, Mr. Hepplewhite, I'd like to go get some dinner and maybe take a walk before I settle in upstairs. Would it be possible to have a key, so I can get back in?"

He sighed. "Some tins of meat in the pantry. And apples in the icebox. Help yourself to the leftover bread. Time enough for keys tomorrow. If you're still here. Gotta go now."

Yeah, rum and metal detectors wait for no man, Kate thought.

Hepplewhite had been acting strangely all afternoon. Inexplicably, whenever the shop had been completely empty he commandeered the kitchen. Yet when customers appeared, he'd hover in the shop. Like he didn't quite trust her with the till.

He wasn't baking. As far as Kate could tell, everything in the kitchen remained untouched.

Watching her from secret security cameras? Hiding something? Or taking a nip?

Several times that afternoon, she'd checked the front porch. With a cheddar biscuit in her apron pocket. But Oliver was gone.

On the bright side, Ball Cap Guy had disappeared, too.

After Hepplewhite left, Kate set about scouting dinner. The upside of eating out of Sam Hepplewhite's pantry: spending zero money. A definite plus, as far as she was concerned.

Besides, there were worse things than being locked in a bakery.

But what was with the "no pastry" edict? She'd tried to get a read on Hepplewhite's cookie preferences a couple of times. She figured she could whip up a batch to break the ice. But she kept coming up blank. Nothing.

That isn't possible. Is it?

Going through a serious case of withdrawal, Kate was craving chocolate chip cookies.

"Makes sense," she reasoned. "The ultimate comfort food. Nicely browned, still warm, and slightly soft from the oven. With the chocolate all melted and gooey. Alongside a tall, cold glass of milk."

Hepplewhite may have told her she couldn't talk about cookies. Or sell them in the store. But he'd never said she couldn't bake any for herself.

However, a quick check of the kitchen revealed not so much as a speck of chocolate. She'd have to wait until she could hit a market tomorrow.

Hepplewhite had sold out of the sourdough. But the focaccia looked wonderful. Covered with thyme, rosemary, and coarse salt, it smelled delicious.

"Tins of meat" turned out to be a couple cans of tuna, a few cans of deviled ham, and half a case of Spam.

Tuna it was.

Ironic, she thought. *I skipped Fish-a-Palooza after I learned they served frozen fish. Now I'm eating the canned stuff and getting minimum wage. And not even real minimum wage.*

She hit the fridge and grabbed an apple, a lemon, and the olive oil. Then she snagged basil and oregano from the pantry. A little chopping, a little mixing, and she had a pretty decent tuna salad. She cut off a healthy chunk of focaccia, sliced it down the middle, and slathered both halves with tuna salad.

With her luggage still MIA and not a magazine in sight, Kate was at a loss. She scoured the kitchen for something to read while she ate. Not so much as a cookbook or recipe file. But with a lot to do over the next few days, she could at least make a list and get organized. She grabbed a notebook from the counter near the phone and flipped it open.

What she found stunned her. A list of questions. Followed by names she recognized. In weird spidery handwriting. She flipped the page. More names. From her references.

That's what he'd been doing in the kitchen all afternoon, she realized. *He must have called them.*

Fascinated, she read as she ate. Part of her felt guilty—like she was eavesdropping. The other part wanted to know exactly what they'd said.

Hepplewhite had outlined his questions on the first page. But they were somewhat limited in scope: "Honest? Trustworthy? Ever stolen anything? Ever been arrested? Ever suspected? Con artist?"

That was followed by page after page of names. And check marks by most of them.

Occasionally there were short notes, too: "Punctual." "Conscientious." "Honest." "Works hard." "Not thief." "Not con artist." "Not crook."

Not much of a comment on my pastry skills, either, she thought dryly.

OK, so the guy wanted to make sure he could trust her alone in the shop. She just hoped he hadn't told them he was paying her less than minimum wage. Or that she was living in his storeroom.

A half hour later, refueled, Kate peeled off her blue-and-white-striped bakery apron. "Time to survey the new digs," she decided.

In the darkened upstairs hallway, she groped for a wall switch and flipped on the overhead light. Half-expecting it to be locked, she turned the handle and cautiously opened the door.

Definitely a storeroom.

Two industrial-sized stainless-steel bookcases flanked the left wall—stocked with buckets and bottles of cleaning supplies, paper towels, and toilet paper. Sam Hepplewhite hadn't just cornered the market. He'd bought enough to last until Armageddon. And then some.

The two large windows at the back of the room were bare. No curtains or even blinds. But they were huge. During the day, this room would be bright and sunny. She might even be able to see the ocean. And she'd definitely be able to smell the salt air.

Take that, Manhattan!

A fair number of moving boxes were stacked haphazardly against the other wall. She walked over, pulled one down, and opened it. What she discovered floored her.

Chapter 4

The carton was a virtual bakery supply store. Cookie sheets. Mixing bowls. Cupcake tins. Whisks. Wooden spoons.

Flummoxed, she closed up the box, replaced it in the stack, and pulled down another. It contained more of the same. Plus a half-dozen cookbooks with titles she recognized—staples for any serious pastry chef. Her own copies were back at the hotel.

What was Hepplewhite hiding?

She heaved the box back into place and looked around the room. With wide-plank hardwood floors and a high ceiling, it definitely had possibilities. Almost a shame that it was only for a couple of nights.

Kate opened a door off to the right, expecting a closet. Instead, it was a tiny bathroom. Artfully arranged to fit a white pedestal sink under a small gilt-framed mirror, and a trim tub/shower combo. Over the tub: a high, round stained-glass window. Bearing the image of a single red flower.

Kate was amazed.

With a layer of dust on the sink, the bathroom clearly hadn't been used in years. And the shower needed a curtain. She turned on the sink tap and flushed the toilet. Both worked.

In the city, Hepplewhite could have called this a studio and rented it out for a small fortune, she thought.

Wandering back into the main room, Kate spotted a large bundle of sticks wrapped in canvas propped against one of the stainless-steel shelves. Tagged with a yellow Post-it note, it was helpfully labeled "cot." She recognized the scrawly script from the kitchen notebook.

Adjacent to that little gift was a door. Opening it, Kate found a walk-in closet. She flipped the light switch. Nothing. If there was a bulb, it had burned out.

She grabbed the cot bundle, unrolled the canvas, and tried to visualize how the wooden parts fit together. It looked less like actual furniture and more like a set of Lincoln Logs.

She took something that resembled a leg and tried to fit it into the main frame. No go. She shoved and it bounced off, clattering onto the floor.

I've assembled six-tiered wedding cakes that were easier, she thought.

Out of nowhere, her ex-fiancé's handsome face popped into her head.

So what was Evan doing now?

Bam, bam, bam! Bam, bam, bam!

Kate jumped.

The pounding continued. "Paradise Cove Resort!" a male voice shouted.

Her bags! She could change her clothes. Brush her teeth. And pore over her cookbooks.

"Coming!" she shouted, galloping down the steep stairs. "Hang on, I'm coming!"

The back door didn't have much of a lock on it, Kate noticed. No dead bolt. Just a twist button on the door-knob.

Hepplewhite had cleaned out the cash register before he left. And there probably wasn't much of a market for stolen baked goods. So absent someone living on-site, the guy probably didn't need much in the way of security.

Kate opened the door to find a teenager in a Paradise Cove bellhop's uniform: black shorts, linen shirt, and a pith helmet. He was standing next to an eight-seater golf cart.

"Kate McGuire?"

"That's me."

He looked around conspiratorially. "I wasn't sure I had the right address. Never delivered bags to the back of a bakery before. Or a bakery, period."

"I, uh, work here."

"Oh. Well, I can drop them off at your house, if you want. That way, they'll be waiting for you when you get home." He pointed to the golf cart.

"Uh, no, this is fine. Thanks, though."

"OK, then just sign here, and you're all paid up," he said, producing an electronic tablet and a stylus. "The resort will apply the charges to the credit card on file. They'll also email you a receipt."

Signing the bill, she regretted not snagging the bittersweet Ghirardelli chocolate bar from her room's minifridge. Or the chocolate-covered macadamia nuts.

As the teenager hauled her possessions—two suitcases, a duffel bag, three book boxes, and three moving cartons full of Kate's favorite bakeware and tools—off the golf cart, it suddenly hit her: She had to tip him. And day-old bread wasn't going to cut it.

"Just drop everything in here!" she shouted, racing

across the kitchen for her purse. She rifled through her wallet and pulled out a ten-dollar bill. Then she remembered the three heavy book boxes and grabbed another fiver.

When she turned, the kid was looking around the bakery kitchen like he'd just landed on Mars.

"It's OK, I'm a pastry chef. I was just staying at the resort until I started my new job."

"Here?" he asked dubiously.

"Yup. And here you go," she said, slipping him the fifteen dollars. "Thanks for bringing my stuff all the way out here."

"OK, but if you change your mind, we pick up and deliver," he said. With that, he tipped his helmet, climbed into the cart, and sped off into the night.

Chapter 5

Kate sat straight up in bed, confused at first.

Absent curtains or bed linens, she'd opted to sleep in the clothes she was wearing: a white short-sleeved blouse and a slim black skirt.

Her throat was dry. Half-asleep, it took her a minute to realize she was thirsty.

There was a crash in the kitchen. Followed by a clang and the sound of something rolling across the kitchen floor. Then silence.

She looked at the watch on her arm: 12:42 a.m. She waited two full minutes. Nothing.

Her throat felt like sandpaper. *The heck with it*.

She climbed out of the cot and tiptoed carefully into the hall, straining to hear more noises. Deadly quiet.

She stepped carefully down the narrow stairs and peeked around the corner into the kitchen.

Empty.

But the paper grocery bag she'd used for a trash can earlier that evening had fallen over, spilling used paper towels, lemon peels, and discarded apple parts across the floor. That clanging? The tuna can from dinner, which had rolled into the center of the room like a discarded hubcap.

Some big, tough New Yorker I am, Kate thought, feeling both silly and relieved as she gathered up the trash, sealed it into a garbage bag, and set it by the back door.

After washing her hands, she grabbed a glass from the cupboard, filled it, and took a long drink.

She refilled the glass and carried it upstairs. Replenished and relaxed, Kate was already drowsy. Maybe now she could finally get a few hours' sleep.

She was just dropping off when she heard it: scratching. Persistent scratching. Coming from downstairs.

Kate was instantly alert. But there was only silence.

Suddenly more scraping. Followed by a sound she recognized: a long, slow groan. Followed by a second one. Then a muffled click.

The back door opening. And closing.

It was way too early for Sam Hepplewhite. But maybe he was checking on her?

Footsteps. A man's staccato steps. Hard shoes walking softly across the kitchen floor.

Not Hepplewhite's sneakers.

Kate's heart was pounding. She was shaking.

Another squeak she recognized. The swinging doors from the kitchen to the shop. Then a scuffling sound.

He was going for the cash register! Would he be angry when he discovered it was empty? What if he decided to try his luck upstairs? What if it was that guy with the baseball cap? What if he came looking for her?

She snatched her purse and fumbled inside for her phone. Clutching it, she hit 911, pressed "talk," and prayed.

Nothing. No service.

The only working phones were the landlines—one on

either side of the swinging kitchen doors. Each just an arm's length from the intruder.

More scuffling, louder this time.

Kate quietly eased over to the storage shelves, trying not to make the ancient floors squeak. She felt around in the dark, and her hand latched onto one of the giant economy-sized bottles of Windex. She pulled it close to her body and twisted the nozzle to what she hoped was "open."

Not much of a weapon, but maybe I can blind him long enough to escape, she thought.

Woof! Woof! Woof! a deep-throated bark cut the quiet night air.

A dog. Close by. The front porch?

Oliver!

Woof! Woof! Woof! Urgent. And louder.

The pup is sounding the alarm!

Woof-woof! Woof-woof! Woof-woof!

Kate heard hard footsteps running across the kitchen. Then the back door groaned twice again.

Open and closed?

Woof-woof! Woof-woof! Woof-woof! Full throated and full volume. He wasn't giving up.

Kate went tearing downstairs.

She tiptoed into the kitchen, window cleaner at the ready. All clear. But the back door was ajar.

She could still hear Oliver, at top volume, on the porch. He sounded big and angry. If she hadn't been pretty sure it was him, she'd have pictured a much larger, more threatening dog.

Kate stepped lightly into the shop. Nothing. No one. Just a weird smell. The scent of cigarettes. And cologne? Plus something sweet. Familiar. But she couldn't quite place it.

The cash register appeared untouched. Looking around, she couldn't see any damage. Or anything missing.

She threw the bolt and opened the front door. Oliver stopped barking and trotted inside.

"You're amazing, you know that?" she said, closing the door and locking it behind him.

Still shaking, she dropped the Windex on the floor and wrapped her arms around him. Warm and solid, he smelled like fresh air. And the beach.

"My hero. My sweet, fuzzy hero. C'mon, let's go call the cops. Then we'll get some biscuits."

Oliver's tail thumped happily.

Turns out, thanks to the actions of Oliver the Wonder Dog, the police were already "en route," the dispatcher informed her. "To investigate a noise disturbance downtown."

When the officer arrived a few minutes later, he seemed surprised that the dog causing all the ruckus was Oliver.

"Known this guy since he was a puppy," said the ruddy blond twentysomething, who introduced himself as Kyle Hardy. "I don't think I've ever heard him bark before," he said, giving the dog's ear an affectionate scratch.

For his part, Oliver, who had just devoured three cheddar biscuits, sat up straight and looked very proud of himself.

"Well, maybe he was saving it up for the right moment," Kate said. "He really rescued me. A man broke in. And I couldn't get a cell signal to dial you guys. Oliver called the cavalry."

"Yeah, cells are tricky in this part of town," Hardy said. "That's why most of the folks down here have landlines. So, you said 'man.' Did you actually see an intruder?"

"Nope. Just heard his footsteps across the kitchen floor. Hard shoes. And heavy. It sounded like a man."

"The dispatcher put in a call to Sam Hepplewhite. He's on his way down here. And what were you doing here at . . ." He glanced at his notebook, "One twelve a.m.?"

"I work at the bakery," Kate said, sensing a shift in the conversation. "I'm moving to Coral Cay, and Mr. Hepplewhite is letting me stay upstairs for a few days until I can rent a place."

"Good luck with that," Hardy said, jotting something on the pad. "Still tourist season. Moving from where, exactly?"

"Manhattan. I'm a pastry chef."

"Sam Hepplewhite hired a pastry chef? That doesn't sound right. Sam doesn't sell pastry. Great breads, though."

"I'm helping out at the shop temporarily."

He gave her a long look. Kate was beginning to wonder if she was a suspect.

"And Sam will back this up?"

"Yes."

"OK, we'll just check with him and we're all set." Hardy looked up from his notes and glanced around the kitchen. "See anything missing?"

"No, not that I've noticed. But you'll have to ask Mr. Hepplewhite. There was a strange smell. Cigarettes. And some kind of cologne. And something else." Kate paused, trying to place that scent, came up blank, and shrugged. "The back door was open a crack. I didn't touch it, in case you wanted to dust for prints."

"Yeah, I don't think that's gonna be necessary."

"What do you mean?"

"This is Coral Cay, not *CSI*. From what you described, it was most likely some kids up to mischief. Summer vacation."

"Kids wearing cologne and hard shoes?"

Just then, Sam Hepplewhite pushed through the back door. In a blue windbreaker and baggy jeans, it looked like he hadn't even paused to run a comb through his sparse gray hair.

He stopped when he spotted Kate. For a split second, she could have sworn she saw relief on his craggy face. Or maybe she was just sleep deprived.

"Hey, Sam," Hardy said. "Looks like you might have had a visit from some young pranksters. Take a look around and tell me if you see anything missing. Nothing in the register, I take it?"

"Nup. Cleaned it out before I left for the night, Kyle. You know that."

"Good man," Hardy said, giving Hepplewhite a slap on the shoulder. "Glad to hear it. Ah, let's you and I go speak in the shop for a minute."

Kate looked down and realized that, in the confusion, Oliver had vanished.

So where does he live?

A few minutes later, the two men were back. Hardy stood in the middle of the kitchen while Hepplewhite did a quick inventory. "No, Kyle," Hepplewhite said, shaking his head. "Nothing's gone."

"That wraps it up then," Hardy said. "No sense even filling out the paperwork."

"How about a hot cup of coffee?" the baker offered. "I'm gonna make some fresh."

"Love to, but I'm headed off-shift. We're shorthanded this week with Ben out. And I wanna grab some shut-eye."

"How's his foot?"

"Doc says he won't even have a limp. He'll be back on duty next week. Walking cast."

Hepplewhite nodded.

Kate had no idea who "Ben" was (or what had happened

to his foot), but she was a little freaked they weren't taking the break-in more seriously.

What if it was Ball Cap Man?

The thought sent ice down her spine. But if she told Hepplewhite she might have a stalker, that would just give him one more reason to sack her. And judging by Officer Hardy's initial suspicion of her—and his haste to blame teen high jinks—she doubted he'd even take her seriously.

As far as they were concerned, she'd probably fallen asleep and dreamt the whole thing. And poor Oliver was just barking to be let into the bakery.

Hepplewhite walked Officer Hardy to the curb. She also noticed that he'd sent the policeman off with a box of sour cream and chive biscuits.

"Too late to bother with sleep now," he said when he reappeared in the kitchen. "Might as well start the morning's baking. Why don't you go upstairs and get some rest?"

No one had to ask her twice. Suddenly Kate was exhausted. And with Hepplewhite ensconced in the kitchen, she felt safe.

Upstairs, Kate opened the storeroom door and found Oliver.

Stretched out on the floor, with his head on her duffel bag, he looked at her through half-closed eyes and wagged his tail.

"Oh, you are a good boy," she said, patting his soft flank. "Such a good boy."

She noticed that his paws were too big for his body. "You're still growing, aren't you? You're just a puppy. A very big, very good puppy."

Ginger snaps.

Kate blinked. Oliver sighed deeply.

"If I had any ginger snaps, I would give them all to you," she said softly, stroking his downy head.

"Tell you what," Kate said after a few minutes. "There may not be any cookies here now, but I'm gonna fix that—soon. For now, there's some deviled ham in the pantry. I know it's not sirloin steak—or ginger snaps. But I bet it would taste pretty good."

Oliver's cream-colored tail stroked the floor rhythmically.

Kate hustled down the stairs and hit the pantry for one of the tins. Then she snagged a paper plate and a small glass bowl. The pup was bound to be thirsty.

She nearly collided with Hepplewhite coming through the kitchen.

"I'm grabbing a few things—for a snack," Kate said, feeling instantly guilty.

"Just keep the dog out of the kitchen. Don't need the health department causing a fuss," he said.

"Thank you, Mr. Hepplewhite. I appreciate it. But you need to know. There really was someone in here tonight. Not kids. A man. He picked the lock on the back door, came through the kitchen, and then went into the shop."

Hepplewhite glanced over at Kate as he floured the counter with a practiced hand. "Yup. Figured as much. Kyle Hardy's a nice kid. I know his folks. Good people."

The baker shook his head. "But that boy's not gonna make detective anytime soon."

Chapter 6

When Kate opened her eyes, sunlight was streaming through the windows.

For a split second, she was disoriented, half-expecting to be in her room at Paradise Cove. Or her apartment in Manhattan.

Oliver, bright eyed, looked at her expectantly. And last night came flooding back.

The storeroom. The break-in. The police.

She checked her watch: 7:05 a.m.

She'd overslept!

The pup gave out a little whine, and Kate realized he needed to go out.

"You good boy. Oh, you've been so patient, haven't you?"

The tail wagged twice rapidly. Definitely a yes.

"The one good thing about sleeping in your clothes," Kate told Oliver as she pulled a brush through her caramel-colored hair, "is that you wake up fully dressed."

She fished through her purse and grabbed her sunglasses. "C'mon, sweet pea, let's get you outside for a nice break."

Oliver raced downstairs. The minute Kate opened the back door, he shot outside. She left it ajar, hoping he'd return, and jogged back upstairs to get ready for work.

Twenty minutes later, brushed and washed, wearing a fresh pair of jeans, a simple white T-shirt, and her favorite white Keds, Kate galloped downstairs and into the kitchen.

As commutes go, she had to admit, this was pretty sweet.

Hepplewhite was heading into the shop with a tray of warm bread. The Cookie House, she noticed, was already open for business.

"Coffee's on the counter in the kitchen," Hepplewhite called over his shoulder. "Some rolls, too."

The entire place smelled like baking bread. And Kate realized she was ravenous.

Next to the coffeepot, Hepplewhite had put out a spread—with a glass mug and dessert plate, a carton of creamer, a jar of orange marmalade, butter, and a platter of popovers still warm from the oven.

After two mugs of strong coffee and three popovers slathered with butter and marmalade, Kate felt like she was ready for anything.

"Left a clean apron on the counter," Hepplewhite said as he reloaded a tray with corn muffins. "Soiled ones in the pantry hamper. Clean ones on the shelf."

She found it. Neatly folded on the counter next to the coffeemaker. With wide navy and white vertical stripes, it reminded her of one she'd seen in a French patisserie.

She looped it over her neck and tied it in the back with a neat bow. And felt strangely exhilarated.

Brand-new life in Coral Cay: Day One.

For the next few hours, the customers came in a steady stream. Most were locals. Moms running errands. Folks on their way to work. Teens looking for some carbs before they hit the beach.

And they were all as curious about Kate as she was about them. More even.

Seems word had gotten out that Sam Hepplewhite finally hired someone. And that she was living above the store.

For her part, Kate suspected that while Kyle Hardy might not be much of a sleuth, he was a first-rate gossip.

Oliver had vanished again. "Probably home," Kate reasoned.

Wherever home was. But a dog that smart and sweet? Someone must love him.

After last night, she was also on the lookout for Ball Cap Man. But he was MIA.

Sight-seeing with the wife? Or finally giving up after almost getting caught?

Through it all, Hepplewhite kept baking while Kate manned the counter. At one point, when the shop was empty, she saw him grab a liquor bottle under the cash register and carry it into the kitchen.

"Flavoring," he said by way of explanation.

Later, when Kate smelled cinnamon and sugar, she couldn't contain her curiosity. With her empty coffee mug as a prop, she hustled into the kitchen in time to see Hepplewhite take a batch of sandwich bread out of the oven. Along with a pan of cinnamon rolls.

"My snack," he announced bluntly as she refilled her mug. "Not for the store."

Eyeing the rum bottle on the counter, Kate wondered what, exactly, he'd use to wash them down.

Just as the morning rush had tapered off, Kate grabbed a clean towel and started wiping down the counters. She glanced out the front windows in time to catch a long black limousine gliding to a stop in front of the Cookie House. A driver in a black suit and cap hopped out, ran to the car's side door, and threw it open.

Kate knew that the area was catnip to the very wealthy, as well as more than a few celebs. But in laid-back Coral Cay, most of them at least attempted to keep a low profile. And downplay their net worth.

Not this one.

Fascinated, she watched as a well-dressed man exited the limo. Short and squat, with high cheekbones and a tan, he looked like a businessman or senator straight out of central casting. Complete with a full head of expertly barbered gray hair.

The cut of his blue blazer screamed "money." As did the blue-and-white-striped Turnbull & Asser–style shirt paired with a lavender silk tie. When he shook his finger in the driver's face, Kate caught the glint of gold on his white cuffs.

Her ex-mother-in-law-to-be, who hailed from money fresh off the *Mayflower,* would have dismissed him with one acid-drenched word: "arriviste."

When the driver opened the shop door his passenger marched in like he owned the place.

The man sized up Kate with a smirk. "And here I thought old Hepplewhite didn't fancy sweets," he said loudly, with a British accent that betrayed his East End origins. "I don't suppose you know what a crumpet is?"

"It's similar to what we Yanks call an English muffin,"

Kate replied pleasantly, smoothing her apron. "While we don't currently have any, the popovers are delicious."

"If I'd known you were here, I'd have popped over a lot sooner," he said, leering. "I'm Stewart Lord. I'm going to be your new boss."

Hepplewhite burst through the swinging doors with a pan of iced cinnamon rolls in one hand and a spoon dripping white icing in the other. "You can take your break now," he said quietly to Kate, setting both pan and spoon on a low caddy against the wall.

She was all too happy to flee. Something about Stewart Lord gave her the creeps.

"Well, well, Sam, got some pretty new help, I see," the man jibed. "But you're only delaying the inevitable. And at your age, you shouldn't have to work. Just think, if you accept my generous offer for this shop, you can spend all your time on the beach. With that . . . metal detector you love so much. Yo-ho-ho and all that."

Kate couldn't resist eavesdropping from the kitchen. Angling herself the right way, she discovered she also had a line of sight on part of the shop.

"What do you want, Lord?" Hepplewhite asked tersely.

"Oh, let's see," the businessman said, pacing in front of the case. "Hmmm, are those cinnamon rolls I see? I heard you didn't sell pastries. Y'know they look just like the ones my gran used to bake. And I haven't had any really good ones since she died. Of course, Gran never allowed dogs in her kitchen. I certainly hope the Board of Health doesn't hear about that. Lovely people, they are. I snap my fingers and they come running."

Stewart Lord leaned in and lowered his voice to a ragged whisper. "You should take my deal before I drop the price."

"This is a bakery, Lord. Order something or get out."

"Is that any way to treat a paying customer?" he said genially, as if he was playing to an invisible audience. "If my employees did that, I'd fire them on the spot. Of course, I know what it is to run a corporation. I hire and fire legions. And you just have the one employee. So is that charming girl really your 'niece'? That's the story that's going around town, you know. Of course, *I* wouldn't doubt it for a minute. I'll bet those buns are a special treat just for her. They smell delicious."

Hepplewhite pulled a flattened white box from under the counter and neatly assembled it. Then he grabbed a knife, loosened the cinnamon rolls from the tray, and lifted them into the box. He closed the lid and handed it across the counter to Lord.

"Time for you to leave," Hepplewhite said quietly. "Now."

Kate noticed the baker never put down the knife.

"Luckily for you, my time really is money," Lord said, flashing his gold Patek Philippe. He opened the bakery box, pinched off a roll, and downed it in two oversized bites.

It's like watching a cobra swallow a rat, Kate thought as she peered in from the kitchen.

"Ah, good stuff!" Lord said, licking his fat fingers. "See you soon. And thanks for breakfast."

The rest of the morning was fairly uneventful.

But after the break-in and Stewart Lord, a brass band marching through the bakery would be positively soothing, Kate thought lightly. *New York's got nothing on this place.*

Carl Ivers, an ex-cop who ran the hardware store, showed up to install a dead bolt on the back door.

"Can't say for certain this one's been picked, but from the scratches I'm seeing, that'd be my guess," he pronounced. "Want me to give any of these parts to Kyle?"

"Wouldn't do any good," Hepplewhite said.

"Yeah, 'fraid you're right about that," Carl agreed. "But I might hang on to 'em, just in case. In the meantime, this is the dead bolt I have on my own home," he said, holding up a brushed-silver model.

"That'll be fine," Hepplewhite said.

When Carl finished, he presented Kate with a new key on a shiny chrome key ring. "Welcome to Coral Cay. And don't let what happened last night give you the wrong idea," he said, dropping his voice. "Truth is, crime is rare here. Very rare. That was one of the reasons my wife and I moved the family here from Atlanta. Well, that and the beach."

"You like it?" Kate asked as she centered herself and mentally focused on the ex-cop.

Snickerdoodles.

"Love it," Carl said, oblivious. "Love. It. Can't buy a decent piece of sweet potato pie, but other than that, it is heaven. Especially for an old cop like me."

Sam finished the baking a little before noon and announced he had to run a few errands and would bring them lunch from the deli down the street. Since the rum bottle had moved from the kitchen counter to the trash bin out back, Kate suspected one of his first stops might be a liquor store.

But, she had to admit, Hepplewhite always seemed perfectly sober. And she never smelled a drop on him.

Maybe it was just "flavoring" after all?

After he left, Kate heard a police siren. Followed by what sounded like a fleet of emergency vehicles.

She was filling an order for Amos Tully, who ran the corner market, when Justin came running into the store.

Still wearing board shorts—this time in orange—the surfer looked shaken.

"Oh my God, did you hear?" he said, eyes wide.

"What happened?" Tully asked, taking a bakery bag from Kate and handing her a twenty-dollar bill in return.

"It's Stewart Lord. The guy just had a heart attack in the back of his limo. He's dead!"

Chapter 7

That night, Kate turned in early. If Ball Cap Man tried to break in again, he was in for a surprise. Thanks to Carl Ivers, that back door was beefed up with a dead bolt.

And, for the first time in her life, Kate owned a land-line phone. A fire-engine-red slimline that magically appeared on a shelf in her storeroom-slash-bedroom.

One of Hepplewhite's "errands."

And the light in the closet worked, too. Now that someone had installed a pink bulb in the socket.

Still, she slept fitfully. And it wasn't the cot.

When Hepplewhite showed up in the bakery again at 2:00 a.m.—whistling loudly, slamming cupboard doors, and banging pans—Kate finally relaxed.

The next morning, armed with her own key and a workday that didn't begin until noon, she vowed to get out and explore Coral Cay. She made it as far as next door when she spied Oliver.

Maxi was planting some kind of bush out front, and Oliver was, literally, running circles around her.

"Did he at least help you dig the hole?" Kate called from the curb.

"He's super good at digging," she said, laughing. "He's not so good at stopping."

Oliver bounded over to Kate, raced around her several times, then planted his front paws, ducking his head, and wagging his tail. Clearly, a game. Even if the clueless humans didn't know how to play.

Maxi tenderly patted the ground under the bush, then leaned back and peeled off her garden gloves. "I don't know about you, but I could use some coffee. And it's nice and cool on the porch. Wanna join me?"

The front yard of Flowers Maximus was a marvel. Kate had never seen most of the colorful flowers that filled the wide beds ringing the shop.

But some blooms she recognized. Like the purple bougainvillea overflowing from hanging baskets that rimmed the porch. And the two lemon trees, thriving in oversized clay planters on either side of the door.

Kate was mesmerized. It smelled like a tropical paradise.

Oliver ignored all of it, in favor of the yellow water bowl on the far end of the porch. And the pup splashed almost as much as he drank.

"This is incredible," she said when Maxi reappeared with a tray. "It's like an explosion of color. How do you do it?"

"Time and patience," Maxi replied with a smile, setting the tray on a table between two wicker rockers. "And the weather doesn't hurt. It's warm and humid—like a jungle. The challenge is to keep them from taking over."

Oliver trotted over, spun around a few times, and stretched out next to the table between them, looking up hopefully. Kate guessed she wasn't the only one who smelled the platter of lemon cookies on the tray.

Kate helped herself to a cookie and nibbled thoughtfully. "Wow, these are wonderful," she said, savoring the lemony flavor, sharp and sweet at the same time.

Maxi beamed. "My *abuela's* secret recipe. So 'secret' that she only shared it with anyone who asked her for it."

"If you ever give up gardening, you could give the Girl Scouts a run for their money."

"The garden is what makes them good," Maxi confessed. "The lemon syrup comes from these two trees," she said, pointing to the container pots. "Last year's harvest. Along with some herbs from my garden."

"Too bad Mr. Hepplewhite won't sell cookies in the bakery," Kate said, taking two more from the tray and slipping one to Oliver. "These are amazing."

"Gracias," she said, smiling widely. "Coming from you, that's a very big compliment. So you're from New York? What made you decide to come to Coral Cay?"

"I got voted off the island," Kate deadpanned. "Unfortunately, the island was Manhattan."

Maxi giggled.

"The restaurant I was working for folded. Turns out the owner had been embezzling. My apartment building went condo. And I called off my wedding."

"Sounds like a rough year," Maxi said.

"All in the same day," Kate said sheepishly.

"No!"

"A month before the wedding," Kate said, grinning.

"*¡Arroz con mango!*" Maxi said, her black eyes wide.

"Exactly. So I decided, what the heck—time for a change."

"That is super gutsy."

"Or super stupid. Jury's still out on that one. So tell me, what should I know about Coral Cay?"

"Ay, where to start. Right now the big news in town

is Stewart Lord. I saw his limo in front of the bakery yesterday. You met him, right?"

"Briefly," Kate said, wincing at the memory. "Apparently, he wanted to buy the place. What did he do for a living?"

"He called himself an 'entrepreneur,'" Maxi said, carefully pouring coffee into two tiny china cups. "Which, for him, meant making lots of noise and throwing around lots of money. Bought up blocks of property cheap, cheap, cheap. Then he would either build something and sell it off quick or flip the land. The locals used to call him Lord Stewart Lord. But only behind his back."

"Because it would have ticked him off?" Kate asked.

"Because he would have loved it," Maxi said, shaking her head. "He craved attention, that one. Good or bad. And it was usually bad."

"Yeah, he seemed like a real charmer. So what do you know about him?"

"Not much," Maxi said. "He was originally from London, of course. You could hear it in his voice. Just like you hear a tiny bit of Santiago de Cuba in mine," she said, smiling. "He became a big shot in South Florida after the hurricanes a few years ago. Blew in with cash when people were so desperate. He made a fortune."

"So basically a total slimeball?"

"He wanted downtown Coral Cay," she said quietly.

"Which part?"

"All of it," Maxi said. "Every bit. He had some kind of big plan to 're-energize downtown,'" she said, forming air quotes with her hands. "The rumor was he really wanted to level it to expand the resort area. More hotels. Condos, casinos, maybe even a private airport. Is it horrible to think that it's not so bad he's gone?" She quickly crossed herself.

Kate took a sip of the inky black liquid in her cup. Hot and bitter, it numbed her tongue.

"Oh, *corazón,* no! You can't drink it like that. It needs sugar," Maxi said, laughing as she ladled a few teaspoons of large brown crystals into the cup.

Oliver, on the alert, raised his head.

"Lots of sugar—and a little coconut cream," she said dropping two large spoonfuls of white fluff into the steaming liquid. "Now try it."

"Ooooh, that is good. I could seriously get used to this."

"It's addictive," Maxi said with a grin. "And super good with chocolate, too."

"You're a bad influence," Kate said, surreptitiously slipping another cookie to Oliver and grabbing a third for herself. "Like I don't have enough chocolate in my life. Another caffeine-laced delivery system is all I need. So what did Stewart Lord want with the Cookie House? It doesn't seem like his kind of place."

"He thought it was the weak link," Maxi said, settling back into her rocker. "Because of Sam. Lord figured if he could get one piece of property downtown, he could collect the rest. Like that board game. The one with the candy-colored money."

"Monopoly? But why would Hepplewhite be the weak link? I mean, the place is a little run-down. Outside, anyway. But he does a good business."

Maxi shook her head, frowning. "Not the bakery so much as Sam himself. When Cookie died, he changed. I think he kind of gave up."

"Cookie was his wife?"

"Yeah. The Cookie House was their dream. Retire to a beach town. Open a bakery. And just enjoy the heck out of life. And that's exactly what they did. Ay, I wish you could have seen it then. The place was known for its desserts. Even the resorts bought stuff there."

"Desserts? Hepplewhite sold desserts?"

"That was Cookie," Maxi said. "Her real name was Ginger. She was magic. She did all kinds of cakes and tarts and pastries. So good! She really knew her pastry. And she absolutely charmed the customers. Sam baked the breads and kept the books. The place was a landmark. Everyone who visited Coral Cay stopped at the Cookie House."

"Those must have been her things I found," Kate said. "Packed away in the storeroom. Boxes of pastry-baking tools and books."

Maxi nodded. "She died three years ago. And it was like the light went out of Sam. He couldn't bring himself to make her sweets. And he didn't want to see someone else doing it, either. It hurt too much."

"I'm surprised he didn't sell the place and leave."

"The Cookie House is the one piece of her he has left. He's not about to give it up."

Maxi took a long sip of coffee. "Have you seen the stained-glass window upstairs?"

"In the bathroom? The red flower?"

"It's a ginger flower. When they first bought the shop, Sam and Cookie lived over the store. And Sam had that installed as a surprise for her."

"That is seriously romantic."

Maxi giggled. "I know, right? You'd never know it to look at *mi padrino,* but he's a real sweetheart."

"So what's with the metal detector on the beach?"

Maxi smiled. "That's easy. The two of them used to love beachcombing together. Do that alone and you look like a lonely old man."

"But carry a metal detector and you're a treasure hunter."

Maxi nodded.

Kate shook her head. "I had no idea."

She looked down. Oliver was dozing. With a little smile on his face.

As Maxi refilled their cups, a police cruiser sped down the street, stopping in front of the Cookie House. Kyle Hardy climbed out of the car, straightened his belt, and marched purposefully toward the bakery.

Alarmed, Kate glanced over at Maxi, who paused mid-pour.

"Maybe I better get back," Kate said, rising.

"I'll go with you," Maxi added quickly.

With Oliver at their heels, the two crossed the front lawn.

"You wait here," Kate said to Oliver, pointing at a bench on the bakery's front porch. "We'll be right back."

"Where is she, Sam?" Hardy was asking when they walked through the front door. Hands on hips, he turned sharply when he saw Kate. "Ms. McGuire, we need to talk."

"Don't be a donkey, Kyle. She has nothing to do with this."

"Nothing to do with what?" Kate asked.

"Those cinnamon pastries that Stewart Lord got here," Hardy said. "You're a pastry chef. Did you make them?"

Kate started to answer.

But Hepplewhite cut her off. "I made them. They were for me. A snack. For the beach."

"Don't give me that, Sam. I know you don't make pastries. And this one," Hardy said, jerking his thumb at Kate, "that's her specialty. Why are you covering for her?"

"I made them, Kyle," Hepplewhite insisted. "Used scraps from the morning's bread dough. She doesn't bake here. Just minds the counter. And that's what she did all morning. Never even came into the kitchen when I was baking them."

"What about when you were icing them?" Hardy asked harshly.

Hepplewhite shook his head. "I was in the kitchen alone. Only came out when Lord showed up and started raising Cain. Brought the rolls with me and sent her out."

Hardy exhaled, looking back and forth between the baker and Kate. "Whose idea was it to give the rolls to Stewart Lord?"

"His idea," Hepplewhite said. "Lord's."

Kate nodded. "I was listening from the kitchen. Lord was awful. He goaded Mr. Hepplewhite into giving him the rolls. But what difference does it make?"

"Is that true, Sam?"

Hepplewhite nodded. "I packed 'em up and handed 'em over. Didn't even charge the double-dealin' snake."

"Think about this very carefully, Sam," Hardy pronounced sternly, planting his hands on his hips. "Your statement is that you made the rolls, you iced the rolls, and you were the only one who came near the rolls. And you were the one who packaged them and gave them to Stewart Lord?"

"That's what I've been saying, Kyle."

"But why does this matter?" Maxi asked. "The man had a heart attack down the street. Why does it matter who gave him sweet rolls first?"

"Stewart Lord didn't have a heart attack," Hardy said, reaching for the handcuffs on his belt. "Steward Lord was poisoned. And the poison was in those cinnamon rolls."

He stepped toward the baker, deftly spun the old man around, and cuffed his hands neatly behind his back.

Hepplewhite's eyes went wide. His mouth dropped

open as his shoulders sagged. He knew what was coming but could only shake his head mutely.

"Samuel Hepplewhite, I'm arresting you for the murder of Stewart Lord. You have the right to remain silent."

Chapter 8

"Kyle! You don't have to handcuff Sam!" Maxi said, confronting the baby-faced officer. "You know him. He's not going to run."

"Procedure, Mrs. Más-Buchanan," Kyle said briskly. "He may have had a good reason, but he killed a man."

"But he didn't," Maxi insisted. "You know him. You know he didn't do it."

"That's not what the evidence says. And we have to follow the evidence. You're married to an assistant state attorney. You of all people know that," he said, marching a mute Sam Hepplewhite out to the squad car.

Maxi and Kate followed them down the walkway. Oliver hopped off the bench and trotted after them. The breeze had picked up, and Kate could smell ozone on the salt air. Off in the distance, she glimpsed dark clouds. A storm was coming.

"Your evidence is wrong," Sam rasped. "I didn't do it!"

"I'm gonna lock up the place, Sam," Kyle said quietly when they reached the curb. "Where're the keys?"

"My pocket," Sam replied, his voice like gravel.

"Sam, don't worry about a thing!" Maxi called, running up to Sam. "We'll get you a lawyer. And I'll meet you at the station."

Hepplewhite nodded.

Kyle gently retrieved a ring of keys from the baker's baggy jeans pocket, tucked him into the car, and firmly shut the door.

Oliver, sitting on his haunches on the grass near the curb, watched the car and whined softly. The little noises went up in pitch at the end. A question?

Kate saw Kyle fish something out of the front seat and sprint past her back up the walk. When he got to the porch, he shut the door firmly and locked it. Then he peeled off strips of yellow and black, pasting them across the doorframe.

Crime scene tape.

Kate looked at the police car and saw Hepplewhite's face collapse. The baker crumbled forward in his seat. She was afraid he might have fainted.

She bounded up the walkway behind the cop.

"Kyle, is that really necessary?" Kate asked quietly. "This is going to kill Sam. And his business. Look at him. You're hurting him."

He turned and stared at her. His face was bright pink, his crew cut like mown straw.

"You want to confess, Little Miss Pastry Chef? Because I don't for one minute believe you're innocent. As sure as I'm standing here, you had a hand in this."

"I didn't. I don't even know Steward Lord."

"Yeah, well, we'll see about that. Here's what I do know: It was you, or it was Sam. Or maybe it was the two of you together. Maybe you lured a lonely old guy into doing your dirty work for you. Right now, as of this minute, I have enough evidence to haul him in and close the bakery. But don't get too comfortable. With any luck, I'll be back for you soon."

"Isn't this the part where you tell me not to leave town?" Kate said deadpan.

"I was kinda hoping you would," he said, looking at her through slitted eyes before lowering the Ray-Bans back onto his face. "Because that would give me probable cause to arrest you, too."

Kyle Hardy turned his back on Kate, strode to the edge of the porch, planted his feet, and put his hands on his hips. "This place is a crime scene," he announced loudly to no one in particular. "Until our investigators are done with it, no one goes in or out. The Cookie House is closed until further notice!"

Chapter 9

As the squad car crawled away from the curb, Kate's eyes followed it down the street. When she finally turned back and faced the front door of the Cookie House, bandaged in yellow and black tape, another thought struck: She was homeless.

All of the belongings that were most dear to her—from her toothbrush to her recipe journals—were locked in that upstairs room. All she had were the clothes on her back.

As if reading her mind, Oliver was standing next to her, his shoulder to her leg. He leaned against her and looked up. She reached down and stroked his soft, silky flank.

Across the yard, Maxi was pacing with a cell phone to her ear. She gestured with her left hand as she spoke. Kate couldn't hear the words. But whatever the florist was saying, she was emphatic.

She clicked off, fast-walking toward Kate and Oliver.

"One of the few places I can sometimes get a signal," Maxi explained with a shrug. "I think it's the tree."

"More bad news?" Kate asked tentatively.

"No, I called Peter. *Mi amor* is an assistant state attorney. And he likes Sam. He's calling in a lawyer he knows to meet *mi padrino* at the police station. Still, I want to be there, too. Want to ride with me?"

"Yeah, that might be a good idea," Kate said, remembering the steaming wreck that was now her most valuable worldly possession.

Three hours later, they were still sitting in the lobby of the Coral Cay police department. Kate was just happy she wasn't in an interrogation room. But she could feel Kyle Hardy's laser gaze every time he walked into the room.

With its stucco façade and terra-cotta tile roof, the Coral Cay police station could have passed for a smaller, slightly more worn guesthouse. Which it kind of was, Kate reasoned.

No one would let her or Maxi speak with Sam. Or even tell them what was happening. But they knew Sam's lawyer was with him. Somewhere in the bowels of the building.

Kate remembered the notebook full of her work references from his kitchen. Sam didn't care if she could bake. But it mattered to him that she was honest. Someone planning a murder wouldn't care. A killer would just as soon have someone who was a little shady to take the blame.

And she remembered something else. The look of relief on Sam's face when he came into the bakery after the robbery. At that point, he hadn't known if anything had been taken from his shop. Only that she was OK. And he'd stayed in the bakery that night—and come in early the next—just so she'd feel safe.

Whatever else was going on, Kate was rock-solid certain of one thing: Sam Hepplewhite was no killer.

Chapter 10

Maxi plunked the paper cup of cold coffee decisively on the worn wooden table. "We need to see Sam," she said. "He needs to know that we're here. That we're on his side."

Kate nodded. But she half-expected to hear that Sam couldn't—or wouldn't—have visitors.

"Given the fact that Kyle seems to believe I'm involved, it might be better if you asked about us visiting Sam," she reasoned.

"That *bobo*!" Maxi said. To Kate's puzzled expression, she added, "He's a moron."

Maxi stepped up to the glass partition, drew herself up to her full height, and smiled brightly. "Hi, Ray, we're here to see Sam Hepplewhite. We've already cleared it with his lawyer."

"Hey, Maxi," the cop behind the desk greeted her cheerfully. He pulled out a clipboard and ran his finger down the list. "Yup, you're good to go. Sam's lawyer put you on the visitors list. Along with someone named Kate McGuire. She here, too?"

"Yes—that's me."

A few minutes later, they were seated on folding chairs in front of Sam's cell. And Kate now understood why people called jails 'graybar motels.' Everything was, indeed, gray. The walls, the ceiling, the floors. The bars. And Sam.

Steel shelves that served as benches lined three walls. And there was a stainless-steel commode shoehorned into one corner.

Sam, in a faded navy jumpsuit, sat alone in the cell on the far-left bench. Near the bars. Farthest from the toilet.

As if he was waiting for a ride home, Kate thought. Had they told him he didn't make bail? That he'd be staying until the trial? Or longer?

"Hey, Sam, we just wanted to stop by and see if there's anything we can bring you," Maxi said brightly.

"Nope. I'm fine."

"Oh sure, you say that now. But tonight I'm making spicy *fricasé de pollo,* fluffy rice, and fried plantains. How about I bring you some of that for an early lunch tomorrow?"

He shook his head vigorously. "Don't need it. 'Sposed to get three squares here."

"What about a few of your things?" Maxi said gently. "A couple of books? Maybe your shaving kit?"

Sam shook his head again. "Doesn't matter. Don't think it's allowed, anyway."

Kate noticed the old baker never made eye contact. He seemed to be addressing a spot on a far wall instead of them.

"They shut down the Cookie House," Kate said quietly.

Sam's eyes went wide. He looked at her for the first time. Like he actually saw her. "No," he mouthed.

Kate nodded. "They declared it a crime scene. Kyle won't tell us anything, other than it's closed for now."

"Kyle is a damned—" Sam said before he caught himself. "He can't. That's the only part of her I . . ." Then he stopped again, looking down.

"I didn't do it," he said finally. "What good would that do?"

"We know that," Maxi said soothingly. "And the whole town's going to know it, too."

"Not that lawyer of mine," Sam spat. "Wants to tell the world I'm nuttier than a fruitcake."

Whatever ailed Sam Hepplewhite, his mind was in perfect working order. Clearly, though, the rest of him had given up—body and soul. He didn't care what he ate. Or how he looked. Or even if he had a few belongings to brighten his cell. And the only thing that did matter to him was swathed in crime scene tape.

"What if we could keep the bakery up and running?" Kate said. It popped out of her mouth before she even realized she'd said it. "Just until you get out."

Sam's body sagged against the gray wall. His face relaxed. He opened his blue eyes and looked straight at her. "You'd do that? Could you?"

Maxi smiled and looked at Kate. "I could help," she said. "The flower shop is right next door. Of course, that dead bush in your window box? That *chica* is so gone!"

Kate took a deep breath. She looked at a tentative, hopeful Sam, then back at Maxi.

"Well, I am kind of between jobs right now. If you're OK with me being there and running the place, I can do it. But I don't know when the police will let us reopen. Or what kind of hoops we'll have to jump through first."

"I'm not some charity case," Sam said defiantly. "I can pay you. I have a little money in savings. . . ."

Kate smiled. If Sam's pride was returning, that was a good sign.

"Woo-hoo!" Maxi said, grinning. "We're gonna run a bakery."

"I'm going to hold you to that, partner," Kate said, shaking her hand. "We're going to run a bakery."

Chapter 11

"Could you drop me off at the resort area?" Kate said as they climbed into Maxi's battered Jeep. "I'm gonna book into the hotel tonight. Just until I can get back into the Cookie House."

"I've heard bad things about that ritzy resort," Maxi said. "Bedbugs the size of roaches. Roaches the size of rats. And rats the size of dogs."

Kate grinned. "Yeah, that explains all the celebrities I've seen around the pool this week."

"Seriously, those resort cooks couldn't fry a plantain if their lives depended on it. The place is too white bread. You need a taste of the real Coral Cay. How about an authentic home-cooked meal served on a big picnic table under a grapefruit tree?"

"I can't ask you to do that. It's already so late. And you've got a family."

"Right, so what's one more person at dinner? Obviously, I was teasing about the bugs and the rats, but if you're gonna stay, you need to start eating local. The resorts are great, but they're ex-pen-sive. And bland, bland, bland. A little *cubana* food will put a smile on your face. And the guest bedroom is lovely, if you don't mind Star Wars drapes."

"I can't put your kids out. Or your husband. The resort is just for tonight. Then I can get back to the Cookie House. All my things are there in the storeroom, anyway."

"Whoa, girl, I hate to tell you. But I was talking with Ray. And he says the bakery's gonna be closed for a few more days, at least. And some of your stuff's at the crime lab. But look at the bright side."

"What's that?"

"I know a very stylish *cubana* who can loan you some threads. Only—what is it the rich ladies say—'gently worn.' And our local drugstore stays open late, so you can pick up some toothpaste and stuff."

Kate remembered Ball Cap Man. What if he was after her? What if he followed her to Maxi's house? If this whole situation with Sam was somehow her fault, that was bad enough. But she couldn't get Maxi's family involved.

"I can't. I'm sorry."

"OK, is it the spicy Cuban food or the Star Wars drapes?"

Kate laughed. Why did she feel like she could tell Maxi anything without being judged?

"The truth is, I think I'm being followed. I know it sounds paranoid. But I'm afraid it could be connected with the break-in at the bakery. I saw the guy sporadically for a week or so before that. But that afternoon I saw him a bunch of times. He was driving a rental about a half a block back when my car conked out. And later when I walked to the bakery, he was on foot, too. Like he was trailing me. Then, during my job interview, he parked himself on a bench right across the street. I really hope I'm wrong. But if I'm not, I don't want him following me to your house. I'll be safe at the resort. They have lots of security. And your family will be safer that way, too."

"Did you get a good look at this guy?"

"Not really. Just from a distance. I think I've seen him a lot over the past week. Always wears big sunglasses and a different hat. It's possible it's all my imagination. And when Kyle was so convinced the break-in was a teenaged prank, I didn't mention it. I was hoping I was wrong. I wanted to be wrong. I should have said something."

"Stop blaming yourself. And Kyle is an idiot. Why they're letting him anywhere near Lord's murder is the real mystery."

"It's possible this guy is just some tourist visiting the same small town who wants to see a lot of the same things I do," Kate reasoned. "But I don't know. And after the break-in, I admit I'm spooked. I don't want to take any chances. And you have a family to protect."

Maxi nodded. "You need to talk to Peter. He works with this stuff all the time. Come for dinner. You can talk to him, then we'll drive you to your hotel. Deal?"

"Deal."

Chapter 12

The minute they opened the front door to Maxi's house, the florist was mobbed by a gang of children. Most of them, it turned out, her own.

"Can Zachary stay for dinner?" begged the larger of two boys. Kate pegged his age around seven. "Mama, please? Please? I told him how good *fricasé de pollo* is, and he doesn't be-lieve me! Please?"

Kate looked over and saw the other boy—also around seven—standing off to the side. Looking eager. Zach.

"Mama! Mama! Mama!" said a younger boy of perhaps five while bouncing on sturdy short legs. "I got a sticker at nap time! On my arm! Wanna see? Wanna see? Mama! It's got a truck on it!"

Meanwhile, the youngest, a little girl of maybe two, grabbed the leg of Maxi's white jeans and hung on for dear life. She looked up at Kate with wide, dark eyes and grinned.

"And Zach's never had fried plantains. Can you be-lieve it? Not even once!"

"Well, Miguelito, we need to expand Zach's culinary education," Maxi said as she swung the little girl up onto her hip, and planted a kiss on her cheek. "Zach, we would love to have you stay for dinner. Call your mom and make sure it's OK. And tell her we can bring you home after."

"Yahoo! I told you she'd say it was OK!" Michael hooted. "C'mon, you can call her in my room!" And with that, the two raced off.

Still cradling the little girl, Maxi bent down and examined the sticker on her younger son, who had traded hopping for rocking up and down on his tiptoes. On closer inspection, Kate realized the "sticker" was actually a Band-Aid.

"Well, that is lovely, Javie! How did you get that?" Maxi asked, kissing him on the forehead and ruffling his wavy black hair.

"Jessica bit me," he reported glumly.

"Did she now? I'm guessing there's a note from your Miss Maxwell?" Maxi asked.

Javie nodded. "She says you need to sign it. And I'm s'posed to bring it to her tomorrow."

"Mmmm," Maxi said. "Is this the same Jessica who stole your cupcake at Bobby's birthday party?"

Javie bobbed his head. "Miss Maxwell says she likes me. But I think she's yucky!"

"I know a Jessica myself," Kate said sotto voce. "My ex-fiancé's new 'friend,'" she explained with air quotes. "I'm with Javie on this one."

Sensing a kindred spirit, Javie looked up at Kate, nodding earnestly.

Maxi giggled. "OK, for you, my young sir, peroxide and lots of it. Go wash that out, and I'll meet you in the bathroom. And 'wash' means 'use soap.' *Jabón*!"

"Yes, Mommm," he replied, springing away.

When he left the room, Maxi said, "Let's hope Miss Jessica has had her shots."

"Amen to that," Kate said with a smile.

Looking around, Kate was amazed at how much Maxi's house was like Maxi herself: bright, happy, and comfortable. Sun streamed through sparkling windows. And every nook and corner seemed to host a thriving plant or colorful flowers. While there were toys all over the place—and constant noise—it was happy chaos.

The fragrance wafting from the kitchen made Kate's mouth water. Savory and spicy. Meaty. That's when she realized that they had both missed lunch.

"So has your *abuela* gotten you a snack, Elena?" Maxi asked the elf in her arms. "Could you eat a little sliver of something while I finish dinner?"

The littlest Más-Buchanan nodded vigorously.

"I thought so," Maxi said. To Kate she said, "You must be starved. I know I am."

"I'd love to help with dinner," Kate volunteered. "How'd you like a trained sous chef? Then maybe I could learn the secret to *pollo,* uh . . ."

"Spicy *fricasé de pollo,*" Maxi added with a grin. "It's like chicken stew. Only better. And it's my mother's recipe. She's been simmering it all afternoon. It should be falling off the bone by now. Oh, it smells so good! After I tend to Javie, I'm gonna put on the rice, fry up some plantains, and spell her in the kitchen for a while. If I can get her to leave. Course, if I tell her she's being replaced by a professional chef we're going to have one angry *cubana*. Better you just drink a glass of wine and keep me company. And we can do a little pre-dinner 'tasting' to make up for lunch."

"Well, if you insist."

"If it makes you feel better, you can help set the table."

"From pastry chef to busing tables in two short

weeks," Kate said, grinning. "My teachers at the institute would be absolutely horrified."

"Hey, the plates and glasses may not match, but the food is *muy buena*. None better. *Mi mami* is a first-class cook."

"Oh yeah," Kate said when she finally got a taste of the spicy chicken stew. "Your mom could open a restaurant. This is seriously good!"

"Right?" said Maxi as she slipped a forkful into her mouth and closed her eyes. "It's not just Cuban food. It's goood Cuban food."

"*Deja algo para la cena!*" A female voice from the den. Stern.

Maxi giggled. "She's telling us to leave some for dinner," she said softly. "Flashback to high school. *¡Si, mami! ¡Es tan buena! ¡Muy buena! ¡Y nos perdimos el almuerzo!*" To Kate she said, "I told her we missed lunch. And that we love her cooking."

"Definitely. She could teach a class. I've worked with pros who never made anything this delicious. But are you sure she's OK with having extra people at the table?"

"We always have extra people at the table. Peter, the kids, *mi mami*—somebody's always bringing friends. It's part of the reason we put a large table in the yard."

"Part of the reason?"

"Under that big tree in the evening, you get the best breezes. Even in the heat of the summer. Like natural air-conditioning. You have to be careful in November and December, though."

"Why?" Kate wondered if there was another spate of hurricanes late in the year.

"Grapefruits. You're sitting there minding your own business—and plunk! She drops one right on your head. Like big, hard softballs. I threatened to make the kids wear helmets. Peter talked me out of it. So we just keep her plucked—like constantly—during the season. On the bright side, lots of grapefruit juice and grapefruit ice and grilled fruit. Grilled is the best. Peter cuts them in half and throws them on the grate till they have those char marks. And I pop them on a platter and drizzle them with a little honey. Yum!"

They both heard the front door open and slam. "Hey, babe! Whatever that is, it smells great!"

"Ah, *mi amor*," Maxi said with a grin. "I'll be right back."

Kate cradled her half-empty wineglass, looked around the warm kitchen, and wondered: Could she and Evan have ever ended up like this? Contented and cozy? If she could have convinced him to visit Coral Cay? If he hadn't met Jessica?

Doubtful.

Evan was Evan. That's why she'd fallen for him. And why it never would have worked. Not long term, anyway.

He must have realized that, too. Lately his phone calls had tapered off. At first, right after she'd thrown the engagement ring at him that horrible night, he'd phoned a dozen times every day. And sent flowers. Gradually, as she refused to answer (and refused the flowers), that dropped to a few calls a day. Then once every day or so. And in the past week: nothing.

Technically, she'd ended the engagement. But it was still painful. Raw.

She was almost glad that her phone was locked in the Cookie House. If she couldn't see it, she didn't have to deal with it.

The heck with it, and the heck with him, she decided. *This isn't what could have been. This is where I am* right now. *And I'm going to eat dinner under a grapefruit tree. Evan Thorpe can't do that in Manhattan. No matter who he's with.*

"OK," Maxi said, reappearing. "Peter's going to get the troops washed and march them out to the table. And you've already set that, so we're good to go."

She grabbed the wine bottle from the fridge, turned to Kate, and grinned. "Pastry chef or no, one good Cuban meal can change your whole life."

Chapter 13

Maxi's dinner was every bit as good as promised. The light, savory rice sopped up the rich, spicy stew—which brought out the sweetness of the fried plantains. Everyone at the table had at least two helpings. Kate noticed that both Michael and Zach went back for thirds.

"Esperanza, your *fricasé* is *muy delicioso,*" Peter told his mother-in-law, refilling her wineglass. "*Fantástico!*"

"Gracias," she said, smiling shyly.

Kate was amazed at their outdoor "dining room." It looked like pictures she'd seen in Tuscan cookbooks. A big farm table under the trees, with a lush carpet of green and blooming flowers everywhere. The tree itself—herself?—sported a healthy profusion of shiny leaves. And if the verdant cloud was any indication of this year's crop, the Más-Buchanan kids might actually need those helmets.

But Maxi was right. The cool, salt-air breeze—laced with the scent of tropical flowers—was better than any air-conditioning.

Was it just a few weeks ago she was braving exhaust fumes and killer work hours in the city? She smiled. Coral Cay was definitely a move in the right direction.

With the kids gone from the table, followed by Esperanza (who went inside to watch her "stories"), the three of them had lingered. Enjoying the cool of the evening.

"Maxi says you have a bit of a problem," Peter said quietly. "A stalker."

"I don't know what he is. Or who he is. I only know I started seeing him a day or so after I arrived in Coral Cay. Regularly. The afternoon of the break-in, I saw him more than usual. And that break-in? It wasn't teenagers."

"OK," Peter said encouragingly. "And you know this because?"

"Because no teenager I've ever met wears hard shoes. I heard the footsteps across the kitchen floor. It was a man. One heavy-footed man."

"This guy you saw. When you spotted him that day, what was he wearing?" Peter asked.

"Tan ball cap, khaki shorts. Some kind of a Hawaiian shirt. Medium blue, I think. And sunglasses. Always big sunglasses."

"So probably no hard shoes."

"You're right," Kate said. "Unless he went home to change. And you wouldn't put on dress shoes for a break-in. Just the opposite."

"So your stalker probably isn't your robber," Peter concluded.

"Wait, you believe me? About the stalker? You don't think I'm crazy?"

"The man lives with me, my mom, and three kids," Maxi said, leaning forward. "He's seen crazy up close and personal. No offense, but you don't qualify."

Peter smiled and sipped his coffee.

"Look, in my experience, women have pretty good

radar," he said finally. "And this guy's tripped yours, for some reason. The animal part of your brain—the part that senses danger—is trying to tell you something. My advice is 'listen to it.' Take some precautions. Don't go off by yourself. And I'll talk to Ben. That way, if you see the guy again you can phone the station. Ben doesn't have to pick him up or arrest him to have a chat and find out who he is."

"What about the burglar?" Maxi interjected.

"Unfortunately, that was Kyle's case. And he bungled it. Didn't even take fingerprints."

"*Bobo*," Maxi concluded.

"Grade A prime *bobo,*" Peter agreed.

Now Kate was smiling. Seeing these two together, she couldn't help herself. Peter was calm and unflappable. Maxi was a hummingbird—constant motion and energy. Yin and yang.

"The bakery is closed for now," Peter said. "And I hear they're gonna be patrolling that block pretty heavily, too. Regular crawl cars. So if your burglar wants to try it again, let him."

"What about Sam?" Maxi said. "Can we get him released? At least before the trial?"

"You know I can't talk about that."

Maxi gave him a look.

"I'm just glad it's not my case. I'd have to recuse myself."

"Only if you wanted a wife to come home to," Maxi said with a smile "He didn't do it. You know he didn't."

"I can't picture the Sam I know doing that. He's family. He's sat right here at this table more times than I can count. And Stewart Lord was a sadistic bully. It wasn't enough for him to get what he wanted, he liked to break people. He'd been after Sam—and the bakery— for a while. Maybe Sam just snapped. I mean, in this case, I almost wouldn't blame him."

"Temporary insanity?" Kate asked.

"More like temporary sanity," Peter said. "Lord was what his own countrymen call 'a nasty piece of goods.' Did you ever meet him?"

"Once. I was working the counter when he came in that morning. He started leering, and suddenly Sam was there shooing me out of the room."

Peter nodded. "That's both of them in a nutshell."

Kate wrapped both hands around her coffee cup as a birdcall pierced the night air. If she hadn't left—if she'd waited on Stewart Lord—would Sam be safe at home right now?

"So if the burglar is after the bakery and not you, why don't you stay here until the bakery reopens?" Maxi asked. "Trust me, no one in his right mind is gonna break into this place."

"Only if I can help out around the house," Kate said. "How about I start by baking up a batch of cookies? I mean, if you don't mind someone else in your kitchen."

"Are you kidding?" said Maxi. "Anyone who wants to cook in my kitchen is welcome to it."

Chapter 14

"If you don't mind cartoon characters, I can find you a new toothbrush," Maxi said. "You have your choice of SpongeBob or Batman. And I've got some pj's and a robe that should work. Brand new from my Tar-zhay collection. Stylish, yet practical."

"Definitely Batman," Kate said. "And I don't know how to thank you. Your poor boys are getting kicked out of their room. They're going to hate me."

"Say it with cookies. Seriously, they're so excited. We're calling it a 'camp-out sleepover' in the living room. Complete with a tent. Which Peter is struggling to put up right now. Zach's mom even said he could spend the night."

"Camp-out sleepover, eh? That calls for some special cookies. Maybe something with a s'mores theme. And chocolate chip cookies as a backup. Everybody loves chocolate chip."

"I'm just gonna sit here at the bar and watch you work," Maxi said with a grin. "Sweetest deal ever."

"Your kitchen is great," Kate said, appraising the surroundings. "I haven't been able to bake since I packed up and left Manhattan. And I've really missed it."

"Did your home have a big kitchen?" Maxi asked, pulling cookie sheets, mixing bowls, spoons, and a sifter out of the cupboards. She opened a different door and lifted out flour, two kinds of sugar, and two yellow bags of Nestlé's chips.

"Tiny. It was one corner of an efficiency apartment. All in one room," Kate added. "Nineteen fifties white Formica everywhere. But the fridge and the stove were new. And I loved it. It's where I perfected my recipes before I baked them at the restaurant."

Kate surveyed the ingredients and smiled. "Got any marshmallows or chocolate bars?"

Maxi walked to the pantry, retrieved a step stool, and put it next to the refrigerator. She climbed up, opened a top cupboard, and produced a bag of marshmallows, along with three giant chocolate bars.

"My secret stash," she explained.

"It's for a good cause, I swear," Kate said with a grin. "I made these once before. For a Halloween party. The kids loved them. The base is like a snickerdoodle, without the cinnamon. And with a lot less sugar. But the cookie has the same tang and the same texture. And on top, melted chocolate and a toasted marshmallow. Last time, I used a blowtorch from the restaurant. But I think we can get the same effect with the broiler, if I do it right."

"That sounds delicious. I'll eat any of the burned ones."

"Good, because I'm in a new oven at a different altitude. I might scorch the first batch. But don't tell anyone."

"Please! Around here, we eat the mistakes. Peter calls

those my 'flop cakes.' They taste good. They just look weird."

Kate quickly learned that it's impossible to keep baking cookies a secret in a house full of children. Twenty minutes later, she had a full audience in attendance.

"That smells good," Michael said. "What is it?"

Kate looked at Maxi, who nodded. "We're calling them camp-out cookies," Kate said. "They're topped with melted chocolate and toasted marshmallows."

"All right!" said Zach.

"Cool!" said Michael.

"Yeah, cool!" said Javie.

"Cookies!" said Elena. "Cookie, cookie, cookie," she sang.

"That's right, love," Maxi said. "Cookie, cookie, cookie."

Kate pulled out the first batch. So far, so good.

"OK, who wants to help me top them with chocolate and marshmallows?" she asked as she put the cookie sheets onto tea towels she'd set out on the counter.

The kids answered her with a chorus of "me, me, me!" and Maxi gave each one a hand wipe. "Can't be too careful," she said, winking.

"OK, now the cookies are really hot, so you don't want to touch them. Just drop a piece of chocolate on top, and then one of these big marshmallows."

"Then can we eat them?" Javie asked.

"Then we pop them back into the oven for just a couple of minutes. Then we can eat them."

"That's the part I like," he said solemnly. His sister nodded.

"Soon, baby," Maxi said, hugging him. "Very soon."

With two adults and four kids, they were done in no time. Kate slid the two trays into the broiler, cranked it up, and crossed her fingers. This could go either way, she thought.

"OK, guys, check this out," she said. "If you peek through the window in the oven, you can watch the marshmallows toast. They're going to turn brown. That's when they're gooey and good."

For the first thirty seconds, nothing happened. Then, like a flower blooming, golden patches appeared on the tops of all the marshmallows, gradually deepening until they were a rich brown.

"Done!" Kate declared. "Everybody step way back."

"OK, kiddos! Everybody take a seat at the table," Maxi said protectively as Kate grabbed another tea towel and pulled the cookie sheets out of the oven, placing them carefully back on the counter.

"Can we eat them now?" Javie pleaded.

"Not quite yet," Kate said. "There's nothing hotter than a hot marshmallow. It'll really burn your mouth. Just give them a couple of minutes to cool and we're good to go."

"Just enough time to pour some milk," Maxi said. "Who wants some?"

When every hand shot up—including Elena's—she gave everyone a jelly jar and carefully filled each with cold milk.

Kate gingerly touched one of the cookies. It felt cool enough to try. She broke off a piece. Warm, melty, and wonderful. Done.

She grabbed a spatula, loaded the cookies onto a platter, and placed them in the middle of the kitchen table. "I think we have lift-off," she told the crowd.

"They smell good!" Zach said. "And they look like s'mores."

"Oh man!" Michael said, grabbing a cookie and taking a big bite.

"Dunk!" Elena declared, submerging the cookie in her glass. "Ooh, good cookie!"

"I don't think she's ever met a bad cookie," Maxi said with a wink. "But neither have I. Oh, *muy buena*! I watched you make these, every step, and I still don't know how they can taste this good. And the cookie part is so light!"

Kate beamed.

"I like camp-out cookies!" Javie said, snagging another one. "And I like camping out!"

Maxi put four cookies on a tray with two fresh glasses of milk and carried it into the next room "for *mi mami* and the tent builder." While she was gone, the kids polished off the remaining cookies.

When Javie grabbed the empty platter with both hands and licked it clean, Kate nearly strained a muscle trying not to laugh.

"Javier Peter Más-Buchanan, you put that down!" Maxi said charging back into the kitchen. "You know better than that. Now, all of you, what do you say to Miss Kate?"

"Thank you!" they all said in unison.

"Cookie, cookie, cookie," Elena cooed happily.

"OK, bath time for Javie and Elena! Miguel, you get a pass tonight, since you have a guest. And your father said to tell you the tent is ready and you can grab the sleeping bags from your closet."

"Awesome!" Michael said as he and Zach raced into the next room.

While Maxi readied her younger kids for bed and Peter entertained Michael and Zach with ghost stories, Kate kept baking. It felt good to be creating something again with her own hands. Useful.

She made a few batches of Toll House cookies, knowing the kids would love those, too.

As she mixed more dough, Kate thought about Sam—

and how he'd perked up when she volunteered to keep the bakery going. So just how was she going to do that?

Maxi planned to take him an early lunch of spicy chicken stew, plantains, and rice. Home-cooked comfort food. Cookies for dessert would be perfect. Normally. But what kind of cookies do you make for a man who hates cookies?

In all her years selling Girl Scout cookies and baking professionally, she'd never run into anyone who didn't love cookies. Whether they admitted it or not. One renowned Michelin-starred chef even kept a secret stash of Thin Mints in his tony restaurant's walk-in fridge. For emergencies.

Yet when Kate tried to get a read on Sam, she'd come up totally blank. A first.

For some reason, Oliver's soft, fuzzy face popped into her mind. She smiled.

Ginger snaps.

Did Maxi have all the ingredients? Kate did a quick check of the fridge and found a big jar of molasses. And in the pantry she discovered an industrial-sized jar of powdered ginger, along with plenty of cinnamon and cloves. And another one-pound bag of brown sugar.

Good to go.

She had just rolled out the dough and was cutting it into little rounds with a small glass when Maxi reappeared. The ends of her black pageboy were damp. And there were telltale wet spots on her fuchsia T-shirt.

"Bath time is a battle," she reported. "Even when they love the water. Oooooh, that smells good. Spicy."

"Ginger snaps. For Oliver and Sam."

"Oliver loves his ginger snaps," Maxi said. "And Sam loves them, too. Or used to. Before Cookie . . . um . . . passed. How did you know?"

"Call it a hunch. I figured I'd make a big batch and we

could tuck some in with Sam's lunch. And drop the rest off with Oliver's owner. Who is his owner, anyway?"

"Oliver owns Oliver," Maxi said. "He's sort of the town dog."

"But he has to live somewhere," Kate said.

Maxi shook her head. "Nope. He just showed up downtown one day. That was, gee, about three months ago. Oh, you should have seen him! He was just this little ball of cream-colored fluff," she said, holding her hands about a foot apart. "We didn't even know what he was exactly. Maybe a Labradoodle. Or a Goldendoodle. Even now, nobody knows for sure. And Oliver's not telling. But everybody wanted him, and a couple of folks tried to adopt him. He'd accept their hospitality for a couple of days. Then he'd take off. Course I thought what he really needed was a family with little kids. So then I brought him home. And he stayed more than a week—almost two. But one morning—poof! He was gone. Oliver loves everybody. But he never stays in one place too long. So he's become the town dog. Everyone puts out water for him. And feeds him. I give him regular baths at the flower shop, 'cause I have a hose and a big sink. He'll stay at different houses, a night or two at a time. Like a hotel. And there's a mobile vet clinic that comes through regularly. So I take him there for checkups and puppy shots. Annie Kim, our pharmacist, she gives him a heartworm pill once a month. But Oliver has basically decided he doesn't *belong* to anyone. He's kind of his own dog."

"That's why his tag says 'Coral Cay.'"

"Sam got that for him. Wanted to make sure people know he isn't a stray—that he has a home. He's microchipped, too. The address and phone number are the town hall. And we all paid for that. Heck, the last time Oliver got a round of puppy shots, ten different people were giving me money to cover it. So now the town clerk keeps an 'Oliver fund.'"

"And I thought New York had some odd stories," Kate said, smiling.

"You ain't seen nothing yet," Maxi said, covering a yawn with her hand. "Sorry, I was up so early. And I still have stuff to do. I'm gonna make some coffee. Cuban coffee. You want some?"

Kate remembered the strong, dark liquid from this morning. Was it only this morning? A little caffeine right now was exactly what she needed.

"That would be great. So have you told Peter that we're going to be running the bakery for a while?"

Maxi shrugged as she carefully measured the rich, pungent grounds. "I think he suspects something's up. Better I tell him later when we can talk. Right now, he's telling the boys scary stories. Using flashlights for a campfire. And I can't tell who's having more fun."

"I've been thinking," Kate started as she rolled out more dough. "If we're going to get people to come back to the Cookie House, we're going to need some pretty fancy marketing."

"I know what you mean. Sam *is* that bakery. Without his breads, the locals aren't going to come."

"Not only that," Kate added. "Everyone keeps mentioning 'bakery' and 'murder' in the same sentence. That's not exactly good for business."

"We need to clear Sam's name," Maxi declared, carefully setting the coffeepot on the stove.

"Exactly. I've only known the man a couple of days. But he's a gentle soul. Besides, poison? That's the weapon of a sneak. Whatever Sam's flaws, he's not a sneak."

Maxi giggled. "*Mi padrino* doesn't know how to be sneaky. He's too blunt. One more reason he's family to me. But there's something else. Something you need to know. Sam? He loved Cookie so much. She was his *corazón*. His heart. Using the Cookie House to kill someone? He'd never do that. Not even that horrible Stewart Lord."

Kate nodded. "That makes sense. Not in a way you can present to a jury. But I get it. Do you think the people here in Coral Cay believe he's innocent?"

"From what I know about this town, I think they're in two camps," Maxi said, holding up two fingers. "First, people like us, who know he didn't do it. And second, people like my Peter, who think there's a tiii-ny possibility but wouldn't blame him one little bit."

"So who really killed Stewart Lord?" Kate asked aloud.

Maxi snapped her fingers. "I have an idea. But we're gonna need more cookies. A lot more."

"Bribing a jail guard?" Kate said lightly.

Maxi shook her glossy head. "Better. I belong to a book club. Most of the members are local business owners. We read mysteries. And thrillers. A little true crime, too. We call ourselves the Coral Cay Irregulars. It's a good bunch, and it's fun. We get together once a month or so. Eat a little, talk books, talk business, talk mysteries . . ."

"Drink a little wine," Kate suggested.

"Oooh, the wine! That's the best part. Harper Duval hosts it. I don't think you've met him yet. He runs the local wine shop, and he's rich. Very wealthy. His house is . . . magnificent. He has a wine cellar, where we meet. Racks full of wine everywhere. Like a cave and climate controlled. Only, because it's South Florida, not a real cellar, like under the house. But it's fantastic," Maxi said, spreading her hands. "Like something from a movie. And the food! He puts out the most wonderful cheeses and meats. My favorite last time was this special aged ham, imported from Italy. And a buttery cheese from Denmark. So good. When we meet, everyone brings dishes to share. Only their very best. That's why we need your cookies. And *rápido*. The next meeting is Sunday afternoon. The day after tomorrow."

"I'll make as many as you need," said Kate, puzzled. "But how will that help Sam?"

"These people are smart. They see everything. They know this town. And they love mysteries. Who killed Stewart Lord? It's a mystery. A real mystery. And it happened right here. On our Main Street. We all knew the victim. We all know Sam. If you and I can persuade the club to look into it, maybe we can all put our heads together and solve this one."

Chapter 15

Harper Duval's house was everything Maxi had described. Only more.

A whitewashed Florida-style mansion with a baronial front porch, surrounded by pin oaks dripping in Spanish moss and a wrought-iron fence, it looked like it had been part of the landscape for at least 150 years.

Maxi swore it was less than a decade old. "Harper and Caroline built it right after they moved to town. Their dream house. You can't tell from here," she said, angling the car onto a grassy spot near the overcrowded driveway, "but it's on a bluff that overlooks the beach. You can see the water from almost every room."

"Wow, I'm guessing money was no object," Kate said.

"Nope. They're loaded. So when Harper volunteered to be the club's permanent host, we were thrilled. His home's almost as good as his food. The man has excellent taste. The funny thing is, I thought he might want to take a break while Caroline's away. But I think it helps him to keep busy."

"Away? Where did she go?"

"Rehab," Maxi said quietly. "For drinking."

"He runs a wine shop and his wife's an alcoholic?"

"I know, right? The shop has always been more his thing than hers. And they haven't decided what they're going to do with it when she gets back. But I'm guessing the wine cave will definitely have to go."

They fell silent for a moment, digesting this, as Maxi shifted the car into park, straightened the wheel, and pulled out the keys.

"Are you sure your club is OK with my crashing the party?" Kate said, smoothing an unruly lock of her caramel-colored hair. "I'm not a member. And I haven't read the book. I don't even know what the book is."

"*The Mysterious Affair at Styles.* And of course they won't mind. You're bringing them two things they can't resist: dessert and a mystery. Trust me, they'll love you."

Kate hoped her friend was right. She and Maxi had done some math and calculated they'd need about four dozen Toll House cookies for the meeting. So while Maxi spent Saturday morning at the flower shop, Kate hit Amos Tully's market for supplies.

After they dropped off Sam's lunch Saturday afternoon, Kate planned to go hunting for Oliver. To deliver her gift of ginger snaps. But when they walked out of the police station, he was there rolling in the grass. Like he'd been waiting for them.

After he scarfed the first three cookies, Kate managed to lure the half-grown puppy into Maxi's car.

"He'll stay for a while, just don't expect anything permanent," Maxi warned as they'd pulled into her driveway.

"I just wish someone had told me the same thing about Evan," Kate said with a smile.

She devoted most of the afternoon and evening to baking for the book club. With a few extra batches thrown in for the family, of course.

Besides, a certain amount of tasting was integral to the process, Kate reasoned. She had to make sure she hadn't lost her touch.

They'd packed their precious cargo into a collection of Maxi's large Pyrex dishes with colorful silicone lids. "It's the same stuff I use when we take food to Miami for family dinners," Maxi confessed. "Plenty big."

Now, as Kate stood in front of Harper Duval's palatial door, the butterflies in her stomach felt more like pterodactyls. She didn't know any of these people. She was invading a stranger's home to ask for a favor. A big favor.

Then she remembered Sam. Sitting alone in that gray cell. He'd looked so hopeful when she'd volunteered to run the bakery. He was counting on her. Counting on them.

Kate took a deep breath, squared her shoulders, stood up straight, and fixed a smile on her face. "Fake it till you make it," one of her culinary instructors always said. Well, she'd fake it until they succeeded. Until they freed Sam.

"Relax, partner, we can do this," Maxi said as she pressed the doorbell.

"Yup, we've got this," Kate agreed.

The man who opened the door was about four inches taller than Kate, though he probably had at least twenty years on her. His wavy light brown hair was thick and stylish, his clothes casual but expensive. He sported a blue blazer with white linen slacks. A lemon-yellow dress shirt, open at the neck, emphasized his tan.

"Maxi, welcome!" he said, stepping back. "So glad you could come. And you've brought a friend—fantastic!"

"Harp, this is Kate McGuire," Maxi said, walking into the two-story foyer replete with marble floors, a gold filigree mirror, and an enormous crystal chandelier. "She just moved to Coral Cay from New York. She's a pastry chef. Kate, this is Harper Duval, our host. He also runs In Vino Veritas, the best wine shop in Coral Cay."

"Of that I am guilty. And it's the only wine shop in Coral Cay. But I'll take my compliments where I can get them. And please, call me Harp."

"We come bearing cookies," Kate added shyly, holding up the dishes.

"Then by all means, please allow me to relieve you of your burdens, ladies," the man said affably, lifting the containers out of her hands. "And your timing is perfect. We're just opening the wine. Let me get you both a glass."

As their host turned to lead them into the house, Maxi and Kate exchanged glances. Maxi shrugged.

"We're set up in the wine cellar," Harp called over his shoulder, his deep voice offering just the suggestion of a refined southern accent. "And I hope you've brought your appetites, because we've got quite the spread. Maxi, I procured a hickory-smoked artisanal turkey from Vermont that I think you're going to love. And there's a beautiful roast of Wagyu beef. So tender you can cut it with a spoon. And Annie Kim brought some delectable-smelling scallion pancakes."

They walked into a caterer's kitchen. Kate scoped out the space and realized it was easily three times the size of the kitchenette in her Manhattan apartment.

Harper Duval grabbed a carafe from the counter and poured three glasses.

"See what you think of this," he said, handing them each a glass of the ruby liquid. "A very nice Napa Valley Zinfandel. Goes well with red meat, smoked foods, and, in my humble opinion, just about everything. If such a thing were possible, I'd have it flowing from the taps like water."

"For me that would be coffee," Kate said with a smile.

"Oh, this is good," Maxi said tasting it. "*Muy delicioso.*"

"It's lovely," Kate said, taking a sip and feeling its warmth spread from her mouth down to her core. "Thank you."

"The least I can do. Besides, what good are the finer things without friends to share them?"

Harp took another sip and smiled contentedly. Setting down the wineglass, he produced a large, round teak platter from the counter behind him. Opening each of the glass containers, he deftly arranged the cookies, adding layer on layer in a spiral until the result resembled a giant cookie flower.

"These smell magnificent," he said, stealing a glance at Kate. "Am I correct in assuming we have our new resident pastry chef to thank?"

"Absolutely," Maxi said. "Her cookies are fantastic. She's staying with us, and my kids are ready to adopt her."

Kate felt a blush spreading on her cheeks. She hoped it wasn't noticeable. "Nope, I had a lot of help with these. We wanted to make enough so that everyone could have a few," she explained.

"That's very generous. And we have a full contingent tonight. I think you'll get a kick out of it. Do you enjoy Agatha Christie?"

"I love her, but I have to admit, it's been a while."

"Don't worry about it. If you appreciate good food and a good mystery, you'll do just fine."

Harp picked up his glass in one hand and balanced the platter in the other. "Well, ladies, shall we commence to the cave?"

Chapter 16

If Kate hadn't known better, she'd have sworn they were standing in an actual cellar. Only steps from the caterer's kitchen, the Duvals' wine cave lived up to the name. The walls were plaster, the floor stone. The room was crafted with the kind of roughhewn handiwork that required piles of money to achieve. And it was cavernous. Truly a cave. Kate estimated at least a dozen guests, yet it didn't seem crowded in the least.

Wooden racks loaded with bottles lined the walls. Some were actually set into the walls. And while the wood glowed with polish and care, many of the bottles bore a light blanket of dust.

The air was chilly. The climate control that Maxi had mentioned? And there wasn't a single window. The only thing missing from a true cellar was a set of stairs.

Even with the abundant size of the room, Kate felt the same tingle of claustrophobia that had always shadowed her in Jeanine's dusty basement.

Fake it till I make it, fake it till I make it, she chanted silently in her mind as she took another sip of wine.

"Kate, this is Sunny Eisenberg," Maxi said. "She runs the yoga studio just off Main Street."

"We met at the bakery," Sunny said, clasping Kate's hand genially. "But you still haven't accepted my offer of a free class."

"Be careful," Maxi warned. "If anybody can get you hooked on yoga, it's Sunny. I drop in a couple of times a week."

"One of my prize pupils," Sunny said with a grin. "Horrible about the bakery. Word around town is they've arrested Sam? What on earth are they thinking? That man's no more a murderer than I am."

"We feel the same way," Maxi said, nodding. "In fact, we've promised to help him keep the bakery going until this mess gets straightened out."

"Good for you girls! Just let me know when you re-open; I'll stop by to pick up some goodies. Don't tell anyone, but I think Sam's yeast rolls are the real reason people show up for my six a.m. class. I put out a little spread afterward with local jam and butter. The students think I don't hear them, but they call it Stretch and Starch. And they pick the platters clean."

"Can a pastry chef make yeast rolls?" Maxi stage-whispered as Sunny moved out of earshot.

"Yeah, although I'm going to need to run a few practice batches of my breads. It's a lot more humid here."

"That matters? I thought that was—what's the phrase?—an old wives' tale."

"It matters like you wouldn't believe. But I know how to adjust. I'll just need a few run-throughs."

"My kitchen is at your command." Maxi giggled. "And I call dibs on any flop cakes. Oh, good. Rosie and Andre are here. You'll love them. They run an antique store. There are a couple in Coral Cay, but theirs is the best. As Time Goes By. Some really expensive stuff, but some bargains, too. Beautiful things you can really use. Not old tchotchkes. Oh, and some very nice jewelry."

Kate looked across the room and spied a handsome couple. Both looked to be in their mid-thirties. She was willowy and beautiful, with mocha-colored skin, close-cropped hair, and—at least to Kate's eyes—not a hint of makeup. Her husband was just as tall, olive skinned with a stocky build and a dark, slightly receding hairline. Each with a glass in hand, they leaned toward each other, laughing. A private joke. An intimate moment.

Kate smiled. "Do they know Sam?"

"Everyone here knows Sam. But yeah, they like him. And he's helped them out a couple of times. You've met Carl Ivers, right?" Maxi said, eyeing the ex-cop talking with Amos Tully and a statuesque African-American woman in a yellow watered-silk dress.

"Yeah, he changed the locks on Sam's doors after the break-in. Is that his wife?"

"Minette. She's a hoot. And a great cook. If you're lucky, they'll invite you for dinner. She brought a mac-and-cheese dish tonight that will make you cry. She crumbles crispy bacon over the top. And there's another flavor I can't place. It's the best. Anyway, Carl is gonna be primo for our mission. If we can get him on our side . . . ," Maxi added, letting the thought hang in the air.

"For what it's worth, he was decidedly unimpressed with Kyle's investigation of the break-in."

"See? That's a good sign."

"I hesitate to even ask, but is Kyle Hardy a member of your group?"

"Uh-uh. We have a strict 'no *bobo*' rule. Written right into the bylaws. Seriously, I don't think that boy is much of a reader. Ben drops by sometimes, when he can. But with everything going on in town, I don't think we're gonna see him for a while. And I'm kinda relieved."

"How come?"

"I don't think he's happy with Kyle, either. But he's very loyal. And he might feel he has to stand by the department. Whether he agrees or not."

"Who's the man talking with Harp?"

"That's Dr. Patel. Rakesh Patel. He's our town G.P. It would really help to get him on our side, too. He's super logical. What's the word Peter used? . . . 'Methodical.' And see the woman adjusting the dishes on the buffet table? That's Annie Kim. Her parents own the drugstore, and she joined them as the pharmacist a couple of years ago. She's also killer on a surfboard. That girl can dance on waves. She's won a couple of competitions. Huge Agatha Christie fan. In fact, she suggested tonight's book. It was Christie's very first."

"That's why it sounded familiar. I know I've read it. But it's been years."

Across the room, Harp smiled and raised his glass to them.

"Uh-oh, somebody likes you," Maxi said under her breath.

"He's married. And that's definitely not my type."

"I'm not saying he'd actually try anything," Maxi intoned, barely above a whisper. "But in the kitchen? He was looking at you like you were one of those bottles of red wine he likes so much."

"No, I think he was just being a good host," Kate protested. But the knot in her gut told her otherwise.

Harp was handsome. And he definitely had charisma. But the notion filled Kate with dread.

Truth be told, she still loved Evan. She'd left him.

She'd put fourteen hundred miles between them. And she wasn't going back. But she still loved him.

Besides, the last thing she needed was another playboy.

"Who's that?" she asked, inclining her chin toward the buffet table, where Annie was chatting with a solidly built woman with short salt-and-pepper hair.

"That's Barb Showalter. She owns the bookstore. Coral Cay Books. This club is her baby. Even though Harp is the host, she's the leader. La presidenta. And that young couple over there talking with Gabe? You definitely want to meet them. They run a really popular local pub. Right on Main Street. Oy and Begorra. One of Sam's biggest clients."

Gabe spotted Kate and Maxi and waved. Kate smiled and returned the gesture.

"Oy and Begorra?" Kate asked.

Maxi noticed her friend's puzzled expression. "Bridget O'Hanlon and Andy Levy. Newlyweds. Their restaurant is great. Like a real Irish pub and a great Jewish deli. All rolled into one. Peter and I eat there all the time. The brisket melts in your mouth. And it's affordable. Not like those places in resort town. The coffee's good, too. Not as good as mine. But close."

Kate took a deep breath, trying to release the tension she felt. What if they couldn't do this? What would happen to Sam?

She followed up with a small sip of wine.

Maxi patted her arm and smiled. "It's gonna be OK. These people are friends. We're just gonna share some good food and chat."

Kate nodded, repeating the mantra in her head.

"All right, ladies and gentleman," Harp intoned to the group. "The buffet line is officially open. Please help yourselves to this delicious repast." He held a half-empty carafe aloft. "And as you undoubtedly know already, around here the bar is never closed."

There were titters from the guests. Maxi and Kate exchanged a knowing look.

As the club members milled around the buffet table, Kate stepped back and appraised it from a food professional's point of view. The selection was dazzling. At least four kinds of meats and an equal array of imported cheeses shared space with a bountiful selection of chutneys, mustards, relishes, and pickles. Guests had also loaded the table with offerings, including Minette Ivers' famous mac and cheese, two different kinds of quiche, and an enormous pan of fragrant lasagna. There was also a variety of potato salads, cold salads, and slaws. A drinks table sagged under the weight of pitchers of lemonade, iced tea, and sangria and several bottles of wine. An ice chest beside it on the floor held a treasure trove of imported beer.

"Puts a Tudor monarch to shame, no?" Gabe said, handing her a white china plate. Today the mechanic was wearing a sky-blue Hawaiian shirt and pressed chinos. The reflective sunglasses were perched atop his head.

"I've never seen anything like it outside a restaurant or a hotel," Kate admitted.

"Harp doesn't do things halfway. And he uses these events to publicize products from his shop. That way, it's a write-off, too," he said, shrugging. "You settling in OK? I heard about the thing with Sam."

"I'm fine. But I am worried about him. And he's more concerned about the bakery than anything else. Maxi and I promised we'd run it for him temporarily."

Gabe smiled. "That sounds like the Sam I know. And I'm glad you guys are keeping it going. In the interim," he added quickly. "But you'll have your work cut out for you replicating his sourdough. Oh, and by the way, Gwendolyn is just fine. Coming along nicely, in fact."

It took Kate a few seconds to remember: Gwendolyn was what he'd nicknamed her ailing car.

"You've been working on it? Her?" She didn't know whether to be grateful or horrified. She wanted her car. Needed it, in fact. But she had no money, and her only prospect for a paycheck was sitting in the local lockup.

"Nothing big. Just flushing some of the systems and removing a bit of the gunk. In my spare time and off the books. I can't run a bakery. But I can help someone who's helping a friend."

"Wait, you already knew about that?"

He grinned. "This is a very small town. The cell service might be iffy, but we're wired in other ways. Look, if I can assist Sam in any way, just say the word. That guy is like his sourdough: crusty on the outside, soft and warm on the inside. But I never said that."

Kate relaxed. Maybe this would be all right after all.

She smelled the food and, for the first time all day, was genuinely famished. She recalled a foodie friend's sage advice on buffets: Skip the bread basket and sample a tablespoon of everything. Then double back for seconds of the really good stuff.

Eyeing the table, Kate suspected it was all really good stuff.

When she caught up with Maxi, her friend had snagged seats next to the Armands.

"Rosie, Andre, this is Kate McGuire. Kate, this is Rosie and Andre Armand. They run As Time Goes By. Kate's a pastry chef. She's moving to Coral Cay, and she's probably going to need to pick up a few things."

"Oh, decorating a new place is always fun," Rosie said, smiling. "Where are you moving from?"

"New York," Kate said. "Manhattan."

Andre smiled at his wife. "We've had some great buy-ing trips in the five boroughs," he said with a slight French accent. "Last year, we even got last-minute tickets to *Hamilton*. Have you seen it?"

"My fiancé and I—my ex-fiancé and I—went last spring. It was fantastic." It had been a magical night, Kate remembered with a familiar pang. All the more lu-minous because she and Evan were just falling in love.

"So are you decorating a house or an apartment?" Rosie asked, slicing off a bite-sized piece of lasagna with her fork.

"A room, actually."

"She's bunking at the bakery until she can find a place," Maxi explained. "Sam's letting out a room upstairs."

"We heard about the incident with Stewart Lord," An-dre said. "How is Sam?"

"About as well as you'd expect," Maxi said. "He's worried about the Cookie House. He asked us to keep it open. Just until he gets everything straightened out."

"Good," Rosie said emphatically. "There's no way Sam would hurt anyone. Not even Lord Stewart Lord."

"The man was a snake," Andre said, his mild French accent catching on the last word. "He wanted to turn this town into some kind of vacation playground for the very rich. People who live and work here? He wants us gone. Zap! No place in his plans for the likes of us."

Rosie patted her husband's arm reassuringly. "One of our customers worked for him. Muriel Hopkins. Did you ever meet her?"

Maxi shook her head.

"Let's just say she shared a few stories," Rosie drawled. "That man was an ogre. The way he treated his employees? Forget humane. He wasn't even human."

"Have you talked with her in the last few days?" Kate

asked. "I'm curious what happens to his big plans now."
And who inherits his fortune, she thought.

Andre shook his head sadly. "She is dead," he said
simply. "Last month. A heart attack. She was not terribly
old, but she had always the bad heart."

"It was stress, pure and simple," Rosie added. "That
man worked her to death. He expected her to be at his
beck and call twenty-four-seven. Whatever crazy thing
he wanted, whenever he wanted it. And half the time,
he'd change his mind at the last minute and demand
something else. I think the *coullion* did it on purpose."

"That's awful," Maxi said.

"Coullion?" Kate asked simultaneously.

Andre laughed heartily, his face turning pink. He
nudged his wife's shoulder with his own.

"Sorry, that just slipped out," Rosie said with a rueful
smile. "French slang. Let's just say if we were talking
about a bull, it's the part you probably wouldn't eat. I'm
sorry, but if they want mourners at that man's funeral
they're going to have to rent them by the hour."

Maxi, finishing a bite of mac and cheese, nodded.

"We don't think Sam did it," Kate said. "But Stewart Lord did have a lot of enemies. We were hoping that
maybe the Coral Cay Irregulars could take a look at it.
And figure out what really happened."

"Solve an actual mystery?" Rosie asked.

"Why not?" Maxi said. "It happened in our town.
And they're saying one of our own did it. It's like the
puzzles in the books we read. It happened in a closed
bakery kitchen. But Sam was the only one in there. And
we know it wasn't him—"

"A mystery in a locked room!" Andre exclaimed.

"Exactly," Kate said. "So who's the real culprit, and
how was it done?"

Rosie and Andre exchanged a look and both smiled in unison. "Count us in," she said.

Kate did a quick count in her head. With Gabe and Sunny, that made five—plus herself. Out of fourteen Irregulars. They still had a ways to go to win over the group. And Maxi was right: Dr. Patel and Carl Ivers would be crucial. Having Harp or Barb on their side wouldn't hurt, either.

"So how do Sam and Barb get along?" Kate asked softly as Rosie and Andre hit the buffet line for seconds.

"Cats and dogs," Maxi said. "They never agree on anything. Except Stewart Lord. And Cookie. Barb and Cookie were friends. Honestly, I don't think Cookie ever met a stranger."

"What did she do before they came here?"

"Cookie was a teacher. Elementary school. And she was great with kids. Even my boys were on their best behavior around her. Kinda like they are with you."

Kate grinned. "They'll get sick of me soon enough. Or sick of sleeping in the living room. Do you think Barb will support Sam?"

Maxi smiled. "She went to visit him this morning. Took him a bag of books and magazines to pass the time."

"I'm surprised he accepted them," Kate said.

"She told him they were overstocks and she either had to throw them out or pay to send them back. At least, that's the story I heard."

"It sounds like she's in his corner."

"Barb is practical," said Maxi. "Whether she believes Sam's innocent or not, she's happy Lord is gone."

"Who isn't?" Kate said quietly. "That suspect list is getting longer by the minute. I'd love to know what happens with Lord's plans for downtown now that he's out of the picture. I don't suppose there's been anything on the Coral Cay grapevine about that?"

"All kinds of theories. No real news. Not yet."

In spite of themselves, Kate and Maxi hit the buffet line again. Kate carved a few slices of Harp's smoked turkey and dropped them onto one of the scallion pancakes. She followed up with a healthy slice of caramelized onion quiche, while Maxi dove into the lasagna.

"Nutmeg," Kate whispered to her friend as they split what little was left of Minette's mac and cheese.

"What?" Maxi asked, mystified.

"The subtle flavor you couldn't quite place. Minette uses a dash of nutmeg. It brings out the sweetness of the cheese."

Maxi sampled a forkful from her own plate and sighed happily. "Mmmm, that's it. So good. Well, at least we solved one mystery."

As they polished off brunch, Kate realized Maxi had been right. While the resort meals had been first-rate, she'd never eaten better in her life than the past couple of days. Between her friend's house and the book club spread, Coral Cay—the real Coral Cay—was a foodie paradise.

Good thing she didn't have a car. A little extra walking would burn the calories.

When Barb Showalter stepped to the front of the room, Maxi and Kate exchanged a nod.

"OK, people, now that we've cleaned our plates and drained poor Harp's wine collection, time to discuss the real reason we're all here—one of the classics from the Queen of Crime herself—"

The florist raised her hand.

"Maxi, something to add? You've got the floor."

She stood. "Ye-es, but it's not about the book. You all live here, so you've all heard the news. Sam Hepplewhite is a friend of ours. He's a kind, gentle man, not a killer.

He and Cookie have helped a lot of us over the years. With money, with time, with advice. Sam's a big part of Coral Cay. And a big part of our downtown community, too. So instead of talking about a murder mystery in a book, I say we talk about the real murder mystery that happened right here in our own town."

Barb's eyebrows went up, and she scanned the room. Some members seemed equally baffled. Others nodded in agreement with Maxi.

"OK, let's do this right," the club leader said. "How about we put it to a vote? All those in favor of devoting part of this meeting to the Stewart Lord murder, raise your hands."

Kate looked around anxiously. Every hand in the room shot up. Except one.

Carl Ivers.

Minette elbowed him in the ribs. He put a hand shoulder high. A low wave.

"All right, it's unanimous," Barb concluded. "We have a topic. Who wants to share first?"

Carl fully extended his arm. Barb nodded.

"Look folks, crime—real crime—is a whole different animal. I've been a cop and a detective for most of my working life. It's not what you read in books or see on TV. The clues don't always line up flush. We don't have whiz-bang, Dick Tracy forensics. And murderers aren't always monsters. Sometimes they're just regular folks who get pushed too far."

"Who's Dick Tracy?" Kate heard Bridget ask Andy. He shrugged.

"What I'm sayin'," the retired cop concluded, "is that this is one time when you want to leave the work to the trained professionals. It's not like painting your living room or changing out a bathroom faucet. Trust me, when it comes to police work, you don't want DIY."

"What if the professionals have arrested the wrong man?" Sunny challenged.

Minette nodded, glaring at her husband.

There was a general grumble of agreement.

"That's what the courts are for," Carl said from his seat. "They'll hear all the facts. If Sam's innocent, he'll go free. Maxi, you're married to an assistant state attorney. You know that's true."

"But sometimes mistakes happen," Maxi countered. "And sometimes people—real people—fall through the cracks. I'm not saying everyone should grab a magnifying glass and crawl through the bushes. I'm just saying that, in this room, we have the eyes and ears of Coral Cay. Kinda like those security cameras they have all over London? Only with people. We can share what we know. And if we come up with anything, we take it to Ben."

Carl nodded.

"OK, when you put it that way, that could actually be helpful. But remember, we're witnesses. Not detectives."

He said that last part gently to Minette, who scowled at him, then turned her head.

"Hang on, I've got something that might help," said Harp, ducking out of the "cellar" and leaving the door open behind him.

He returned lugging a large A-frame chalkboard. "I got this for signage in the shop. But it might come in handy for this. I can jot down what we learn."

"A very logical approach," Dr. Patel said, nodding.

"I've got a question," Barb said brusquely. "Everyone says Sam was alone in the bakery when he made those rolls. But he wasn't. You were there," she said, pointing at Kate. "So how do we know you didn't do it?"

"Now, Barb—" Harp started.

"No, she's right," Kate said, standing. "And that's

a fair question. First, Sam hired me strictly as counter help. Even though I'm a pastry chef, he never let me bake. That wasn't what he needed. Second, he checked my references and my credentials thoroughly. I mean he called nearly everybody I've worked with in the past eight years. Along with several of my instructors at the culinary institute. He didn't even care about my pastry skills or my degree. He wanted to verify that I'm honest and trustworthy. And he did that. Last, and maybe most important, he was alone in the kitchen baking all that morning. I was working the counter. When Stewart Lord came into the shop, Sam stepped out carrying the finished rolls and asked me to leave the room. So you have Sam's word—and mine—that I was never alone with those cinnamon buns."

"And all of that's in the police report," Carl added, nodding.

"What the police report doesn't say is that I moved here from Manhattan about a week ago. Sam gave me a temporary job and was letting me live upstairs until I found a rental. And a permanent gig at one of the resorts. That morning was the first and only time I ever met Stewart Lord. I'd never even heard of him before. But I know Sam is a good guy. And I know he didn't do this. I just don't know who did. And neither does Sam. He's as baffled by all of this as the rest of us."

When Kate finished, her knees buckled, dumping her into the chair. Maxi smiled over encouragingly.

Barb nodded, apparently satisfied. And Harp gave her a small smile.

"OK, so what do we know?" he asked, chalk at the ready.

"Lord treated his workers very poorly," Andre said. "We knew his assistant. We would talk. Some of the stories . . ." He shook his head.

"OK, Lord was a bad boss," Harp said, neatly printing "employees" with "bad boss" in parenthesis next to it on the board. "That means his workers might have a motive. This assistant, has she talked to the police?"

"Muriel Hopkins died last month," Rosie said. "She'd been ill for years. Heart condition."

Harp nodded.

"But the truth is, Stewart Lord worked her to death," Rosie blurted. "Bullied her to death."

"What about all the owners of homes and shops he bought out on the cheap after every storm?" Amos Tully asked. "There was a rumor he was making deals with some of the insurance companies to drag out the claims process. So folks didn't have a choice if they wanted to survive. They had to take Lord's lowball offers. He'd get land on the cheap. Insurance companies got to skate on payouts. Win-win for everybody but the property owners. That was me, it'd make my blood boil."

"OK, so we put 'former landowners' on the list," Harp said. "But given the scale of the man's business dealings, we're going to need a much bigger board."

"Shorthand it for now," Barb said. "Let the police sort it out."

"Fair enough."

"If that's really true, any of the insurance people in on the deal might have a motive, too," Andy said. "Especially if a reporter or regulator suspected what was going on."

"Lord would be a loose end," his bride agreed.

Harp printed "insurance execs" with two question marks.

"Since Lord was a successful businessman, a money motive would make sense," said Dr. Patel. "Did Sam have anything to gain financially from his demise?"

"He didn't," Gabe said. "Lord had made a couple of

lowball offers on Sam's shop. Even though I think Sam was seriously considering unloading the bakery, he was adamant he'd never sell it to Lord. He didn't even want to turn the place over to someone who'd possibly sell out to Lord. And, from a practical standpoint, Sam would have gotten a lot more money from just about anyone else."

Off to the right side of the board, Harp wrote: "Sam ≠ selling to SL." Under that, he printed: "Sam ≠ $."

Kate remembered listening to Sam and Lord from the kitchen. The taunting. The threats. No way she was sharing that.

"*Sí*," Maxi added. "Sam warned me about Lord, too. He was afraid the guy would try to buy Flowers Maximus for much less than it was worth. Like we'd ever sell."

"Who inherits Lord's money and business now that he's gone?" Minette asked.

Carl Ivers folded his arms across his chest and shook his head.

"He wasn't married," Rosie said. "We learned that from Muriel. And his parents were gone."

"In Christie's books, there's always a long-lost relative," said Annie. "And yeah, I understand this is *real* life. But Lord could have a sibling or a cousin we know nothing about. It would be nice to learn more about his family. And if he has a will."

"Hundo P!" Andy exclaimed. "A couple of bad cinnamon rolls and somebody's gonna get filthy rich."

"And you can bet that skunk won't be leaving a nickel to charity," Tully said.

"So we put down 'family' with a question mark," Harp said. "And I'm writing 'will' in all caps. I'd like to get a look at that myself."

"I, as well," said Dr. Patel, inclining his head slightly. "'Follow the money,' as the journalists say."

"We need to know more about the women in his

life," said Sunny. "After all, poison is often a woman's weapon."

"Or a sneak's," said Kate. "Another reason it wasn't Sam. He's not a sneak."

"And he'd have never used Cookie's bakery to kill someone," Maxi added. "He loved her too much."

"That's actually a pretty good point," Barb conceded.

"Unless he just saw red and did it on impulse," said Tully.

"The police haven't released the name of the poison that was used, but judging by the effects, it wasn't some everyday household chemical," Annie argued. "Most likely a drug of some sort. And not a common one. Not something you just have lying around. That kind of murder takes planning."

"Another reason poison is favored by women," Sunny concluded.

Harp added "poison = planning" to the list on the right.

"You said his assistant died last month?" Bridget asked.

Rosie and Andre nodded.

"Did he replace her?

"I have not heard," Andre said. "We knew Muriel because she came into our shop. She loved antiques. And she was charmed by Coral Cay. She talked about buying a little house and settling here when she retired."

"A new assistant would have access to him," Bridget said. "And his food. Maybe she didn't want to end up like her predecessor, so she wrote a new script."

Sunny smiled, clapping her well-manicured hands. "Girl power."

Harp wrote "new assistant" with a question mark.

"There wasn't any assistant with him that morning," said Tully. "I saw him in that stretch limo he always swans around in. But he had a driver. Did the chauffeur go into the bakery?"

Kate shook her head. "No, he waited outside. Lord ate one of the rolls in front of Sam and took the rest with him. So the driver could have gotten his hands on them later."

Harp wrote "driver" on the chalkboard.

"Did Muriel have any relatives?" Gabe queried. "Someone who's angry about her death? Maybe wanted to get even?"

"Family vengeance?" Kate asked.

"An ancient and time-honored motive," Gabe replied. "Look at the *Iliad*."

"I don't think Muriel had much in the way of family," Rosie said.

"She had a cat," Andre supplied helpfully.

"And a job that took up seventy hours a week," Rosie finished. "That's why it was such a special occasion when she had a few hours to come out here."

"Sam may have had the opportunity, but it doesn't look like he had a motive," Harp said, studying the chalkboard.

"Depending on the poison, he may not have had the means, either," Annie said. "I'd love to see the forensic report." She looked at Carl. "Is that possible?"

He shrugged. "That's up to Ben. Or Kyle. And the state attorney's office."

Kate looked at Maxi, who gave an infinitesimal nod.

"Mmmm-hmmm, not exactly the slam-dunk case we keep hearing about," Minette announced to no one in particular.

"Shall we put it to a vote?" Harp asked Barb. "To see where we stand?"

She nodded decisively.

"OK, just based on what we've learned so far," he said to the room, "who thinks Sam is innocent?"

Fourteen arms shot up.

"Who thinks the case needs more evidence—one way or the other?"

Carl Ivers raised a lone hand.

"And who's convinced that Sam Hepplewhite killed Stewart Lord?"

They all looked around the room. Kate's face relaxed into a smile. Maxi bounced excitedly in her seat.

Not a single hand.

Chapter 17

Late that afternoon at the jail, Sam seemed buoyed by the news that his friends and neighbors were convinced of his innocence. That and the leftovers from the buffet.

"This lasagna is mighty good," he said, shoveling it in like he hadn't seen food in a week. "Who made it?"

"Andy and Bridget," Maxi said.

"Figures. Those two know their way around a kitchen. Spring onion pancakes are pretty tasty, too. Especially with this roast beef. Not like the meat they serve here. Hamburger today was like shoe leather. Tough and dry. Tell everybody 'thanks.' Still don't know what's gonna happen. But thanks all the same."

"What's going to happen is we're all comparing notes and looking at a few new angles on Stewart Lord's murder—and that was all Maxi's doing," Kate said. "Somewhere, the police are missing something. And now you've got a whole team of people in your corner who want to find out what really happened—and get you out of here."

"And a big ol' birdie told me that the investigation unit is releasing the bakery tomorrow," Maxi said. "So we can give it a good scrubbing and get it reopened in the next few days."

Sam stopped in mid-bite. He stared at Maxi and back at Kate. Then down at the floor. For a moment, he was completely still. Finally, he wiped his face with the sleeve of his navy jumpsuit. "Tomato sauce," he muttered.

"Well, I hope you saved room for dessert," Kate said matter-of-factly. "'Cause Minette made a sweet potato tart and some banana pudding just for you. She even crumbled vanilla wafers over the top of the pudding."

"Yeah," Maxi added. "And word is, Carl's on the warpath because she didn't make any for him."

Chapter 18

Kate rolled over and glanced at the Millennium Falcon clock on the bedside table: 4:45 a.m.

She couldn't help it. She was too keyed up to sleep. Apprehensive. But also excited. And Sam was counting on her.

Today they would get their first look at the bakery since Kyle had shuttered it. She'd learn what, if anything, could be salvaged. And what would need to be replaced.

It was already a given that all the foodstuffs would have to go. If they weren't already gone. They couldn't take a chance on using anything. But what about the pots, pans, tools, and mixers?

And what of her own belongings?

Kate felt a knot in her stomach. She'd already liquidated most of her possessions just to move here. So what, exactly, would she have left?

A warm, furry lump shifted at the foot of the bed. And yawned. Oliver.

He looked up at her with bright onyx eyes.

"You want to go out, don't you?" she said, ruffling his soft head. "OK, but we have to be careful not to wake Michael and Javie. Or the rest of the house. Very quiet. Promise?"

Oliver made a soft *chuff, chuff* sound.

"I'm going to take that as a 'yes,'" she whispered, stroking his ear.

Quickly she pulled on the new baby-blue terry cloth robe Maxi had loaned her. It matched the blue T-shirt top and pastel-striped pajama bottoms that went with it. Though on Kate, the pj bottoms looked more like pedal pushers.

She grabbed the dayglow-yellow lead and clipped it to his collar. "Come on, baby boy. Let's get you a little break. And if we use the kitchen door, no one will even know we're up."

Kate stealthily opened the bedroom door. And smelled coffee. It couldn't be. Could it?

She looked down at Oliver. "Remember," she whispered. "Sssshhhhh!"

The pup lunged for the door, pulling her along for the ride. When they arrived in the kitchen, Maxi was sitting at the breakfast bar, reading the paper.

"Good morning, sleepyhead," she said with a smile. "Or should I say 'sleepyheads'?"

"I couldn't sleep, and Oliver needed to go out," Kate said. "I can't believe you're up. Are you nervous, too?"

"Nah, this is when I normally get up," Maxi said. "But don't tell anybody. It's my deep, dark secret."

"Getting up before the crack of dawn is your deep, dark secret?" Kate asked.

"One of them," she said with a wink. "How about some coffee *cubano*?"

Kate nodded. "Tell you what, I'll take this little one

out, and then I'll pour us both a cup. You keep reading the paper."

"The yard's all fenced, isn't it, Oliver? Just open the back door and this little guy knows exactly what to do."

"What if he . . . um . . . waters one of your bushes? You know, hits something he shouldn't?"

"I trust him. Besides, he's got to go somewhere. Right, sport?"

Kate had to admit, Oliver looked like he agreed with her. She bent and carefully unclipped the leash.

"Just leave the door open. When he's done, he'll come back. I guarantee he won't take off before breakfast."

Maxi reached down, patted Oliver's fluffy head, and gave one plush ear a good scratch. "This little guy is a chowhound. Aren't you, sweet boy?"

Oliver dogged Maxi's steps to the door. The minute it swung open, he dashed outside.

"Now, time for a second cup for me and a first cup for you," she said, pouring them each measured portions of the hot, inky liquid and setting the fluffy coconut cream in front of Kate.

"Would it be OK if I baked a little something?" Kate asked as she ladled several tablespoons into her coffee.

"Oh yeah! *Mi cocina es tu cocina.*"

"I don't even know how to thank you. Baking, well, it calms me down. And helps me think. And with the whole bakery thing today, I could really use it."

Maxi laughed. "Sheesh, you can thank me by coming into my kitchen at five in the morning and baking anytime you want. I can't believe I have my very own kitchen elf. Look out, Harry Potter. I mean, *mi mami,* she cooks. But not at five a.m. So what are you going to make?"

Kate took a long draw on her coffee cup and felt the caffeine gallop into her bloodstream. "I kind of have a craving for monkey bread. It's pretty easy. And it goes great with coffee."

"Ooh, that sounds perfect."

"Best of all, kids usually love it. Partly because of the name, mostly because it's sticky and good."

"If it's food, *mi chiquitos* will love it," Maxi said. "Not a picky eater in the bunch."

As Maxi read the newspaper, Kate spent the next few minutes collecting ingredients. Just as she had everything lined up on the counter, Oliver pranced into the kitchen, turned three circles next to Maxi's barstool, and settled himself on the floor at her feet.

Retrieving the glass measuring cup from the dishwasher, Kate remembered something she'd once read about measuring the quality of a friendship not just by the honest conversations but also by the companionable silences.

Maybe that's why it seemed like she and Maxi had known each other for years, instead of just a few days.

With the windows open, Kate caught the scent of jasmine and salt water in the cool morning air as she mixed flour, salt, and sugar.

For some reason, those white blossoms reminded her of weddings, which naturally led back to Evan. The good times. His devilish blue eyes. His dimples. What was he doing now? Did he still care? Had he ever really loved her?

She threw the dough onto the floured counter with a hard *thunk*.

Maxi looked up and grinned. "What's his name?"

"Evan. How did you know?"

"I've punched a few balls of dough. Before Peter. And after."

Oliver rolled over, stretched, yawned, and closed his eyes.

"I was angry when he was calling all the time to apologize," Kate explained. "Then I was even madder after I left New York and he stopped calling."

"Well, yeah."

"I know. It makes no sense. I'm being totally irrational."

"You're grieving," Maxi said. "You don't have to be rational. You don't miss him. You miss the man you thought he was. And angry is good. Hang on to angry for a little bit. It keeps a girl from making the same mistake twice. Or going back to the lunkhead."

Kate smiled in spite of herself. "You're right. On both counts. So get ready for one angry batch of monkey bread," she said, reaching for a bag of shelled walnuts and a rolling pin.

Twenty minutes later, Kate slid the Bundt pan into the oven and shut the door. "I've been thinking about it. If we're going to reopen Sam's bakery and keep it going, we're going to need some marketing. I mean, not only is Sam not going to be there baking his signature breads, but some of the tourists might actually believe that Cookie House rolls poisoned someone."

"Mmm, yeah," Maxi said, draining her small cup. "Half of Sam's customers come just to buy his sourdough. *Muy delicioso.* Can you make that?"

"I've made it before. But it's not my specialty. And my bread won't taste like Sam's, even if I follow his recipe perfectly. With sourdough, the secret is the starter. It's the stuff that leavens the bread. And it's a big part of the taste and texture. The baker keeps a little bit back every time they make a batch—letting it grow for the next time. Some bakeries have been using the same line of starter for decades. Or even centuries. But after what happened at the bakery, we're going to have to destroy Sam's starter. If the police haven't already."

"Is there any way we can get more?"

"Well, I could find out where he got his starter in the first place. And if they're willing, we might be able to buy some of that. But it still wouldn't be a perfect match. Starter changes over time. Adapts to the environment. And good bakers all have their secrets—things they do to grow it, change it, and make it better."

"Just like plants. So we get another cutting from the momma tree?"

"Exactly. But depending on how long Sam's been growing it and what he's done to it over the years, his plant could be a whole lot different than the original."

"Still, that seems like a really good idea. And pretty much our only idea."

"The starter will help. But my strengths are sweets and pastries. And we're running a shop named the Cookie House. Call me nuts, but I think we should sell cookies. Make it what we're known for—our calling card."

"Oooh, Sam's not going to like that," Maxi said, raising her eyebrows.

"When Sam comes back, we need to hand him the keys to a thriving business. At that point, he can do whatever he wants with it. But if we don't do something drastic now, the place is going to fold. I'm not Sam. I don't have his bread skills. But I have my own talents. And I think we can make this work."

Maxi slowly nodded. "The tourists, they're always surprised when they can't buy cookies at the Cookie House. I mean, we natives? We know better. We don't even ask anymore. I wish you could have seen the place when Cookie was there. There were lines out onto the porch and down the sidewalk. Especially during tourist season. And the house looked so different. The outside was pretty and clean. It was painted this super pale pink with white trim and lots of flowers in the yard. It was so beautiful."

"What if we did that?"

"What do you mean?" Maxi asked, pouring each of them another cup.

"Take the Cookie House back to what it was when everyone flocked there. A little paint, a little pressure washing, a little yard work on the outside. On the inside, a new, improved Cookie House that actually sells cookies—along with Sam's breads. All kinds of cookies. Maybe a few cakes and pastries, too. I mean, sure, people come into a bakery for bread. But nothing says they won't leave with bread for dinner—and a little something for dessert. Or they'll buy their kids cookies on the spot as treats. And all those tourists who come into the Cookie House looking for cookies? Let's give the people what they want."

Maxi cocked her head to one side. "We could actually use this time to help Sam by giving the bakery a makeover."

"Inside and out," Kate added.

"And if he wants to change it back . . ."

"It's his business. He can do what he wants. But once he sees what the Cookie House can be again, he might actually like it. I can do the cleaning myself."

"I can do the landscaping," Maxi added. "A little grass, a few flowers."

"And after we reopen, we can get estimates on painting the outside. Maybe with the right payment plan and the extra money from selling desserts, we could swing it."

"My head says it's a super good idea," Maxi said slowly. "My heart says we should do it without telling Sam."

Chapter 19

After a morning of scrubbing every surface in the bakery, Kate collapsed on the settee in the floral shop with a fresh cup of *café cubano*.

Maxi was finishing three different flower arrangements simultaneously. But, somehow, with flying fingers, she made it look effortless.

Oblivious, Oliver occupied himself with a bright red rubber Kong left behind on his last visit. His new favorite game: dropping the cone-shaped rubber toy and watching it bounce oddly on the hardwood floors. When it finally landed, he'd race over, grab it in his mouth, and fling it again.

"I'd like to put the word out that the Cookie House will be selling cookies now," Kate said, feeling the caffeine and sugar lift her spirits. "I was thinking of having us drop off fresh batches at some of the businesses around town. Hit a handful of different ones every day. Give them each a dozen or so and see if we can build up a demand. Maybe even leave a few business cards? The problem is, it won't be cheap. And I'd have to do the baking in your kitchen. At least, for now."

"Ay, that's horrible news. All those good smells coming from my kitchen—what will the neighbors think? Seriously, that's a super excellent idea. And I can help out with the baking in the evenings. And with some money for the ingredients. But at this rate, I'm going to need a lot more of Sunny's yoga classes."

"Speaking of Sunny, what if I started baking some rolls for her—just for the early morning class?"

"Oooh, we could drop those off with the cookies. Sunny talks to everybody. That would really spread the word."

Kate released a deep breath and smiled. "I'm just so happy to be baking again. I don't know if Gabe ever told you, but I was heading for a job interview at Fish-a-Palooza before my car broke down."

"Ugh!" Maxi said, decisively snipping an inch from a rose stem. "A total waste of your talents. Frozen fish. And, word is, they do the same thing with the desserts. It's the same mushy stuff you can get on the freezer aisle."

"With all the great food around here, how do they stay in business?"

"It's what we natives call 'a tourist trap.' Tons of ads aimed at visitors. And they cozy up to the bigwigs at the resorts and hotels, too. They have a fun atmosphere, like a party. Lots of tropical drinks. And the setting is beautiful. On the mainland, right on the water. But they spend their money on rent and booze, not food. By the time you pay the bill and figure out what you got for it, you're out the door. And I don't think they care if you ever come back."

"Yeah, we have a few restaurants like that in New York, too. Luckily, most of them don't last long. New Yorkers don't hesitate to tell total strangers what we think of a place—whether they ask or not. And once the word is out among the cabbies, that's it—game over."

"Do you miss it? The city?"

"Oddly, no," Kate said, shaking her head. "I always thought the pace was exhilarating. Energetic. But toward the end, I was burned out. Fall and winter were so cold and gray. Spring too, for that matter. I mean, there's wonderful culture—art, and food and music. And for a chef, the markets and the neighborhoods and food trucks are a wonder. But I was working sixteen-hour days. When I started dating Evan? He'd talk me into playing hooky once in a while. Taking a day off here and there. Going to shows. And clubs. And some wonderful restaurants. The guy really knew how to have fun. And everyone around him always had fun. I actually started to think about what I wanted to do next. If I could do anything. If I could go anywhere. That's when I realized that it wasn't New York."

"So did the 'if I could do anything' part involve running a bakery that doesn't make cookies?"

"A restaurant. A little hole-in-the-wall place."

"In Paris or Rome?"

"Here, actually."

"For real?"

Kate nodded vigorously. "I'd been hearing about Coral Cay for years. From foodie friends. Other chefs. Things I'd read here and there. So I wanted to come here for at least part of our honeymoon. I was secretly hoping Evan would fall in love with the place and say, 'Let's never go back.' We'd buy a little café and run it together. And spend all our spare time at the beach. Stupid, right?"

"OK, so instead of a handsome rich guy, you got a cranky old baker who's accused of murder. Other than that, exactly the same."

"It's stupid because it was *my* dream and I was waiting for *him* to suggest it. I mean, how lame is that? And he wouldn't have wanted to work in a restaurant. Or work, period."

"You fell for a guy with no job?"

"Independently wealthy."

"That's just rich-people speak for 'the boy is livin' out of his momma's purse.'"

"Yes, but it's a Gucci purse."

"Sorry, chica, you did the right thing. He doesn't *have* to work? Fine. But he *doesn't* work at all? That's just bone lazy in a better zip code."

"For a while there, I think I was working enough for both of us. When Rosie and Andre were talking about Muriel Hopkins, I almost wanted to cry. Before I met Even? I swear, I was just like that."

"You're nothing like that," Maxi said. "I mean, look at you. You took your whole life and—boom! You changed it."

Kate looked down. Oliver was standing in front of her with a green leash clutched in his mouth. He sat back on his haunches and peered politely up into her eyes.

"Uh, does Oliver have a green leash?"

"Yup," Maxi said. "That's one of many. Sometimes he shows up here, sometimes at the house. So I keep a few of them in both places. I think they're less for him and more for the human he wants to walk."

"OK, little guy, you don't have to ask me twice. Let's go for a nice stroll around downtown. Maybe we can decide who we'll cookie bomb first."

Chapter 20

As Kate walked down Main Street with Oliver, it finally hit her: Her cell was still MIA.

It had been on the steel shelf, next to the red landline, when she left the bakery that fateful morning. She'd had no need to carry it. It didn't work in downtown Coral Cay. And there wasn't really anyone she wanted to call.

But it was gone when she and Maxi went through her room. Along with who-knows-what-else.

The police probably had it now. Ben, she hoped. She cringed at the thought of Kyle Hardy reading her texts. Going through her phone log. Calling Evan. Or Jeanine.

Could he *do* that? *Would* he?

Or worse, would he phone Evan's mother? Amanda Throckmorton Thorpe definitely did not suffer fools gladly. So why did the thought of her ex-almost-mother-in-law verbally deflating a pompous Kyle Hardy make Kate smile?

The heck with it. She'd deal with it later. She only had

two things to do now: find out who really killed Stewart Lord and jump-start Sam's bakery.

Mmrowr. It came out as a cross between a whine and a question as Oliver's tail dropped between his legs.

"OK, three things," Kate said aloud to Oliver. "And the most important right now is making sure we get a nice walk."

Ruff! Oliver's tail wagging gained speed. Springing on the balls of his feet, the puppy practically bounced down the street.

"While we're at it, let's pick up lunch. We can take it back to Flowers Maximus and have a picnic on the porch."

Was it her imagination, or did Oliver's tail accelerate a notch?

As she passed a store window, something behind her caught her eye. Across the street. She turned. Along with the usual throngs of tourists, she spotted a familiar bulk in a lime and white swirled Hawaiian shirt with the same khaki shorts she'd seen him wear days earlier. Today he also sported a Panama hat with his big sunglasses.

Ball Cap Man!

This time, instead of a shopping bag, he carried binoculars.

Instinctively, she brushed the outline of her pocket. But she didn't have her phone. And cell service was erratic, anyway.

Did he know that? Was that why he lingered downtown? Was this his hunting ground?

She glanced back again. He was gone.

Kate planted herself on the sidewalk and did a full 360. Nothing. Tons of people—mostly tourists, with a few locals mixed in—but the Panama hat was gone.

She could feel her heart banging in her chest. Someone knocked into her from behind. Kate whirled around.

"Sorry!" said a woman in a sundress with an impossibly large Birkin bag as she bustled past.

Behind them, a woman with a little boy stared at Oliver.

"Mommy, look at the cute doggie," the boy said, pointing.

"Stay away, Neddie, you don't know him. He could bite. And you're allergic."

"Aww, Mom! I am not! Jimmy has a dog, and we play all the time. I jus' never tell you."

"March, young man!" the mother said, giving Kate a sheepish shrug.

Kate reached down and stroked Oliver's downy head. "You don't bite, do you, sweetie?" she murmured. "Not unless they really deserve it."

Oliver stepped closer to Kate, a mischievous twinkle in his eyes. Just touching his soft, fluffy coat made her relax. She stood and took another look in all directions. Nothing.

She thought about returning to the flower shop. But she didn't want to lead the guy back to Maxi. Besides, Oliver needed a walk. And so did she.

What was it Peter had said? Trust your instincts and don't go off alone. Well, no chance of that. Even on a weekday afternoon, Coral Cay was full of people. So she'd stick to Main Street, among the multitudes, and continue her outing. With Oliver by her side. And once she was reasonably sure Hat Man was truly gone—and not just playing hide-and-seek—she'd grab lunch and take it back to the flower shop.

Who was this guy? What did he want? And, in a place where she knew virtually no one, why her?

Chapter 21

For the first leg of the new Cookie House marketing campaign, Kate opted for two recipes that were old favorites with friends and restaurant customers alike: Toll House and (for those few curious souls who didn't appreciate chocolate) rum butter cookies.

Kate figured she and Maxi could make the rounds in the morning. Each shop would get a dozen—half and half—in a bakery box with the Cookie House address and phone number.

Maxi had picked up stick-on labels and treat boxes from a party store off Main Street. And printed out the first batch of labels on her home computer. In light blue ink, they featured a line drawing of the Cookie House.

"Maxi, these look great," Kate said, clearly impressed.

"Part of being a small-business owner." Maxi patted the monitor. "This old girl helps me with invoices, stationery, marketing, and, in a pinch, those little cards that go with a delivery. When you run your own shop, you learn to do a little bit of everything."

"I figured I'd start on Sunny's rolls tonight and we'd deliver the first batch the day after tomorrow. That way, I can proof the dough a couple of times."

"I feel like the Easter Bunny," Maxi said with a grin. "All I need are some of those plastic ears."

The front door slammed.

"My guy," Maxi declared, getting up. "I can't believe he had to work through dinner."

Peter Buchanan appeared in the kitchen, his face serious. "Hey, we need to talk," he said quietly.

"I'll join Oliver and the kids in the yard," Kate said, moving toward the back door.

"No, you need to hear this, too." He turned to Maxi and guided her to the kitchen table. "Baby, you want to sit down."

Kate's heart dropped. Sam. It had to be Sam.

Peter set his briefcase by the bar and dropped his suit jacket over one of the kitchen chairs. "There's no easy way to say this. . . ."

Maxi's hands flew to her face. "Peter, just tell us," she pleaded.

He nodded. "Carl came to our office this morning. He actually called last night, but that's another story. Anyway, he'd heard that someone else connected with Lord had died recently. Died the same way Lord did." Peter stopped, taking a deep breath.

"Muriel Hopkins," Kate said. "His assistant. We heard about it at the book club meeting yesterday."

"She had heart problems," Maxi said. "For a long time."

Peter nodded. "She did. Her doctor said it was a chronic condition. But she was managing it well. She watched her diet, took her meds, walked regularly. Bottom line, he was surprised when she died so suddenly."

"Rosie said it was from the stress," Maxi said. "Working for Stewart Lord."

"Yeah, the doctor mentioned that. He was also afraid he might have missed something in her last exam. Some complication related to her health. And that's been weighing on him. He's truly convinced that she shouldn't have died so young."

Kate felt a thudding in her own chest. Maxi had gone silent, her eyes wide and worried.

"The bottom line is, after talking with her doctor, the assistant state attorney handling Lord's murder believes that Muriel Hopkins' death deserves a second look. And, unfortunately, after hearing the facts, I agree with him. The office is going to move to have her body exhumed. There's a chance that Muriel Hopkins might have been poisoned. It's possible she might have been murdered by the same person who killed Stewart Lord."

Chapter 22

Kate punched the dough, flipped it, and hit it again. Then she started pummeling it.

"If you're not careful, those rolls are going to have you arrested for assault," Maxi said.

"Haven't you heard? We pastry makers are a violent bunch. We beat eggs and whip cream. But don't tell Kyle. Seriously, what are we going to say to Sam?"

"Peter's idea is to say nothing," Maxi said, sipping coffee out of a tiny cup. "Not yet. And I think he's right. We don't know anything yet. One doctor feels guilty because maybe he missed something. And maybe he did. Or maybe he didn't understand just how awful it was to work for Stewart Lord. All the hours. All the pressure."

"Or maybe Muriel wasn't being as good with her diet and exercise routine as she told her doctor."

"That too. Until they do tests, there's nothing to tell Sam. He'll just worry. And that *will* hurt him."

"But you know Coral Cay," Kate said, cleaving the doughball in two, placing each half in a separate mixing bowl, then deftly covering them loosely with plastic wrap. "That little piece of bad news is going to be the talk of the town, literally, before the week is out. And Sam is sitting right there in the police station jail. Gossip central. He's going to hear something."

"I wonder if this will maybe help him. Help his case."

"What do you mean?" Kate asked, pushing the bowls up against the far side of the counter—well out of the reach of curious little hands.

"Well, Sam knew Stewart Lord. And really didn't like him. So someone could say that he had a reason for that one. Even though we know he didn't do it. But Muriel Hopkins? I don't think he even met her. So why would he kill her? And how?"

"You're right. If it turns out she was murdered and we can show Sam didn't do it, that should go a good way toward proving Sam didn't kill Lord, either."

"It also means the *bobo* has to leave you alone and find another suspect," Maxi said.

"What do you mean?"

"From what Rosie and Andre said, she died a month ago. You were still living in New York then, right?"

"Oh yeah. With an apartment and a job and a fiancé. I wonder when she died?"

"Well, let's fire up my old girl and ask," Maxi said, walking into the living room and sitting down at the computer. "*M-u-r-i-e-l* and *H-o-p-k-i-n-s.* I'm gonna put in 'Florida,' in case there's more than one."

"Add 'obituary,'" Kate suggested. "That should narrow it down."

Maxi hit "Enter," then scooted back in her seat. "Oooh!"

"What?"

"This is from the Hibiscus Springs newspaper. It says Muriel F. Hopkins, fifty-two, administrative assistant at Lord Enterprises Limited, died of a heart attack." She paused, scanning the text. "On the sixteenth of last month."

"Whoa," Kate said.

"That mean something?" Maxi said, looking up.

Kate shook her head. "Remember how I told you I lost my job, my apartment, and my fiancé all on the same day? That was the day. And if this doesn't make me stop feeling sorry for myself, I don't know what will."

Chapter 23

The next morning, Kate and Maxi hit downtown armed with cookies—and the news that the Cookie House would be reopening with an expanded menu.

"About time!" Amos Tully declared as they shared coffee out of paper cups in his storeroom. "That old fool was tying his hands behind his back. What's a bakery without sweets? Really like these. What did you say they're called again?"

"Rum butter cookies," Kate said. "Similar to a traditional butter cookie, but with a kick."

"Heh! Don't want to let Sam get too close to these. That man likes his rum. Well, gotta get back to the store. Lemme know when you girls are open again. We'll order up some more of these. And the chocolate chip, too."

As Kate, Maxi, and Oliver walked the block in the cool morning air, Kate realized she recognized many of the faces. Even if she didn't yet know their names. More often than not, folks waved or nodded. And were usually greeted with an enthusiastic wave or "Hiya!" from Maxi.

But the town was strangely devoid of tourists.

"Too early," Maxi explained. "This is what we call local hour. Although it's really more like two. Tourists don't show up much before ten."

Overhead, Kate heard the scream of seagulls on the briny breeze, as the sweet scent of tropical flowers mingled with the aromas of food—coffee, bacon, onions— from shops and restaurants prepping for the day. She felt a tingle of excitement.

"Let's hit the pharmacy next," Maxi said. "Annie's researching Lord's family tree to see if anybody interesting falls out. I'm curious to see if she found anything that could help Sam."

"Any word on Lord's will? There could be a few clues there."

"Peter swore me to secrecy. So you can't say anything. But they can't find one."

"You're kidding. A guy with that much money? That doesn't make sense."

"They're still looking. Could be they just haven't found it yet. But Lord's personal lawyer says he never made one. At least, not that he knows. And the guy who heads up his company's legal department says Lord had one, but that he'd never actually seen it. It's all a mystery. That's why I want to find out what Annie discovered. But remember, the stuff Peter tells us we can't share. At least, not yet."

Kate mimed locking a key over her mouth. "I swear, on three dozen of my best cookies. Especially the Toll House."

"Yeah, well a couple of those 'dozens' were nearly a few cookies short. I caught Javie and Michael trying to sneak some out of the boxes this morning. Peter had to have a little talk with them about respecting other people's property. That big legal degree of his comes in handy sometimes."

"Well, we did put cookies in front of children. That's basically entrapment."

"That's what Peter said. Something called 'attractive nuisance.' Of course, he had chocolate chip cookies on his breath when he said it."

A little bell tinkled as they opened the door to Kim's Drugstore. Annie popped out of the storeroom. Her shoulder-length hair was damp.

"Hey, guys! Anything new on the Stewart Lord case?"

"We were gonna ask you the same thing," Maxi admitted, presenting Annie with a box. "But we're reopening the bakery this week, and we brought a little sample of some of the new stuff."

"Cookies! Oh, this is great. I just got back from the beach, and I'm starving."

"Two kinds," Kate said proudly. "Chocolate chip and rum butter."

"These are heaven," Annie said, happily munching one. "Hey, how about some tea? Moms made a whole pot before she took off. *Nokcha*—green tea."

"I'd love that," Kate said.

"And I have a few treats for you, big guy," Annie said, bending to scratch Oliver's ear. "I can't believe how fast he's growing."

In the back room of the pharmacy, Annie motioned them to a beautiful low teak table with matching chairs. Complete with a red area rug bearing a gold and blue geometrical pattern, the setup could have been straight out of a comfortable living room.

Annie saw Kate taking it all in and grinned. "We spend so much time at the shop, it pays to make it homey and comfortable. But you'll discover that soon enough."

She unrolled a straw mat onto the table, set out three delicate blue and white china teacups, and filled each from a pot of the same design.

"It's the weirdest thing," Annie said, putting the cookie box in the middle of the table. "I haven't been able to find a thing on Lord before he came to this country. I mean, the last few years, all kinds of stuff in the papers. About him and his company. Most of it good, oddly enough. The business press loved him. And so did the banks. But nothing from his earlier life in London. Or the U.K., period. Did you guys manage to learn anything about Lord's will? That might give me a few other names to search. Especially if he mentioned family members."

"Nothing yet, but I'm hoping to hear something soon," Maxi said quickly.

"What about the poison that killed him? Any idea what it was?"

Maxi paused, clamping her lips together. "I don't have a copy of the report from the exam . . . the autopsy," she said slowly, clearly caught between her conscience and her desire to clear Sam. "Not yet. But from what I hear—from a very good source—it was a drug, like you thought. A heart drug."

"That would make sense," Annie said matter-of-factly. "In the right circumstances, they calibrate heart function. In the wrong ones, they can wreck everything."

"Someone at the book club said Lord starting popping up in the headlines around here about five years ago?" Kate asked.

"Yeah. South Florida got hammered during one really bad hurricane season," Annie said, setting a bowl of water on the rug in front of Oliver, alongside three bone-shaped treats. "It was just one storm right after another. That's about the time he moved in and started buying big. Before that, I found just a few scant references to him here and there. Mostly in business journals. He was part of some group that bought a couple of hotels. He had a minor partnership in a Missouri casino. Very minor, from the sound of it. He and a bunch of other investors bought and sold a few resorts and some condo buildings out west. But about five years ago, he went bigtime. Buying on his own, instead of going in with other people. Putting his name out there. And that's about the time he seemed to discover South Florida."

"How old was he?" Kate asked.

Annie smiled. "I can't even get a straight answer on that one. Some of the stories say he was forty-five or forty-seven when he died. Others, fifty or fifty-three. And I saw one blurb from years ago that, if you do the math—and I did—would have made him about fifty-seven. I never actually met him, so I have no idea."

"No way he was forty-five," Maxi declared.

"Yeah, from the view I had that one time at the bakery, I'd have said your fifty-seven was closest to the mark," Kate said. "I wonder why the discrepancy?"

"Vanity," Annie countered. "Plus, I hear the corporate world's almost as bad as Hollywood. Once you hit a certain age, if you haven't made your fortune a lot of doors close."

"And fifty-seven is a little late to be the next wunderkind or hot new flavor of the month," Kate mused.

"How's Sam doing?" Annie asked quietly.

"Better," Maxi said. "Now that he knows people are behind him. He has hope."

"Moms and Pops are going to stop in and see him this afternoon. Moms wants to take him a home-cooked meal. She makes a ground-beef rice bowl that's heaven. And she's also fixing him some of her glazed chicken wings. Those things are seriously sick."

"He'll love that," Maxi said. "With any luck, we might be able to fatten him up a little by the time he gets out. That man is too skinny. Not a good advertisement for a bakery—a scrawny baker."

"Sam doesn't know about the cookies, does he?" Annie asked, smiling.

"Nope," Maxi replied, draining her teacup.

"I wouldn't tell him just yet," the pharmacist said in a hushed voice. "Plenty of time for that later."

Chapter 24

That afternoon, Kate and Maxi sat in folding chairs in front of Sam's cell and watched the baker devour a healthy portion of *enchiladas de mariscos*—seafood stew. Along with several large wedges of skillet corn bread.

Life behind bars was giving the man an appetite, Kate noted approvingly.

Earlier Ben had confessed to Maxi that they were getting Sam out for walks once or twice a day.

"The backyard of the station house isn't exactly the beach," the detective had admitted. "But at least it's green, and it gives him a little fresh air and exercise."

A stack of books and magazines occupied half of Sam's metal bench. And a crossword puzzle book was open next to him, adjacent to a thick new dictionary. Barb.

There were a couple of fat pillows and a plush plaid blanket on the second bench. Gifts from other visitors, Kate speculated.

A navy throw rug carpeted the previously bare tile floor. Kate was guessing that was from the Kims. Or possibly Rosie and Andre.

Dorm room chic aside, the biggest change was in the baker himself. The hollows and creases in his face were filling out. He had a kiss of sun on his forehead and cheeks. And his attitude was downright upbeat.

"How's the bakery?" was the first thing out of his mouth when he saw them. "Open yet?"

"Not quite," Kate said. "I gave it a good scrubbing this morning. Now we're trying to schedule a health inspection. And we have to order supplies."

"Gold Coast Supply. Got an account. You call 'em, they'll come. Ask for Roberta. Had the account since we opened."

Kate pulled a small pad from her pocket and dutifully scrawled "Gold Coast Supply" and "Roberta."

"Is there an account number or PIN code I need to give her?" she asked.

"Don't need that foolishness. Tell her you're my assistant. Running the place for a bit. She'll send what you need. Knows the right amounts, too." To Maxi he asked, "How are the kids?"

"Well, they miss their Tio Sam," Maxi said. "We didn't tell them—"

"Course not. Too young to understand."

"Looks like you've had some visitors," Kate said lightly.

"Whether I want 'em or not," Sam said. "Won't let me out. But they'll let anybody in. Sunny Eisenberg and some pal of hers in here this morning. Yakkin' about some consarned TV show. Genuine housekeepers of somewhere or other."

He sighed. "But they did bring some of Bridget's egg-and-cheese biscuits. From the pub," he said, shaking his head. "Worth it."

Maxi looked at Kate, who was straining not to smile.

From what Kate learned this week, Sam had always helped others when they needed it. Usually on the Q.T.

Clearly, receiving help in return was sheer torture.

"Heard anything more about who killed that snake Lord?" he said between bites.

Kate looked at Maxi, each thinking the same thing: Inside the jail, what had he heard? What should they say?

"The police are following up on a new lead," Maxi said. "But it's too soon to know anything for sure."

"We're looking at a few things, too," Kate admitted. "Just to be sure the police don't miss anything."

Sam nodded.

"No one can find any record of Lord before he came to the U.S.," Kate admitted. "You ever hear anything about his private life? If he had a family, or where he lived?"

"Didn't know anything about him. Didn't want to. Seemed like he knew a lot about me, though. And what he didn't know he made up."

"What do you mean?" Kate asked.

"Doesn't matter."

"Samuel Hepplewhite, it very much does matter," Maxi scolded. "Everyone in this town is trying to figure out who killed Stewart Lord. Because whoever did it made it look like you're the culprit. So if you know anything, mister, you spill it!"

Kate stared at her friend in amazement. Sam looked up and blinked, a surprised expression on his face. He was quiet for a long moment.

"Run a small business, some months are better than others," he started haltingly. "You know."

Maxi nodded encouragingly.

"The lean times. Lord would show up. Make an offer."

"Always a lowball offer?" Kate asked gently.

Sam nodded. "Don't know how he knew. But he always did."

"If you wanted to sell the bakery, you could have sold it for more than he was offering," Kate said.

"Won't sell. Never."

"But why did he think you'd take less?" Kate asked. "I mean, he was wrong about you wanting to sell. But if he hadn't been, you still could have gone somewhere else and gotten a better deal. Why did he think you'd ever say yes to him?"

"Fast cash."

"Actual cash?" Maxi asked, her eyes wide. "Like greenbacks? Benjamins? Bills in a suitcase?"

"Yup. And the weasel would show up when . . . things were bad," the baker said slowly. "Wave money around. Promise to solve my problems. Or make them worse."

"Worse how?" Kate asked.

Sam shook his head. "Never said. Kept sayin' that the business was only worth the ground it was sittin' on. Saying he could make that go down. Then he'd laugh. Some kinda inside joke. Said if I was smart, I'd get out quick. While I could."

Kate nodded. It was pretty much a replay of the conversation she'd overheard at the bakery. "Was he going after any other businesses?"

Sam's spoon stopped halfway to his mouth. He returned it to the bowl.

"Who?" Maxi asked.

Sam exhaled deeply. "Harp. Heard he talked to Harp."

"That makes sense," Maxi said. "When Caroline gets back, they're probably going to have to sell the wine store or turn it into something else. If Lord heard about that, he's the kind who'd swoop in to try to take advantage."

Sam nodded. "Don't know what Harp said. Can't think he'd be fool enough to take that blowhard seriously."

"There could be a few others around town, too," Maxi said thoughtfully. "When you run a small business, things can go from great to awful like the blink of an eye. Even the time of year, that can make a difference."

The baker nodded, picked up his spoon, and resumed eating. "Also get a few things from Sand Dollar Foods," he said, glancing up between bites. "Ask for Betty. Don't tell Roberta."

"Well, of course not," Kate said, nonplussed.

"Cleaning supplies from Casey's Industrial Supply. Talk to Junior. If you get Eddie, hang up. Too slick for his own good."

"We've been getting a few things from Amos Tully's store," Kate said.

"OK to start. But you don't buy retail to sell retail. Won't work. Not for long."

"Truth," Maxi said as she watched Sam mop up the spicy sauce from his bowl with the corn bread.

"Moist. Nice crust."

"Honey instead of sugar," Kate said, smiling.

The baker nodded.

"Um, I hate to mention it, but we're going to have to replace your sourdough starter," she said softly.

"Not Francine?"

"Uh, yeah. The police took everything food related. And apparently that included, um, Francine."

Sam stopped eating and stared at the floor. Kate could see him working his jaw.

"Maybe the place you got it originally could give us another bit?" she prompted. "And if you added anything or grew it a certain way, I can try to replicate that same formula."

"Didn't do anything. Just set her aside every day. Francine did the rest."

He studied the carpet. But unlike the other day, this wasn't dejection or depression. Kate could see the wheels turning in Sam's brain.

"Marco's Bakery," the baker said finally, like he'd made a decision. "In San Francisco. Castro Street. Talk to Marco or Sean. They'll help. Won't be exactly the same. But close."

"I'll call them this afternoon," Kate said. "At this rate, the Cookie House will be reopened for business by the end of the week. Now, if you saved room for dessert, how about a few ginger snaps? I baked a fresh batch."

Chapter 25

As they walked down Main Street, Maxi turned to Kate. "Do you really think we can get the bakery open by the end of the week?"

Kate nodded, slipping a liver treat to Oliver. "The only thing we're missing now is the health inspection. And the guy at their office said he could probably get someone out here on Thursday. If they do—and if we pass—I'll spend all day Friday baking. And we can open on Saturday morning. I might not have all the different kinds of breads that Sam offered, but I can make up a good selection. And some cookies, too. I just want to reach Marco's today and see if they're willing to send us another little bit of Francine."

"Look out, now he's got you doing it," Maxi said.

"Hey, it makes sense. Sourdough starter is a living thing. It deserves a name."

"I'm not poking fun. I do it all the time with my plants. But if you're not careful, you're going to join us crazy folks. Giving names to growing things and trying to make a living from a shop. Nutty!"

"It sounds like Sam had some really rough sledding there for a while. I'm hoping a few sweet treats on the roster might improve his balance sheet."

"I knew it was hard for him," Maxi said barely above a whisper. "But I thought that was because he lost Cookie. I didn't know the money part of it. And I should have."

"Well, we do now, and we're going to help," Kate said as Oliver lifted another treat softly from her fingertips. "What I really want to do is talk to Harp. I'm curious what kind of offer Lord made. And why he never mentioned it at the meeting."

"That did seem a little strange. But I think his wife is a touchy subject right now. My grandmother used to have a saying: *Nunca se sabe lo que realmente está pasando detrás de las cortinas de un vecino.* You never know what's really going on behind a neighbor's curtains." Maxi shrugged. "Course, that goes double in Cuba."

"Cuba sounds a lot like New York. Hey, there he is! Down in front of Seize the Clay. Navy-blue baseball cap and madras shirt. With the big white shopping bag. That's the guy who's been following me!"

"I'll call Ben," Maxi said, grabbing the phone from her purse. "Ay, no signal! Blast it!"

"He's crossing the street. Do you think he knows we saw him?"

"It's a sidewalk full of people in the daytime—and we have a vicious dog." Maxi looked down at Oliver, who stared up at her with a searching expression. "I say we walk up to the jerk and ask him what he thinks he's doing."

"First thing you learn in the big city, never present yourself to criminals or crazy people. They might know what they're going to do next, but you don't."

"Then let's go into a shop and borrow a phone," Maxi said.

"Look! He has to know we've seen him. He's practically fast-walking in the other direction! By the time Ben gets here, he'll be long gone."

"So we go back to the flower shop. Are you sure it was him?"

"Absolutely. And either I'm becoming more observant or he's getting sloppy. He changes up hats and shirts. But he's wearing the same big sunglasses and the same khaki cargo shorts. And the same gray running shoes."

"Maybe he wants you to see him. Like one of those scary clowns. Let's go back to the shop. We can still call Ben. If we tell him what the guy's wearing now, maybe they can pick him up if they see him later today."

"That's a good idea. Besides, I want to call Marco."

"I was thinking," Maxi said as they continued strolling, albeit more slowly. "It might be time to drop off a cookie box to Harp. I have one left from this morning. We could stop by his shop right before closing."

"So we wouldn't be a couple of nosy busybodies," Kate said. "Smart."

"Nope. We're excellent neighbors promoting our business. And then we casually ask him about his super secret business dealings with Stewart Lord."

Chapter 26

As they came to the end of the block and spotted the Cookie House, Kate stopped. And pointed.

Maxi's mouth dropped open. Five different ladders decorated the front of the Victorian house. Most of them holding workmen in white or denim overalls and caps. Bright blue tarps littered the grass beneath the crew.

Out on the front lawn, Carl Ivers, decked out in white coveralls, shouted instructions to the ladder brigade like a conductor directing a wayward orchestra.

"Wally, raise the ladder! Get the top first! Work your way down! Sammy, grab the hand sander! Get rid of those strips of loose paint! Justin, drop that paint can! We're not ready for that yet. This ain't some make-believe DIY show! Prep first!"

"What the . . . ," Maxi and Kate said in unison, gape mouthed on the sidewalk in front of the bakery.

Oliver sat up straight and let out three staccato barks. Announcing their presence.

Carl turned and smiled. "Ladies! We were wondering

when you'd show up," he said, ambling toward them. "Hope you don't mind, but we started without you. S'posed to be dry through Friday, but that's a mighty small window for a place this big."

"You're painting the Cookie House?" Maxi asked, astonished.

"Restoring the old gal to her former glory. High time, too. Heard you girls wanted to get it done at a good price. No price better than free. And no time like the present. Guy who had the hardware store before me had the color chart on file. So here we are."

Kate looked at the crew. She recognized Justin from the shop. But the other men—most of them teenagers— were strangers.

"Who are all these people?" The words flew out of her mouth before she could stop them.

"Friends and neighbors. Well, mostly their kids. On summer break from high school and college. Told 'em we had a once-in-a-lifetime chance to polish up the Cookie House. You know, suit up and get dirty. Most of 'em jumped at it. Or their parents did. But this is just the advance crew. Got the adults coming in later. We'll paint as late into the evening as the light allows. And that team has some experience. These guys, not so much. But they're willing and eager to learn."

"But I thought you believed Sam was guilty?" Kate said, her voice underscoring the confusion she felt.

"Nope, I said the case needs more evidence either way. And we also need to let the cops do their jobs. Sam's a good man. And a good neighbor. And we're gonna help him."

"That's amazing," Maxi said, her voice cracking. "Thank you! From the bottom of my heart. Sam will be so happy."

"Now, that's the other part," Carl said quietly. "We're

gonna keep this under our hats. Let him see the big unveiling when he gets out. Whole crew is sworn to secrecy." The ex-cop grinned. "We'll see how long that holds."

A loud metallic *clank* cut the air. Carl whirled around. "Danny! Stabilize that ladder! Now!

"Can't turn your back on this bunch of rookies," he said under his breath, stomping toward the house. "Not even for a minute."

"You know what this means?" Kate said as Maxi blotted tears from her face.

Her friend shook her head, unable to speak.

"If we're going to feed this crew, we're going to need a lot more food."

Chapter 27

Kate had never seen anything like it.

As word leaked out that the Cookie House was getting a facelift, people started showing up from all over town. Some signed up for work shifts on Carl's crew. Others pledged to bring food for the workers throughout the week.

She and Maxi spent the next few hours standing on the sidewalk in front of the bakery shaking hands and thanking people. It reminded her of the receiving line at a wedding.

Suddenly Kate remembered the reason she had been hustling back to Flowers Maximus: Marco!

How could that have slipped her mind? What if she was too late? What if she failed? What if the bakery had to reopen without its signature sourdough? Who was she to be running a business?

"Uh, I'll be right back," she said hurriedly to Maxi, who was mid-conversation with Andy Levy.

She ducked inside the flower shop, grabbed the orange landline from Maxi's desk, and called Information. As she dialed the California bakery, her hands were trembling.

"This is Marco, how can I help you?"

"Um, my name is Kate McGuire, and I'm a pastry chef at the Cookie House in Coral Cay."

"Hey there! How's old Sam these days? He still making the best sourdough east of the Golden Gate?"

"He is, and that's kind of why I'm calling. We had a bit of a mishap and, well, we lost Francine."

"Oh no! She's Sam's pride and joy. Is Sam OK?"

"He's fine," Kate said, crossing her fingers. "He's actually . . . on vacation. Maxi—she owns the flower shop next door—she and I are running the place while he's away. Anyway, I spoke with Sam and we were wondering, since you guys supplied the original Francine, if maybe you could spare another piece for him? As a replacement? And we'll pay you for it, of course."

She held her breath and prayed Marco was feeling generous.

"Sure, one of us will pack her up and run the box down to the shipper today. If we overnight it, you guys should have it tomorrow. Same address?"

"Same address. The Cookie House on Main Street in Coral Cay. I really can't thank you enough. You have no idea what this means."

"Glad to hear Sam's taking a break. That man could use it. And this is on the house, by the way. It's the least we can do. Because it seems he didn't exactly give you the whole story."

"What do you mean?"

"Sam got Francine—the original Francine—years ago from a historic San Francisco bakery. In business since the 1800s. Made traditional sourdough bread and rolls. Nothing else. Wonderful stuff! Unfortunately, it folded about the same time the housing bubble burst. A few years after that, when Sean and I were opening our place, we went on a road-trip tasting tour. Indie bakeries we'd heard about and always wanted to try. But Sam's sourdough? Off the charts. When he realized we were opening a bakery out here, he gifted us with a piece of Francine. He gave her to us, not the other way around."

"So what you're sending in the mail . . . ," Kate started.

Marco laughed. "We call her Francine Junior."

Chapter 28

"Wow, and I thought I got up early," Maxi said as she wandered into the kitchen sporting faded jeans and a coral T-shirt. "Even Oliver's still sacked out. He's asleep in the tent with *mi niños*. I recognized his little snuffling sounds."

Kate sighed. "I've been up since three. Couldn't sleep. But on the bright side, I just made a fresh pot of your special coffee. Let me know if I got it right. And if you're up for it, you can taste-test the rolls for Sunny's morning class. My only problem is how to actually get them there."

"Taste-testing? That's the job I was born for. I might even put it on my business cards."

Kate grabbed a plate from the cupboard and sliced off a roll from a pan cooling on the counter. She dropped a dollop of butter onto the plate and handed the plate and knife carefully to Maxi.

Her friend pinched off a corner and popped it into her mouth. Maxi's face bloomed into a smile. "OK, these are really good." She cut the roll in half, spread one piece with a little butter, and finished it.

"If you made nothing but these, Sam would be back in business."

Kate grinned. "You're just hungry. But at least I didn't burn them, and the texture is exactly what I was going for."

"If that means they're light and fluffy and taste like more, you nailed it. Sunny's gonna be banging down our door to get her hands on these. Hey, I just realized something. Sunny's six a.m. classes? They don't get out until almost seven thirty."

"Oh jeez, that's got to be one killer class."

"Pretty much," Maxi said, finishing off the other half of the roll. "The only way to survive is to kinda sleep through it. But what I was thinking is, since it's that late, Peter might be willing to make the drop for us. You know, if we give him a couple to try first. As incentive."

"That's fair. As long as he doesn't mind. I made plenty. A few dozen for the class and another two dozen just to test the recipe."

"*Excelente.* That means I can have another one. Oooh, this coffee is good. You might just have a couple of Cubans in your family tree."

"Nah, old sous chef's trick. Watch someone a couple of times and ape what they do. 'Fake it till you make it' is what one of my instructors called it. I just hope that works with sourdough."

Maxi sniffed the air. "Are you baking cookies again?"

"Not again. Still. I thought I'd make some for the crews coming to work on the bakery today. And do a few more of the gift boxes for the people dropping off food."

"Potential customers all," Maxi said happily. "And the best part is we don't have to chase them down, because they're coming to us."

"The batch you're smelling is pecan brownie cookies. I use cocoa powder in the dough. Very rich."

"Ay, hopefully that will be us after this is over. Very rich. And we can pay people to do our work, while we sleep for a week. Oh, that reminds me. The guy from the health department called yesterday. He said either Thursday or Friday. But definitely by Friday."

"That's cutting it close," Kate said, pausing after she poured flour into the bright blue mixing bowl. "If he comes Thursday, I can bake all day Friday and we can open Saturday. If he comes Friday, we can still open Saturday, but we won't have anything to sell."

"So maybe we sell stuff as we bake it. Or give it away as we bake it. Everything fresh and warm. As a way of saying 'thank you' to the whole town."

"Giving away the first batches? That's brilliant. It's going to cost Sam a little in supplies, on top of the cost of being closed for a week. But hopefully we can make it up with the additional sales from desserts and cookies."

"We could do the same thing with some of the restaurant clients, too. Like Oy and Begorra. And even In Vino Veritas. Bread and wine is classic. And wine and cookies? Not so bad, either."

"Which reminds me, we never got over to talk to Harp about Stewart Lord," Kate said, determinedly beating butter and sugar together in a second bowl.

"So we tackle him today," Maxi said. "He's just around the corner. It shouldn't take that long."

"That works. I really want to see what you think of this next batch. I'm mixing up something special. One of my grandmother's recipes. Anise and almond cookies. She always made them at Christmas. I thought it might bring us a little good luck."

"Oh, that sounds good. And we could use a little holiday magic."

A few minutes later, the wet ingredients sufficiently tamed, Kate reached for the extract. Reflexively, she took the cap off the bottle and sniffed it.

And it all came flooding back. The break-in. The footsteps. The fear. Kate's heart pounded.

She set down the anise extract and leaned heavily on the counter.

"Kate! What's wrong?" Maxi called across the kitchen.

Kate shook her head. "It's OK. I'm fine."

"You're working too hard," Maxi said. "Come and sit for a while. Have a little something to eat."

Kate shook her head. "No, it's not that. Hang on a minute." Purposefully, she reached for the extract again. Taking a deep breath and willing herself calm, she brought the small bottle to her nose and inhaled the pungent fragrance.

It was like a front-row seat to the night of the break-in. The memories were vivid. Technicolor. The menacing footsteps across the tile floor. The fear as she tore down the stairs, toward the front door. To safety. To Oliver. The relief that flooded her body as she sat on the floor of the shop, with her arms wrapped around the half-grown puppy. The smell of the beach on his coat. How warm he felt. Solid.

Along with the stench of cigarettes, there had been two other scents lingering in the air after the intruder's hasty retreat. And now she knew. One of them—the familiar smell—had been anise.

Chapter 29

Kate looked over at Maxi, seated at the breakfast bar, her face a tight mask of concern.

"I'm fine, honestly," Kate said finally, white knuckles gripping the counter. "It's just that, well, I remembered something. About the break-in. It was the smell. The anise extract."

Maxi nodded, waiting.

"Remember when I said there was a weird mix of smells in the shop after the burglar left?"

Maxi nodded again. "I remember. You said something was familiar. But you couldn't tell what exactly."

"It was anise. Cigarettes. And anise. And something else. Something I still don't recognize. But I remember it. Sweet. But not food. More like aftershave. Or cologne."

"So what does it mean? We know this man who broke in—he wears hard shoes, he smokes, he shaves, and he smells like Christmas cookies?"

"I know, Kyle Hardy would love that. I can tell him we were robbed by an off-season Santa Claus."

"So we don't tell the *bobo*. Or even Ben. But in Coral Cay there aren't many people who smoke. We already know it was a man, so that helps. And how many guys smell like anise?"

"Not many," Kate admitted, shrugging. "Could Sam have some competition that we don't know about? Another baker? Maybe even a restaurant or shop that sells baked goods? Or someone who plans to sell baked goods?"

"You think someone was trying to steal recipes?"

"Whoever it was didn't take cash. Maybe because they were interrupted. Or maybe because that's not what they were after. Sam is known for his sourdough. Everyone loves it. What if someone wanted his recipe?"

"Good luck with that one," Maxi said. "He keeps it in his head. He's made it so many times, I don't think he ever writes it down."

"OK, what if they were after Francine? His starter is kind of his secret weapon. If they got their hands on her, they might be able to put a dent in his business. Maybe enough that the bakery would go under. We know he's been running the place on a shoestring."

"But they didn't get anything," Maxi said. "And they never came back."

"Scared off? First by the ruckus. Later by the murder."

"And after the police closed the Cookie House, there was no Francine," Maxi added. "And no Sam making sourdough. What is it the pilots say? 'Mission accomplished.'"

"But today we get another batch of starter," Kate

added. "And by Friday or Saturday, we're going to fire up the ovens and start baking again."

Maxi shook her head. "Whatever we do, it sounds like we better be very, very careful."

Chapter 30

As Kate strolled down Main Street with Oliver trotting along on one side and a box of cookies clasped in her hands, she realized all over again just how beautiful Coral Cay really was. Already midday, the sun was high in the sky, but the breeze was cool and salty. Petunias—in shades of coral, hot pink, purple, and yellow—spilled out of giant stone pots up and down the block, while jasmine climbed the lampposts, its scent wafting in the air. Some shops even added to the dizzying display with window boxes and hanging baskets heavy with blooms.

Something told her Maxi and her green thumbs might have had a hand in it. Or maybe Floridians just loved their flowers.

She spotted her destination, In Vino Veritas, and sighed heavily.

Oliver looked up. She could have sworn she saw concern in the black button eyes.

"It's OK, baby. We're just going in to have a nice little talk. Maxi wanted to come, but she's got orders backing up at the flower shop. And someone has to keep an eye on the Cookie House, in case the crews need something. Or any of our deliveries arrive. Or the health inspector shows up early."

In fact, she and Maxi had mulled this over for a good ten minutes. In the end, Kate decided she could handle Harp on her own. And if she could get him talking, he might be more willing to spill about his dealings with Lord. But they agreed she'd take the pup. As a distraction. And, if needed, a convenient excuse to leave quickly in case things got uncomfortable.

"You really are my knight in fuzzy armor, you know that?"

The exuberant puppy stretched his neck high and practically bounced the remaining few steps.

Kate took a deep breath and pulled open the ornate door. From the outside, Harp's shop had a Victorian air, with heavy molding and deep bay windows. Inside it smelled like exotic spices and looked like money. Lots of money.

"Well, if it isn't the pastry chef herself," the proprietor drawled, stepping out from behind a marble counter. Today he'd opted for Ivy League casual: crisply pressed khakis and a blue dress shirt with the sleeves rolled neatly to his elbows. "To what do I owe this very welcome diversion in my otherwise humdrum day?"

"Well, the Cookie House is going to start baking cookies. All kinds of sweets, really. To spread the word, we're sharing some samples with our friends and neighbors," she said, presenting the gift box.

"Well, I certainly hope I qualify as both," Harp said with an easy grin. He flipped open the box lid and inhaled deeply. "Oh my, these look truly superb! So good, in fact, they might become my lunch."

"The dark ones are pecan brownie cookies. And the

ones with powdered sugar are anise and almond. An old family recipe."

"Oh, I love anise. Anything that tastes like licorice, really. I had a great-aunt who used to make anise cookies." He picked one up and took a small bite. "Oh my, this really takes me back."

"That's the great thing about cookies," Kate said. "It's like a little taste of childhood."

"In my case, it's an age I'm not sure I ever left. Mentally anyway." He held out the open box to Kate, who selected a brownie cookie.

"I'd offer you wine, but I am certain you are too much of a lady to be drinking at this early hour."

"Not too much of a lady, but there's definitely too much on my to-do list this afternoon. We're trying to get the bakery reopened this Saturday. We'd love it if you'd stop by. The first day, we're giving away all the baked goods, fresh out of the oven. To say thanks for everything everyone is doing for Sam."

"I heard about the redo. And I'll be happy to attend. Now, how about some coffee to go with these delicious cookies? I've got some wonderful stuff brewing. With chicory, the way they do it in my hometown of New Orleans. Smooths the rough edges off the old coffee bean."

"That would be lovely, thank you."

She and Oliver followed him to a butler's pantry in the back corner of the shop, where a hand-hammered copper coffee urn rested on the white marble counter. As she trailed behind him, she caught the scent of his cologne. Something citrusy. Lime. Either Harp had switched fragrances or he wasn't their burglar.

The pup whined softly.

"It's OK," she said sotto voce. "We'll finish your walk next. I promise. You're being very good."

"I'm afraid I don't have anything for young Oliver,"

Harp said. "This is the first time he's actually favored me with a visit. But I'll be certain to keep a little something on hand for next time."

"He's fine," Kate explained. "He just wants to get back to his walk. Don't you, boy?"

Oliver's curious expression said otherwise. But he stretched out on the floor by her feet like a sphinx. Relaxed but alert.

Harp set down the cookies and, with a flourish, produced two china cups from the mahogany cupboard. Along with matching saucers. He filled the first cup and handed it gently to Kate.

"This coffeemaker may seem like an extravagance," he said as she poured a bit of cream into the cup from an ancient-looking sterling silver vessel. "But it more than pays for itself by fueling the hours I put in here. Or perhaps I am simply spoiled. I do love the finer things."

He ladled several spoons full of brown sugar into his own cup, followed that with a generous splash of cream, and raised it. "Cheers!"

Kate took a sip. Harp was right. With just a little cream, the coffee was velvety. So dissimilar from Cuban coffee it could be an entirely different beverage. But equally delicious.

Kate smiled. "I've noticed that everyone in town seems to have their own way of bringing the comforts of home to their shops."

"Ah, sounds like you've seen the Kims' setup. Truly ingenious! Well, when you run a store, the hours are brutal. Positively grueling. Of course, I would never do anything else." He looked at his surroundings and sighed. "I love this place."

Kate sensed an opening. "But you're thinking of selling," she said softly.

"How did you . . . ?" He grinned and shook his head.

"Ah, there are absolutely no secrets in a small town. And if you're plugged into the local gossip mill, you really are one of us now. I'm afraid there's no turning back. Yes, I was considering it. Still am, in fact. Who knows what the future holds? I suppose you've heard about my situation?"

Kate nodded, sipping her coffee.

"One minute, life is sailing along. Everything is perfect. The next, not so much. Caroline's been in touch. All part of the process, apparently. Informs me that she's simply bored. Bored with Coral Cay, bored with the shop, and, frankly, bored with me. She wants to relocate to one of her old haunts in Europe. Preferably Paris or Rome. Use that as a base of operations and travel again. 'Rejoin the world,' she calls it. So yes, I'm considering selling this place. Even though I don't want to."

"I'm so sorry. I had no idea."

Reflexively, Kate glanced down. Only then did she notice Harp's shoes. An expensive-looking pair of wing tips.

"It's my own fault," he said. "I haven't told anyone. Not until now. You're easy to talk with. Lucky you," he added ruefully. "Of course one can't exactly tell the town fathers that one's wife views their picturesque little hamlet as a— let's see, how did she put it?—'brackish backwater where mosquitos, hurricanes and humans go to die.'"

"Yowch!"

"She doesn't mince words, my wife. At least, I think she's still my wife. I keep getting mixed messages on that one. But I digress."

"Have you received any decent offers on the store?"

"Not yet. To be honest, I haven't been shopping it all that seriously. One interested party proposed an offer. But, as it turns out, he was simply hoping for a fire sale discount. Due to my . . . complicated domestic situation."

"Stewart Lord."

"Ah, good news travels fast. Bad news even faster. The mantra of village life."

"I was just surprised you'd deal with him. He seems like such a . . . well . . ."

"Miscreant?"

"Exactly."

"Yes, but he was a miscreant with the financial resources to solve my present problem. Unfortunately, he didn't wish to part with enough of his filthy lucre. So that was that."

"When you said no, how did he take it?"

"A lot of bluff and bluster. Which, from what I gather, was normal for him."

"Any threats?"

Harp's eyebrows went up. "Well, he did mention something about money now being better than regrets and empty pockets later. And he reliably informed me that absolutely no one was going to make me a better offer. Or any offer. Seemed rather smug about it, too. I take it that's what passed for hard-nosed negotiating in his part of the world."

"Did he ever say what part of the world that was? No one can seem to find any evidence of his existence before he showed up in the U.S."

"Oh, the plot thickens! He always implied that he was from London. The East End. Before all the art galleries and restaurants. You know, hardscrabble boy from the rough streets. The Artful Dodger made good. Wouldn't it be rich if the whole Cockney thing was a façade and he really grew up in a middle-class neighborhood in Sheboygan?"

"Well, something with his story is off. Did he ever mention family?"

"Not to me. But before he made the offer, I'd only

met him two or three times. He'd popped into the shop. When it came to wines, he could talk the talk. But there was something, I don't know, studied about it. I remember he said he loved scotch. Claimed his everyday tipple was MacKendrick single malt. Vintage Cask."

"MacKendrick's a good name. I'm not a scotch drinker, but I know that much from working in restaurants."

"Well, that particular variety retails for three hundred dollars a bottle and up. It's wonderful to enjoy the finer things. And to have the wherewithal to do it. But I suspect he enjoyed the price tag more than the drink."

"Bragging rights?"

"Precisely. Put cheap rotgut in a glass and tell him it was the good stuff? That man would have never known the difference."

Harp plucked another sugar-dusted cookie from the box. As he did, Kate caught the flash of something on his forearm. The corner of a large, skin-colored bandage.

"You've hurt yourself?" she asked, pointing.

"Oh, that," he said cheerfully. "The patch. With everything up in the air the way it's been, I'm afraid I slipped up my own self. Started smoking again. But never fear, I'm back on the wagon again. Almost a week now."

Chapter 31

Standing on Main Street, half a block from Harp's store, Kate reached down and lovingly scratched Oliver's ear. "So what do you think?" she asked, patting his soft flank. "Is he our burglar?"

She had a hard time reconciling the bon vivant shop owner (and beleaguered husband) with the mysterious figure who terrorized her just a week ago. At the same time, something felt "off." But she couldn't quite put her finger on it.

"C'mon, Ollie, I promised Maxi we wouldn't be long. She's holding down the fort—two forts—on her own. Let's go give her a hand. And a paw."

As they walked up the block, Kate happened to glance across the street. And spotted a familiar form. "Not again," she said under her breath.

Purposefully, she turned in the other direction and hustled through the nearest shop door.

"Welcome to Wheels! Would you like to buy, rent, or browse?"

The upper-crust British accent took her by surprise. So did the girl herself. With large china-blue eyes, blunt-cut blond bangs, and pink cheeks without a speck of makeup on her flawless skin. A perfect English rose.

"Could I use your phone? Your landline?"

"Right over there on the wall," she said, pointing. "So how's Oliver this morning? Are you enjoying your walkies?"

Kate looked over to see the girl had two biscuits in her hand. For his part, Oliver stared into her face entranced.

Kate grabbed the handset of the wall phone and dialed 911.

"I need Ben," she said urgently when the operator came on the line.

"Emergency or nonemergency?"

"It's not life threatening. But it's very important. He asked me to call if I spotted someone. And I've just seen him. But he's going to get away. Please. I need to speak with Ben."

"Detective Abrams is off duty. I can put you through to Officer Hardy. Please hold."

"No! I mean, not Officer Hardy. Detective Abrams. He was very specific that I speak with him only."

"He's at lunch. Let me see if I can raise him. Please hold."

It felt like forever. Meanwhile, she wondered. Did Ball Cap Man know she'd seen him? Would he escape? Again?

Her stomach clenched into a knot. Her throat felt like sand. She drummed her fingers on the handset. Where *was* he?

After what seemed like an eternity, Kate heard a familiar voice on the line.

"Detective Abrams. Who's this?"

"Detective, thank goodness. This is Kate McGuire. The man with the ball cap. He's here."

"Stay calm. Where are you?"

Kate looked around the store. "It's a bike shop. Downtown."

"Tell him you're in Wheels," said the English girl, who had obviously overheard every word. "Ben's likely just down the street at the pub. They've got chicken pot pie today," she added helpfully.

"Wheels. I'm at Wheels. He was right across the street. The shop with the blue and white awning. But I've been on hold forever. He's probably slipped away again."

"What's he wearing this time?" the detective asked.

"Faded olive ball cap. Cream-colored Hawaiian shirt with some sort of pattern. Tan cargo shorts. Big sunglasses. Gray sneakers. White socks. And he's carrying a large brown shopping bag."

"I'm on it. Stay where you are inside the shop. Don't leave. I'll come for you after I canvass the neighborhood. Just sit tight."

"I'm sorry I interrupted your lunch," Kate said, near tears. It was all she could think of to say.

Chapter 32

The girl handed Kate a paper cup full of milky hot liquid. It smelled of bergamot. Earl Grey tea.

"Tea makes everything better," she explained. "Maybe not completely, but it certainly helps. And I put some sugar in it, too."

Kate felt like an idiot. She'd ruined the detective's lunch. And made a fool of herself in the process. She sounded like a hysterical ninny. And at this rate, everyone in Coral Cay was going to hear about it. Small-town secrets, indeed.

"I'm sorry. I feel so stupid. A man's been following me. Since I arrived in town . . ."

"A stalker? That's awful. You'll be safe here. Besides," she said, smiling, "we have Oliver to protect us."

"I'm Kate McGuire," she said, putting out her hand. "I'm helping out with the Cookie House."

"Clarissa St. John. Claire. My boyfriend mentioned you. Gabe Louden?"

"Gabe saved my life when I first got to town. My car broke down on Main Street. And I was on my way to a job interview at Fish-a-Palooza."

"Nasty place. You dodged a bullet there. So how's Sam doing?"

"Better. Although we're still trying to figure out what really happened, so he can come home."

"Gabe mentioned that. I wanted to come to the book club meeting, but I had too much to do here. Stewart Lord was a vile pig. Whoever killed him probably had an excellent reason."

With a clear grudge and a British background, did Claire know more about Stewart Lord than she was letting on? Something about his hidden past?

Then again, anyone who ever met the developer seemed to feel the same way.

"So you sell bicycles?" Kate asked, glancing around.

"Sell, lease, and rent. I also repair them. And I have the grunge on my smock to prove it," Claire said, grinning. "You may not have noticed, but for the locals, bikes are quite a popular way to traverse the town. No noise, no pollution, no petrol. And you can go pretty much anywhere you like. Including over to the beach. Tourists rent them for an afternoon. Makes them feel like they've gone native. And I have those big three-wheeled trikes that the retirees seem to favor. Even a few fat-wheeled ones that they can ride on the wet sand, just above the water."

Kate had seen the racks full of bikes around town. And people zipping here and there on two wheels. But somehow, she'd never made the connection.

"Just out of curiosity, what would it cost to buy a bike? I mean, I was thinking of something with baskets to deliver orders from the bakery."

"I have a couple of models in stock that should be just your size. You're about five-eight?"

"Exactly. How did you know?"

"Bike mechanics are like tailors," Claire said, shrugging. "And if your bike isn't a good fit, you're better off walking. Too small, and you work too hard. Too large, and it's out of balance. Right, Oliver?"

The pup looked up but wisely said nothing.

"The one I'd recommend is practically new," Claire continued. "It came in a few months ago, and I've been using it occasionally for rentals. But I could retrofit it with baskets, or braces for baskets. That way, you could add and remove them as needed. It's not quite how you want to deliver a wedding cake. But for anything else it should be perfect."

A minute later, Claire wheeled a baby-blue ladies' bike from the storeroom.

"The style is retro cool, but it also has five speeds, so you'll have some versatility."

"This is gorgeous," Kate said. "It looks brand new."

"Very low mileage, as the used-car salesmen say. I could put click-in brackets here, on the back carrier, to accommodate different-sized baskets or trays. And it already has the basket in the front."

"I hate to ask, but how much?"

The door opened and Ben Abrams stepped inside the shop. "Ladies," he said with a tip of his Panama hat. "Good news, bad news. The guy slithered away again."

Kate's face fell. Claire, who looked almost as upset as Kate, patted her on the shoulder.

"The good news is, several of the store owners got a nice look at him," the detective said. "I talked with them. And if they spot him again, they're gonna call me. Quietly. And the more eyes and ears we have, the better."

The detective paused, pulling out a small spiral pad.

"I have a general description of this guy. About five-five, five-six. Late forties. Deep tan. Kind of burly," he shrugged. "Lot of that going around. And one of the witnesses mentioned a New York accent. Maybe Brooklyn. Could be the Bronx. Heck, for all Phyllis knows about New York, it could be Yonkers or Bean Town. What I'm trying to say is, you got a couple of ganders at this guy. Is there any chance you might know who he is? Or is there any reason someone might have had to follow you here from New York?"

"No, none," Kate said plainly. "I broke off an engagement. But he's already moved on to someone else. That's why we broke up. I have a sister and brother-in-law in New Jersey. It definitely wasn't my brother-in-law. And besides, they have their own lives. My ex-landlord just sold her apartment building for a small fortune, so she's happy. The last restaurant I worked for went under, so everyone there is scrambling for a job. And that sums up my life in New York. I was working sixteen-hour days. I didn't have time to make enemies. Besides, I have a pretty good memory for faces. You kind of have to in my business. And I've never seen that guy before I arrived in Coral Cay."

Ben nodded. "OK, I had to ask. And you were right to call. Do it again if you see him. Doesn't matter if I'm at lunch or mowing my lawn, the operators will patch you through."

Kate nodded, shaking his hand. "Thank you. And I really am sorry about your lunch."

"No big deal," the detective said, bending to give Oliver's neck a friendly scratch. "I was just finishing up. Only thing I missed was dessert. Strawberry shortcake. And Doc Patel would probably pin a medal on you for that. Oh, I meant to tell you, the crime lab's finished with your cell phone and those books of yours we collected from the bakery. You can stop by the station and pick them up anytime."

"Thank you. I really appreciate that."

"Take care, ladies, Oliver," Ben said, tipping his hat as he turned to leave. "Just keep an eye out. We've got the whole town watching for this clown. We're gonna get him."

Kate nodded, her smile tight. When the door closed after him, she sagged against the counter.

"I'm so sorry they didn't catch your villain," Claire said earnestly. "But Ben's right. If everyone's looking for him, they're either going to collect him or scare him away. Win-win, as you Yanks say."

Kate smiled in spite of herself. And gazed longingly at the sky-blue bike. "You're right. And I'm going to put it out of my mind. Now, how much is this beautiful thing?"

"Rent it first. That's what I always recommend. That way, you can test whether it's a good fit—for you and the bakery. How about we say seventy-five dollars for the week for the bike and a new helmet? If you like it, we'll consider that a down payment. And you could pay off the remaining three hundred dollars in installments."

Kate did some math in her head. Three hundred and seventy-five dollars was a chunk. Especially when she didn't know when or how Sam would be able to pay her. But she could put the first seventy-five dollars on her card. Even her overworked plastic could handle that. A bike would enable her to get those early morning deliveries to the yoga studio. The revenue from that alone would practically pay for it. And if she didn't have the money next week, she'd just have to bring it back.

She fished the plastic card out of her jeans pocket and presented it to Claire, grinning. "OK, you've got yourself a deal!"

Chapter 33

Maxi was on the phone when Kate walked into the flower shop.

"It has been crazy since you left," she said, hanging up the phone. "Cra-zy. The word is spreading about Muriel. About the police investigating her death now. So we've lost a few people from the painting crew."

"But they don't even have any results yet. It's just a theory. One of many."

"I know. But a couple of the parents, they don't want to take any chances. So they told their boys to come home. Or go to the beach. The good part is that most of the crew is still here."

"That is good news, I guess."

"And there is other good news. I talked to Carl. The kitchen is in super good shape. But the storerooms upstairs need fresh paint. He's got some stuff that has no smell. No gassing? And they're gonna get those rooms done tonight. He left a chart, in case you want to pick the colors."

Maxi handed Kate a brochure.

"No VOC? This is perfect for the bakery."

"It's also pet-safe, so it'll be better for you-know-who."

"Oh, these are beautiful," Kate said, studying the chart. "I like this one. The butter yellow."

"That was my pick, too," Maxi confessed. "But I thought maybe that very light blue for *el baño*? It's almost white with just a tiny bit of blue. Super relaxing."

"Oh, that would be pretty. Should we ask Sam? It's his place, after all."

"Nah, Sam wants to delegate. So we let him delegate. Besides, after cleaning up the mess made by the *bobo* this is the fun stuff."

"Speaking of fun stuff, I think I bought a bike."

"You *think*? Did someone take your wallet and say, 'Oh, by the way, here's a bike for you'?"

"Pretty much. I ducked into a bike shop to call the cops after I spotted Ball Cap Man again."

"No! Are you OK? What happened?"

"I interrupted Ben's lunch. They didn't catch the guy. The pub is serving chicken pot pie and strawberry shortcake. And I bought a bike. Well, I'm renting it for a week. With an option to buy, if I can come up with the payments."

"Claire's place?"

"Yeah. I thought I could use it for deliveries around town. For the bakery. She's going to deliver it here tomorrow."

"Oooh, bike deliveries are a great idea. Cookies on Wheels. Cookies to Go. Cookies on the Go. The Cookie House Express. Well, we can come up with a name later. And Claire will give you a good price. Not like those places near resort town. So I'm dying to know. What happened with Harp?"

"He was a perfect gentleman. But he could be our burglar."

"What? No! Harp would never burgle. Harp would hire someone to burgle. And he'd make the guy wear white gloves."

"He loves anise. He wears hard shoes. Granted, some first-class hard shoes. And he smokes."

"I never knew Harp smoked. Caroline hates smoking."

"Old habit, it sounds like. And with all the stress lately, he started in again. But he just quit. He's on the patch. And, by my calculations, he quit just after the break-in."

"What about his aftershave?" Maxi asked. "Was it the same one?"

"Totally different. His is, well, nice. The other one really wasn't. That's what I meant when I said it *could* be him."

"Ay, but why would he do it?"

"That doesn't make sense, either. Harp is thinking about selling the shop. But he seems torn, so he really hasn't put it on the market yet. Lord heard about the situation with Caroline and made one of his famous lowball offers. When Harp turned him down, he went through the same song and dance he did with Sam. Promised him that no one else would ever want the place."

"He was a horrible man," Maxi said. "Squeezing people when they're hurting."

"But everything we've heard about Lord was that he was a very sharp businessman. Telling someone they won't get a better offer? That's pretty standard. Mild, even. But Lord seemed to believe that getting his hands on their property at a rock-bottom price was a sure thing. Almost like it was his right. And when he came into the bakery, he acted like he already owned the place. Why?"

"Because he was awful?"

"No. I mean, yes, he was awful. But I think there was

more to it than that. You said he had plans for redeveloping Coral Cay?"

"That was the rumor. More resorts and some very expensive condominiums. And a casino. Maybe a golf course. Peter even heard he was asking questions about putting in an airport. For those little planes the rich guys fly."

"A private airport?"

Maxi nodded.

"That's a lot of trouble and planning if you've only made a few halfhearted, lowball offers on a couple of pieces of property."

"So what do you think?"

"Lord's specialty was getting land for next to nothing. After the hurricanes. And remember what Amos Tully said at the book club meeting? When that wasn't enough, rumor has it he cut a deal with some of the insurance companies to delay payouts? If that's true, it means Lord stepped up his game and learned how to get even more land for next to nothing."

"You think he learned a new trick?" Maxi asked.

"I do," Kate replied. "I suspect Stewart Lord had a plan. Something big. Something that would have let him scoop up Coral Cay for a song."

Chapter 34

That afternoon, as Maxi carried a late lunch—and the good news about the reopening plans—over to Sam at the jail, Kate kept an eye on Flowers Maximus and the Cookie House.

Pressed for time, they'd opted for one of Bridget's chicken pot pies with strawberry shortcake for dessert.

Before Maxi left, Kate handed her two cookie boxes, both without the new Cookie House labels. "This one's for Sam. So he can enjoy a snack later. And this one's for Ben, if you see him. Apparently, Ball Cap Man and I cost him dessert."

"Ay, you definitely don't want to do that. You know that phrase 'the long arm of the law'? When I hear that, I always see Ben at Thanksgiving dinner, reaching across our table for the cherry pie. That man loves his sweets."

An hour later, Kate didn't see how Maxi managed it. Even without the health department crisis, the florist's phone rang almost nonstop. While most of the calls were fairly simple—people who wanted to see if she had a favorite flower in stock or to get prices for plants or landscaping—many were big last-minute floral orders. Or changes to big last-minute floral orders.

One bride-to-be needed an estimate on flowers for her wedding. But she wanted native seasonal plants only. The date of the wedding? Either next weekend or Halloween. They were still working on that. (Kate promised Maxi would call as soon as she returned from "another event.")

A second bride confessed her father had pronounced the florist's estimate for pink and white roses "too bloody high." What else could Ms. Más-Buchanan recommend that would be stylish and still fit their budget? ("Not to worry, Ms. Más-Buchanan can suggest some lovely alternatives, and she'll be in touch this afternoon.")

And two of the resort hotels phoned. One had a guest planning a last-minute wedding, another needed flowers for an impromptu baby shower this weekend: Could she accommodate them? (Definitely, Kate informed both. And her "boss, Ms. Más-Buchanan, would call for the details and handle the arrangements personally.")

All between taking deliveries for the bakery and the flower shop. And shuttling cookies, cold water, and lemonade to the painting crew.

When she spotted the UPS truck pulling up in front of the Cookie House, Kate opened the door and flew across the lawn to the bakery.

She met the deliveryman just as he was hiking up the walkway carrying a white box with "Marco's" printed on the sides in heavy black letters.

"Hi, I'm Kate McGuire," she said, slightly out of breath. "I think that one's for me."

"Kate McGuire, care of the Cookie House," the young guy said, smiling. "Just take this and sign there," he said, handing her the box with an electronic tablet stacked on top. "Hey, do you guys really make cookies?"

"All kinds. Come back on Saturday. We're having a grand reopening. To celebrate, we're giving away everything we bake. To the community."

She paused for a beat. And focused. "And the peanut butter cookies are outstanding. Salty and sweet."

"With those fork hashtags in the top? Oh man, those are my favorite. My mom hasn't made those in years. OK, you're on. I'll be back here Saturday. Might bring a few friends, too."

"The more the merrier," Kate said, wondering if they might need more supplies.

With ladders forming a virtual cage across the front of the bakery, she headed to the back door. As she rounded the corner of the house, she spied Carl Ivers sitting on the back stoop. Smoking a cigarette.

"Don't tell Minette," he said, inhaling deeply and casting a long glance across the backyard.

Kate's mind worked double-time. A locksmith (and ex-cop) would know how to pick a lock. She remembered Carl installing a dead bolt the morning after the break-in—how safe that had made her feel. Now she suddenly realized it also meant he could have a key to the bakery. And with the painting project, who'd think twice if they saw him going into the place at any hour? He was going to be here tonight. Late. Painting the storerooms. How hard would it be for him to take a "smoke break" to finish searching the place for whatever it was the burglar wanted?

She snuck a glance at his shoes. Work boots. With hard soles.

"I don't really smoke anymore," he explained. "Quite a long time ago. I just bum one now and then. To relax."

Carl finally looked up and met her eyes. "So what's in the box?"

"New shoes," Kate said quickly. "Ordered them online."

Chapter 35

That evening, as Maxi worked the phones for the flower shop, typing away at her home computer, Kate staked out the Más-Buchanan kitchen, baking batch after batch of cookies. While simultaneously researching tricks and techniques for making the perfect sourdough.

Unfortunately, she couldn't put her hands on the real thing for another twenty-four hours. Until Francine Junior Junior had time to adjust to her new home in Maxi's kitchen cupboard—and leaven a bit of flour.

In the meantime, Kate made do by reading every sourdough how-to she could lay her hands on—from professional strategies to hacks from home chefs. She had a library's worth of cookbooks piled on the counter. She'd even bribed Michael into parting with the family iPad so she could access a few online resources.

His price: a post-dinner batch of cookies in the flavor of his choice.

As a result, Michael, Javie, and Elena were conducting

high-volume, high-stakes negotiations in the den, while Oliver supervised from the sofa.

The sound of the doorbell sent them into overdrive.

"Pizza guy!" Michael hollered.

"Pizza man, pizza man!" Javie sang, jumping up and down.

"Piz-za!" Elena exclaimed.

"Got it!" Peter called, heading for the front door, still in his dress shirt and suit pants.

He'd barely made it through the door that evening when Maxi informed him he was on dinner duty. So he'd shed his jacket, pulled off his tie, and ordered pizza.

"Gordian knot solution," he happily informed his wife. "And the kids can help me set up out back."

As they all sat around the outdoor table, Maxi glanced over at him and grinned. "You, *mi amor,* are a wonderful Italian chef. I love it when you cook."

Esperanza, a small smile on her face, delicately cut her slice with a knife and fork.

"Hey, I'm a regular Renaissance man. I cook, I deliver baked goods, I put away the bad guys. . . ."

Maxi looked at him meaningfully. "How did I get so lucky?"

"Well, if that impressed you, I'm going for broke now. Remember how we were having so much trouble finding any information on His Majesty Stewart Lord back in the U.K.?"

Maxi and Kate nodded as Javie reached over and snagged another piece of bacon and sausage pizza.

"Turns out Lord's not his real name. His birth name is 'Larde' with an *e.* Paul Larde. Known around the old neighborhood as Roly Paulie."

"Did he have a record?" Kate asked.

"Some small-fry stuff when he was a teenager. Petty theft. Loitering. Joyriding. Sounds like he was more of a wannabe than anything else. And he already had quite the gift of gab. Always managed to talk his way out of any serious charges. Then, when he was nineteen, his mother passed. Didn't have much of an estate, but the old lady had a nice burial policy. Some kind of holdover from the father's pension plan. Anyway, it was supposed to cover her expenses, with any remainder split between Paul and his sister, Mary."

"I think I know where this is going," Maxi said, taking another piece of veggie pizza and carefully placing it on the paper plate in front of Elena.

Oliver, stationed on the grass near the girl's chair, didn't beg. But he happily accepted any morsels surreptitiously slipped to him. And claimed anything that fell on the ground.

Peter smiled. "Yup. Somehow, Paulie-boy got his hands on that check and both he and it vanished. Sister never saw either one again."

"Did she file charges?" Kate asked.

"Didn't see the point, apparently. She knew Paul well enough to know that money was long gone. Rest of the relatives had to pass the hat to bury the mother."

"That's awful," Maxi said.

"But true to form," Kate added.

"So that real estate empire, he started it with stolen money?" Maxi breathed. "What happens to it now?"

"Barring a will, which we can't find any trace of, his sister gets it all."

Maxi giggled.

Kate grinned. "I know, right?" She raised her water glass. "Here's to karma!"

Chapter 36

Friday morning, as Maxi fielded the phone and finished several orders next door at Flowers Maximus, Kate surveyed the bakery.

The outside was nearly complete. The painting crew was completing the back of the house. And Carl was confident they'd be done by sundown.

Inside, the upstairs was gorgeous. Thanks to whatever Carl had used, the new-paint smell wasn't overpowering. And somehow the pale butter-yellow color intensified the sunshine. For Kate, who'd lived for years in an aging New York apartment where most of the illumination came from fluorescent bulbs and track lights, it was like a glass of cold water after coming in off the desert.

And Maxi had been right about *el baño*. The ice blue looked cool and relaxing. The perfect place to grab a refreshing shower after spending the day in a hot kitchen.

This is just temporary, Kate reminded herself. *Next on the list after the bakery opens and tourist season winds down—get my own place. Still,* she thought, looking around longingly. *This is beautiful.*

She walked to the open windows and looked out across the town, feeling the strong breeze on her face. It smelled like the ocean. She could see so much of Coral Cay. Even a bit of turquoise water off in the distance.

When Kate looked straight down, she was stunned. The dead bush was gone. Replaced by a healthy hibiscus dotted with deep pink blooms. And the second, freshly painted white window box held a twin of the first.

Maxi.

But when did she even have time? Maxi had spent most of the previous day putting in big beds of flowers along the porch and down the walkway of the Cookie House. She'd gotten a little help from Bridget O'Hanlon, who had come to bring lunch and ended up spending the afternoon. Maxi even managed to "borrow" a few of the kids from Carl's crew.

The results were spectacular.

Nearest the house, the petunia beds were either entirely pink or white—"'Cause that will look good against the light pink house," Maxi had confided.

She'd planted ground cover along the walkway. Something with dark green leaves and small, sweet-smelling white flowers. And at the intersection of the bakery walkway and the main sidewalk: two huge beds of petunias in a deep, rich indigo.

"That'll grab their attention," Maxi had explained. "The real estate ladies call it curb appeal. The customers' eyes travel up the sidewalk. And their feet follow right through the front door. Science!"

Even the lawn looked good. Kate thought it was because of the soaking hoses Maxi had crisscrossing the lawn every night.

"Nope," the florist had finally confessed. "That's rye

grass. Rye seed plus a little water and a lot of love equals really green grass. And it sprouts quick, quick, quick."

While everyone had been planting and painting, Kate had given the kitchen and the shop area another thorough scrubbing yesterday. She'd even polished the floors. Everything gleamed.

Now the new supplies were stacked in the storeroom and the walk-in fridge, just waiting on the OK from the health inspector.

Her phone! She'd forgotten to pick it up at the police station. Oddly, after living on her cell for years—especially when she was scrambling for a job—living without it was strangely invigorating.

No jangling interruptions at the worst possible moments. No hectoring demands from Jeanine. No crisp, newsy updates from Amanda Thorpe. Or worse—a profound absence of voicemails from her son. Best of all, no cozy snaps of Evan and Jessica—from Jessica's phone, of course.

It was like baking: She savored the luxury of focusing completely on what was real and solid in front of her. Friends, food, work. It was joyous.

Kate smiled. Maybe, subconsciously, that's why she kept "forgetting" to retrieve that phone.

Next to her, Oliver leaned against her leg. Then he stepped on her foot. When she looked down, the puppy gazed directly up into her eyes and did it again.

"Trying to get my attention, little guy?" She kneeled down and stroked the soft oatmeal-colored coat on his back, finishing with a vigorous scratch behind one ear. His tail wagged faster.

"You know, this is your home, too, if you want," she said softly, settling on the floor. "I mean, I keep hearing that you're not so hot on the idea of a permanent address. And I get that. But this place is pretty nice. And

I am going to be baking ginger snaps just downstairs, so there's that. I know I was plenty set in my ways, too. But in the past week, I've sort of gotten out of the habit of living alone. I don't know how I'm going to bake anything without Michael and Javie fighting over LEGOs in the background. Or Elena singing and bouncing on the sofa. Weird, huh? So, for what it's worth, I'd love to have you as a roommate. You know, if the place meets your standards, and all. But if you elect to stay, we're not advertising that to the health inspector. Which is probably fair, because we're not telling him I live here, either."

Oliver cocked his head to one side and studied her. Then he turned around three times and curled up in a tight ball beside her.

A definite "maybe."

Chapter 37

Three hard knocks on the door downstairs made Kate jump.

"Health department!"

Kate jumped up. "Not now!" she said to Oliver. "They're early. They're not supposed to be here until this afternoon. After three."

The pup cocked his head.

Three more staccato raps sent her heart into high gear.

"Oh no, she's at the back door! How am I supposed to sneak you out of here? If we go through the kitchen, she'll see you!"

Kate grabbed the red landline off the shelf and dialed a familiar number.

"Flowers Maximus, this is Maxi."

"Maxi, it's Kate. The health inspector's at the back door. And Oliver's upstairs. In my room."

"¡Vaya! When it rains, it pours!"

"Just a minute! Coming!" Kate hollered. Into the phone she whispered, "What are we going to do?"

"Leave Mr. Oliver upstairs," Maxi said. "Close the door to your room, and leave the back door open. I'll come get him. While you distract the inspector, we'll make our escape."

"Sounds like a plan."

"Ay, *vaya con Dios!*"

Kate looked at Oliver, who appeared totally sanguine.

"OK, just remember, be very, very quiet," Kate said, ruffling the silky, soft hair on the top of his head. "Maxi will be here to take you out in just a minute."

She sprinted down the stairs and threw open the back door. "Hi, I'm Kate McGuire," she pronounced, slightly out of breath. "Welcome to the Cookie House!"

"Yeah, I'm Stella Branch. County board of health. Let's start in the kitchen."

In a white short-sleeve blouse, shapeless black slacks, and a tight no-nonsense bun, Stella looked like the take-no-prisoners type. If she spotted Oliver, it was over. No bakery. No grand reopening. No business for Sam. He'd lose everything.

As Stella bent to examine the stove and oven, Maxi tiptoed through the back door. She waved at Kate and moved quietly up the stairs.

Kate heard a long creak. An upstairs door opening.

Stella straightened up. "What was that?"

"Old house," Kate said quickly. "It settles. If you're here alone at night, it's really eerie."

"Spooky. OK, let's see the walk-in fridge."

Kate opened the door and held it, letting the health inspector go in first. As she did, she saw Maxi, cradling Oliver, sneak down the stairs and out the back door. The last thing Kate glimpsed as they hustled off was the gangly puppy—front paws resting on Maxi's shoulders—smiling back at her.

From her pocket, Stella produced a thermometer, held it aloft, and tapped it several times. Then she pushed a button on her watch. Half a minute later, it buzzed and she checked the reading. "Thirty-eight degrees. Solid. And very clean. But you really weren't kidding about the noises in this old place."

After a grueling ninety-minute examination that covered every inch of the kitchen, shop, upstairs storerooms, and bathrooms, Stella gave the Cookie House a 99 on its health inspection.

"I deducted a half a point for having to wait to get in, because we're supposed to have immediate access at all times," Stella explained. "And I subtracted another half point for the ladders lying in the grass in the backyard. That's a safety hazard. I understand it's not the regular customer entrance, but we have to examine all access points. Also, you'll have a surprise follow-up inspection sometime in the next thirty days. Got to say though, all those creaks and groans in a big old house? Creepy."

Kate shrugged. "You get used to it."

Chapter 38

Kate burst through the door of Flowers Maximus. "Break out the champagne, and fire up the ovens—we passed!"

"We passed?" Maxi asked, astonished.

"We passed. Ninety-nine out of a hundred. We did it. All of us. The whole town. The Cookie House can open for business."

"Oh, Sam will be so happy," Tears welled up in Maxi's eyes.

"I know," Kate said, handing her a tissue. "It's bittersweet. But we can make sure he keeps the bakery and has a good income. That way, he can keep fighting."

Maxi dabbed her eyes. "You're right. One battle at a time. And this we won."

"Yes, we did, didn't we, Oliver?" Kate said, rubbing his back, then scratching his belly as the fuzzy tail thumped happily. "Oh, you were such a good boy! Yes, you were. And the first thing that comes out of that kitchen will be a batch of your A-number-one ginger snaps. Because you were so good."

"How about me?" Maxi said, hands on hips. "I did the smuggling and the hauling. And that little puppy is heavy. He's been gobbling up the groceries, for sure."

"Any treat you want, just name it."

"I dunno, a few of those ginger snaps sound pretty good. Especially with a glass of lemonade."

"That's a deal. I'll take lunch to Sam. Then I'm going to start baking. I figure, if I begin now, we can stockpile a supply for tomorrow. And maybe I can get the hang of the whole sourdough thing."

"How's that coming?"

"Burned one batch. Another came out OK, if you could get through the concrete crust. And a third one just wouldn't brown. Maybe Francine misses Sam."

"And maybe the Cookie House, too," Maxi said. "Seriously, it's got to be easier to bake that stuff in a professional oven. So maybe we should return Francine's granddaughter to her real, permanent home?"

"Definitely," Kate said. "But I think we should leave a bit at your house, too. Just in case."

"You can't really believe the burglar is Carl? That one, I don't think so."

"Honestly, me neither," Kate confessed. "But this way, we have a little extra insurance. We protect Francine. No matter who it is."

"Fine by me. But if Javie eats her, don't say I didn't warn you."

Twenty minutes and one wobbly bike ride later and Kate was sitting on a metal folding chair in front of Sam's cell. Turns out riding a bike wasn't exactly like riding a bike, she mused as she watched the baker devour his second lunch. And she had a near miss with a newspaper delivery van to prove it.

"I always got one hundred," Sam said. "What happened to the other point?"

"We'll get 'em next time," Kate replied. "They're promising a surprise inspection in the next couple of weeks."

Sam nodded as he spooned some of Esperanza's pork and pepper stew into his mouth and mopped up the sauce with a piece of roll. "Good yeast rolls."

"We're making them for Sunny's morning classes, too. They seem to like them. She has some extra students during the summer, so she's increased the order."

He nodded again.

"About the sourdough," Kate started. "I mean, I know it's a very technical bread. Very unforgiving. I haven't made any in years, but I've been reading up on the process. You know, brushing up on the finer points. I even hit a couple of the baking sites and picked up some good strategies. I want it to be absolutely perfect. But I was just wondering if you had any tips or secrets you could share?"

For some reason, in spite of her degree and eight years of experience, she felt like a gold-plated phony.

"Won't be perfect."

"Well, I know it won't be as good as yours," she said. "Everyone in town loves your sourdough. And mine's not going to be exactly the same. But I'm striving to get it as close as I can. So the customers keep coming back."

He slipped a crumpled piece of paper through the bars. A page from the crossword puzzle book. Down one side was a handwritten recipe. For sourdough.

"Make it every morning. Never exactly the same.

Never perfect. Whatever that is. Wrote down the mix, best I can remember. No secrets. Just love it."

She looked at him, perplexed. Had she heard him right?

He paused.

"Francine knows," he said finally. "The dough knows. If you love it. If you want to be there. Baking. If you do, you'll do fine. Rest of it is nonsense. Buncha noise."

With that, Sam resumed eating.

Galvanized, Kate felt a spark of hope. She just might be able to pull this off after all.

Chapter 39

On the bike ride home, Kate decided it was time to go native. At least until she got steadier on her wheels she was sticking to the sidewalks. While that wasn't quite cricket in many parts of New York, it was totally legal in Florida.

She'd finally collected her phone and the charger from the police. It was—no surprise—completely dead. And she wasn't in any hurry to charge it.

Riding through downtown, Kate planned her first baking session in the Cookie House. In honor of Ginger—and Oliver and Maxi—the first batch would be ginger snaps. Then she'd follow up with a couple of the classics: Toll House and peanut butter.

She was contemplating the merits of tossing a few chocolate chips into one of the batches of peanut butter cookies when she rounded the corner and passed a familiar stocky figure. Ball Cap Man.

Today's ensemble: pale green Hawaiian shirt, tan cargo pants, and a straw hat. With the same humongous sunglasses. Instead of a shopping bag, he had a gray fanny pack. The "I'm just another tourist" look.

Kate wheeled straight past, like she hadn't even seen him. But instead of making for the Cookie House or the flower shop, she turned the corner and headed for Oy & Begorra. Ben hadn't been at the station. And anything before two o'clock was still technically lunchtime. Besides, if she could track him down herself, what did she need with a phone?

As Kate hopped off the bike, she spotted Ben coming out of the pub.

"Detective!"

"Ms. McGuire. Nice ride. Claire?"

"Kate. And yes."

He shook his head. "Sooner or later, that girl will make converts of us all."

"I saw him. Ball Cap Man. He was standing in front of Coral Cay Books. He's wearing a mint-green shirt, big sunglasses, and a straw hat that looks kind of like a bucket. And tan shorts, with a fanny pack."

"I'm on foot. Mind if I borrow your wheels?"

Kate handed over the bike and watched him cut smoothly out into the street and pedal up the block. Even wearing a blazer and a walking cast—and with a bike that was clearly much too small—the detective made it look easy.

Kate fast-walked in the same direction. If the guy ran from Ben, she'd chase him. And tackle him, if necessary. With a sidewalk full of tourists and a cop on a bicycle, she was feeling brave.

As she retraced her route, semi-jogging, she saw Ben. With Ball Cap Man.

Caught!

While the detective was placid, the man was using

agitated hand gestures. Even without hearing their conversation, Kate knew he was upset.

About time.

"Hey, Kate, I'd like you to meet Manny Stenkowski. Mr. Stenkowski is a private detective."

"A totally respectable profession," the P.I. said. "And legal."

"Stalking isn't," Kate spat.

"She's got you there, Manny," Ben said. "You want to press charges, Kate? If you do, we can haul him in."

"Oh man, that is bull," Manny said. "You can't do that! I have a license. I play by the rules."

"I'd rather know who he's working for," Kate admitted.

"I can't tell you that. I took an oath."

"Yeah, Manny, you're a regular priest."

"I tell you and I lose a client. And if they talk, I lose all my clients. I got two ex-wives and a beagle, and they depend on me."

"That thing with the beagle, that's good," Ben said. "Here's the deal. You tell us, I don't arrest you for stalking, loitering, littering, and wearing those shorts, what, every single day this week?"

"It's not the same pair. I've got five of 'em. Wash and wear. They have pockets that hold all of my stuff, and they're tan, so I don't attract attention."

"Should have gotten yourself a whole suit made of the stuff," Ben said. "Then maybe we wouldn't be standing here. So what's it going to be?"

"I have an ethical duty to uphold the canon of my profession."

"*Cannon*? I loved that show as a kid. Now there's a private eye." He grabbed a pair of cuffs from the back of his belt and flashed them in front of Manny. "You, my friend, have the right to remain silent. Anything you say—"

"Evan Thorpe! I was hired by Evan Thorpe."

Kate's mouth dropped open. Ben looked at Kate and gave a small nod.

"Evan? Why? What were you supposed to do? Scare me? Make me run back to New York?"

"No! Nothing like that. The guy is worried about you. You never answered your phone. Then you just up and moved. He's really sweating it. I mean, I think he wants you back. But all I was supposed to do was trail you and make sure you were OK. Nose around and see what you were up to. See if you needed anything. If you did, he wanted to help you, what's the word? 'Discreetly.'"

"How did he even know I was here?"

"He tracked your phone as far as the mainland, then to the resort area. That's when he knew he needed a pro. So he hired me," Manny finished proudly.

"Don't think so," Ben said.

"OK, he hired a buddy of mine. But his wife went into labor, so I caught the case."

Ben nodded.

"Do you smoke?" Kate asked.

"Uh-uh, no way! But what's that got to do with the price of rice?" Manny asked, puzzled.

Ben shrugged.

"You're local?" Kate asked.

"Out of Orlando," Manny said. "But we cover the whole state. Are we square?" he asked Ben.

The police detective nodded.

"But we're not," Kate said, making a snap decision.

"Wait, what?"

Ben shrugged.

"He promised not to arrest you," she said, pointing to the police detective. "But the first thing I'm going to do is call Evan and tell him exactly how I discovered he hired a P.I. And just how furious that's making me."

"Aw, lady, you can't!" he said. "I've got—"

"Yes, I know—two ex-wives and a beagle," she said, smiling. "Lucky for you, I think we can come to an arrangement."

Chapter 40

Kate wheeled her bike up the steps onto the front porch of the Cookie House, wrapped the plastic-encased chain carefully around one of the side columns, and locked it.

As she did, an oatmeal-colored streak charged across the lawn, raced up the steps, and threw himself at her legs.

"There you are, Oliver," Kate said, rubbing the puppy's flanks and ruffling the top of his downy head.

"What is that?" Manny asked.

"This is Oliver. Believe it or not, he's just a puppy. About half-grown now."

"He's gonna be a big one," the P.I. said.

"Come on in, I'll make you some coffee."

Manny followed them into the kitchen. "Hey, this is nice. You running the place now?"

"For a friend. Just temporarily."

"Yeah, I heard about that. The guy who owns it poisoned somebody."

"He didn't, actually. And he's been accused, not convicted."

"You a lawyer and a baker?"

"I'd offer you some cookies, but we're fresh out at the moment," she said as Manny settled on a barstool near the counter. "Come back tomorrow. We'll be giving them away. Literally."

"For real?" he asked as Oliver politely sniffed the detective's knees, then his shoes, before curling up beneath the barstool.

"Tomorrow's our grand reopening," Kate explained. "It should be fun. And you don't have to sneak around anymore. If you want to know something, just ask me."

"OK, so how come you left Thorpe? The guy's loaded. And from what I hear, he looks like some kinda movie star."

"That you'll have to ask him."

"Blonde, brunette, or redhead?"

"Blonde. His real estate agent."

"Sorry."

"Hey, it's OK. I'm happy here. And I hope he's happy there. And that's the way we're going to keep it."

"I don't think he is happy. With her, I mean. You don't hire a P.I. when you're happy. We're kinda like cops. People only call us when something is wrong. Really wrong. I get the feeling he looks at you as the one who got away."

"I did. And I'm not going back. You like cream?"

"Only if you have it. A little sugar, too, if that's OK. I know I'm supposed to drink it black, but the stuff they make today? Too strong. If you don't water it down a little, it's like battery acid."

He reached down and gave the pup a scratch behind one ear. "Wow, his fur's really soft."

"Oliver's a poodle mix. He actually has hair instead of fur." Kate looked up and smiled. "He seems to like you."

"He probably smells John Quincy."

She put the tray down between them on the counter. Manny pulled out his phone, touched it a few times, and held it aloft. "Here."

"What's that?" she asked.

"This is John Quincy. Officially, John Quincy Adams Stenkowski. My dog. I wasn't lying."

Kate squinted at the picture. Manny, kneeling on the grass in what looked like a park, with his arm around a bright-looking beagle.

"This is him asleep on the couch," he said, flipping photos.

"He's adorable," Kate said. And he was. Cuddling what looked like a football.

"Used to be a cadaver dog. His original name was Quincy. After the TV coroner? A whole year of training. Found two bodies, right off the bat. Great nose. But when they took him out the third time, he wouldn't get out of the truck. Just put his head on his paws and sighed. Wouldn't eat. Wouldn't play with his toys. Didn't even want to run with the other dogs. Trainer had never seen anything like it."

"What was wrong with him?"

"He was depressed. Trainer knew my ex. Told her they were gonna take old Quince to the pound. Of course, that's all she needed to hear. Margot's a cop. Hard head, soft heart. She brought him home that night. Renamed him right off. John Quincy Adams, after the sixth president. She wanted to keep it sorta the same, so he wouldn't be confused. Now he's the happiest little guy you've ever seen. And his face lights up when I come through the door at night. Love that. Margot and I split. But we share John Quincy."

Kate doused her coffee with milk and took a long, satisfied sip. Manny dumped in three heaping spoonfuls of sugar and followed that with enough milk to turn the coffee a light tan color. It matched his shorts.

"I need your help," she started. "The man who died? His name was Stewart Lord."

"You mean the guy your friend killed?"

Kate pulled back and glowered.

"OK, OK," Manny said, putting his palms up in surrender.

"He was a real estate developer," she continued. "And let's just say he was ethically challenged."

Manny smiled.

"He wanted to buy Coral Cay."

"What part?"

"All of it, apparently," Kate said as Manny's eyebrows jumped. "The man had absolutely no problems in the ego department. But he seemed to be focusing on downtown, to start. The business district."

Manny nodded.

Kate took a deep breath. "And it's not as outlandish as it sounds. Lord's specialty was buying up property that had suddenly bottomed out in value. He'd come in after natural disasters. Pay cash, but only the bare minimum. Or target owners with personal or financial troubles," Kate added, remembering Sam and Harp.

"From what I'm hearing, Lord believed that the property values in downtown Coral Cay were going to take a nose dive in the not-too-distant future. And he was poised to take advantage of that. But you can't create a hurricane. Much less predict it."

"You think he had something planned," Manny said.

"I do. And I'd like you to find out what."

"Gee, you don't ask for much."

"Look, you don't have to work for free. Keep billing Evan. You said he wanted to help me discreetly. You'd be doing exactly what he asked. So discreetly that even he doesn't know about it."

"OK, I'm pretty sure that's not what he meant," Manny said, shaking his head. "Besides, I'm supposed to be feeding him information on you."

"I'll give you information on me. Heck, I'll even pose for some of those 'candid' telephoto shots," she said, using air quotes. "But what I really need—what everybody in this town needs—is to find out exactly what Stewart Lord set in motion. And whether that plan is still chugging along without him."

Chapter 41

After Manny left, Kate prepped the kitchen for her first project: cookies.

But after hauling umpteen heavy bags down from the storeroom, she was ready for a break. On the bright side, between the bags and the bike, who needed yoga?

After Kate washed up and treated herself to a second cup of coffee, she mulled over the conversation with Manny. The guy had a good heart. And he'd agreed to help.

For a while.

Sooner or later though, they would run out of new details to feed Evan about her life in Coral Cay. Or Evan would lose interest. Either way, she hoped the P.I. was better at gathering information on Stewart Lord's business plans than he was at tailing her.

Kate sighed. At least she no longer had to worry about a stalker. And Manny definitely wasn't the burglar. He didn't smoke. She doubted he even owned a pair of hard shoes. And his cologne of choice was Old Spice. With a side of garlic pizza.

Kate walked into the fridge and grabbed a bag of lemons and a gallon of cold water.

When she looked up five minutes later, Oliver—who'd been charging around since daybreak—snoozed where he'd finally dropped: in a sunny spot in the front of the shop. Every once in a while, she could hear his soft breathing.

She set the pitcher on the tray with a stack of paper cups and opened the door to the backyard. "Hey, guys, how about some fresh lemonade?"

Instantly, she was surrounded by a gang of thirsty teenagers and twentysomethings. Along with a few spry retirees.

"Nearly done," Carl pronounced. "Touching up a little of the trim and that's the whole shebang."

Kate stepped back and took a good long look. The whole house was a soft, barely there pink. Against that, the clean white gingerbread trim and shutters popped. It looked like a dollhouse come to life. Like it had been frosted with buttercream and powdered with sugar for a child's party.

"It's perfect," she said quietly. "I can't believe what you guys have done. This is . . . it's beautiful."

To a one, the crew members grinned.

"How about some more of those cookies?" Justin asked. "I don't know about anybody else, but that's why I signed on."

Another guy, about the same age, punched him on the arm.

"You got it," Kate said. "First batch should be coming out of the oven in about forty minutes. Think you can hold out that long?"

"Oh, we'll still be here then," Carl replied. "We're racing the sun today, but we'll get there. Even if I have to come back next week and touch up a few spots."

"Don't forget," Kate said, "when we reopen the bakery tomorrow, it's all about sharing bread and cookies with the whole town. No charge. As a way of saying 'thank you.' You guys are the ones who deserve it the most."

"Well, I don't know about that," Carl said, refilling his empty cup. "But I wouldn't mind maybe putting a small sign on the front lawn—with the name of the hardware store and our phone number. For referrals?"

"Absolutely," Kate said, topping off cups as the kids clustered in front of her. "That's more than fair. I can't believe how great the place looks."

"Yeah, it really did need a coat of paint," Carl said. "'A little TLC' is what my Minette called it. And she was right about that."

"Sam's going to love it," Kate said quietly to Carl. "It's gorgeous. And the fact that you guys got together and did this? It's going to make him so happy. I can't wait for him to see it."

Carl turned abruptly, grabbed a nearby ladder, and rattled it loudly. "OK, kids, break's over! We've still got work to do and not a lot of time to do it!"

The crew members, looking puzzled, drained their cups, dumped them into the garbage can, and wandered back to their stations.

Kate was equally perplexed.

"Cookies in about forty minutes," she called cheerily. But her voice fell flat on the breeze.

True to her word, she rolled the first baking rack laden with trays of ginger snaps out of the big commercial oven just thirty minutes later.

The bakery smelled of ginger, cinnamon, and brown sugar. Kate rolled the second commercial rack—stacked to the top with trays of chocolate chip cookies—into the big oven. It had been at least three years since the

Cookie House ovens had baked actual cookies. What on earth would Sam think?

Pulled by the smell—and the clatter—Oliver appeared beneath the swinging doors to the kitchen.

"Have a good nap? You're just in time, but we have to let these cool a little first. Otherwise, someone will burn his tongue."

Oliver cocked his head and looked first at the cookies, then at Kate. As if he was actually considering her words.

"It's worth the wait," she said, walking over and bending to scratch him under the chin. "I promise."

A phone rang. For a minute, Kate couldn't fathom where the sound had come from. It rang again. She loped to the counter and lifted the handset off the wall. "The Cookie House. This is Kate."

For a moment, there was only a garbled, incoherent sound. Then a familiar voice. "Kate, it's Maxi. You need to come to the flower shop now. *Rápido!* It's Sam!"

Chapter 42

Barely remembering to shut off the oven, Kate dashed out the front door of the shop with Oliver on her heels.

When she walked into Flowers Maximus, there was no sign of Maxi. Then she realized the form hunched over on the small settee *was* Maxi.

"Maxi? Honey, what happened?" she said, sitting down next to her friend as she tried to quell the panic in her own head. As she reached out to touch Maxi's trembling shoulder, she noticed her own hands were shaking.

"Sam," the florist mumbled. "He's never getting out. They charged him with another murder. They charged him with killing Muriel Hopkins."

"No!" Kate's hand flew to her mouth.

Maxi nodded mutely as tears poured down her face.

Kate got up and snatched a box of tissues from the florist's desk, along with the top sheet from the message pad by the phone. With a fresh phone message, now forgotten. Maxi might need it later.

Kate placed the tissue box gently in front of Maxi on the small sofa and sat down again.

"Are you sure?" Kate knew it was a stupid question, but she had to ask. It just didn't seem possible.

Maxi nodded, grasping a handful of tissues and taking a deep breath. Trying to speak.

"Peter called me. I think he knew it was coming. For days. But he hoped," she said haltingly. "That the evidence. The autopsy. That it would explain. That it would point to someone else."

"Why do they think Sam killed Muriel? He didn't even know her."

Maxi shook her head. "It makes no sense. Nada. But what killed her—it was the same drug that killed Stewart Lord. They're saying Sam was trying to kill Lord and got her by mistake."

"Could it have been suicide? Muriel, I mean?"

Maxi shook her head again. "They think the drug was in some chocolates. Hidden. She ate them, and she died. Like Lord with the sweet rolls. The state attorney is calling it murder. Premeditated. He says if Sam confesses and tells why, they'll give him life in prison."

Maxi doubled over, sobbing silently.

Kate was numb. She felt like she'd been gutted. She studied the phone message. Doodled hearts. With Peter's name. Then, at the very bottom, a long phrase that made no sense. A chemical name. She stuffed it into her pocket.

"And he can't confess . . . because he . . . didn't do it," Maxi squeaked between sobs.

This couldn't be happening, Kate thought. That sweet old baker wasn't some Machiavellian murderer, scheming and plotting and targeting victims. He just wanted to be left alone to bake bread and do a little beachcombing. And half the time he forgot to eat.

"What did Peter say?" Kate asked as Maxi sat up and wiped her face with another wad of tissues.

"It's bad. The assistant state attorney wants to move Sam. Out of the Coral Cay jail to the mainland. He thinks they're being too soft. Too kind."

"Oh jeez," Kate said. She remembered what Sam looked like when he'd first landed in the local jail. Before his friends and neighbors started visiting. Like a hurt, confused child.

"Was Peter able to tell you anything? Can we fight this?"

Maxi shook her head. "Not much. He's working behind the scenes. To try and keep Sam here. But it's not his case. And the other attorney's so angry. And he knows Sam's a friend of ours."

Oliver, who had crawled onto the sofa next to Maxi, put his head in her lap. Absentmindedly, she stroked the soft cream-colored hair.

Suddenly Kate remembered her odd encounter with Carl in the backyard. His attitude had changed right after she'd mentioned Sam. When she'd remarked how much the baker would love the new paint job when he finally got to see it with his own eyes.

Carl knew. The ex-cop had already heard about the second set of charges. And he didn't believe Sam Hepplewhite would ever see the Cookie House again.

Chapter 43

Kate tried to push past the ache and think. The grand re-opening was tomorrow. Should they still do it? And with the owner of the Cookie House charged in two murders, would anyone show up even if they did?

She felt one thing in her bones: If they didn't open tomorrow as scheduled, the Cookie House would never open again.

If she was going down, she was going down swinging.

"Maxi, I think we need to put the word out. That we're opening tomorrow on schedule. Can you call the Coral Cay Irregulars?"

Maxi looked up blankly, blotting her face.

"If there was ever a time we needed our friends around us—and around Sam—it's now," Kate explained. "You know how to reach them?"

Maxi nodded. "I have everyone's phone numbers."

"Call them. I'm going back to the shop. I'm going to

be baking nonstop most of the night just to get ready for tomorrow morning."

"After I close tonight, I'll come over and help. But do you think we should still open? With all this?"

"We have to. Especially with all of this. Face it, if the shop doesn't open tomorrow morning as planned, people will start avoiding it. And that gets easier with every passing day. We have to open like nothing ever happened. Because this second set of charges is just as ridiculous as the first. And we have to broadcast that loud and clear."

"What if no one comes?" Maxi asked.

"They might not," Kate said, shaking her head. "We might have to donate every single cookie and roll and bread loaf to a soup kitchen and close up for good. But right now, in this moment, we still have a shot. For Sam, and for Cookie, and for us, I say we take it."

Maxi took a couple of deep breaths and dried her face with tissues. "I have the phone numbers in my address book. I'll start calling people now."

Kate had another idea. But she didn't want to raise Maxi's hopes.

"I'm heading back over to the bakery. I just put in a batch of chocolate chip cookies. And I promised the crew some ginger snaps."

When she walked through the door, the first thing Kate reached for wasn't the oven. It was the phone.

One call later, she crossed her fingers. With any luck, maybe they could at least help Peter in his efforts to keep Sam in Coral Cay.

Ginger snaps or no, Oliver had stayed behind at the flower shop. With Maxi. Kate sensed that somehow the puppy understood. He knew Maxi needed him.

Kate quickly set the oven and restarted the cookies,

hoping that the interruption hadn't caused any damage. She'd never halted a batch mid-bake.

She grabbed a white china platter from the cupboard. With a spatula, she gently loosened the ginger snaps from one of the trays. She lifted the cookies carefully onto the platter. Instinctively, she plucked one from the top and tasted it.

Sweet with that spicy ginger bite. And the texture was crispy and perfect. And it was a lot easier here than in Maxi's home oven.

She tackled a few more trays, until she had a respectable pile of cookies. Then she carried it out to the painting crew. But not before pasting a smile on her face.

I'm running a bakery, everything is normal, and I don't have a care in the world, she reminded herself.

But at the same time, Kate wondered: Just how many customers would they have tomorrow? Or was she running the only bakery in the world that couldn't attract customers even if they gave away cookies for free?

Chapter 44

Kate was awakened by the sound of someone banging on the front door. Followed by a dog barking. Loudly.

"Wake up, baker-girls! Big day ahead!"

"That's Peter!" Maxi said, rubbing her eyes. "And Oliver! Ay, what time is it?"

Kate sat up from the kitchen table where she'd inadvertently dozed off. "Six a.m.! Oh my gosh, it's six a.m.! I have to get yeast rolls in the oven for Sunny! And we have to open in two hours! I'm so not ready."

Maxi stretched like a cat as she headed for the front door. "It's like Christmas. It comes whether you're ready or not. But in this case, we're ready."

"I don't have any sourdough yet. Lots of cookies and plenty of other breads. But no sourdough. That's Sam's signature. I've been too freaked out to even attempt it."

"So we go without sourdough," the florist said, smiling. "Look at this place. We've got enough stuff to open a bakery."

Kate looked around, amazed. There were racks lined

up cooling. And almost every available inch of counter space was covered with breads, rolls, and cookies. It had taken the two of them working flat out all night. But Maxi was right. Except for the sourdough—and Sunny's rolls—they were all set.

"How's my girl holding up?" Peter asked, handing Maxi a large paper cup as Oliver rushed past them.

"I think I slept sitting up," Maxi confessed. "I haven't done that since Elena was teething. Oh, is this what I think it is?"

"Esperanza's special double-strong mocha espresso with lots of cream and sugar. Brought one for each of you. Figured you could probably use it. Along with some bacon and egg sandwiches. Got a suitcase with fresh clothes in the car."

"*Mi amor,* right now I'd marry you all over again."

"That's just the caffeine rush talking. Oh, and I promised Javie I'd relay a message. 'What does a baker have in common with his dough?'"

"Mmmmm, I don't know," she said, sipping happily. "What does a baker have in common with his dough?"

"Both have to rise early in the morning," he finished, shrugging. "I swore to him I'd tell you that, so message delivered."

"That's awful, truly awful," she said, "but this coffee is wonderful."

"So are the sandwiches. Made 'em myself. The secret is extra butter on the toast."

Kate slid two trays with Sunny's yeast rolls into the small oven. As she turned from closing the door, Oliver jumped up and put his front paws on her knees. His curved, fluffy tail seemed to have a mind—and rhythm—of its own.

"I missed you, too," she told the puppy softly, stroking his flanks and scratching him under the chin. "But

I know you had fun with Michael and Javie and Elena. Yeah, that's my guy!"

She grabbed a ginger snap from the counter, placed it on her palm, and held it in front of him. Nimbly, he lifted the cookie gently into his mouth and crunched it. Kate could have sworn his black eyes twinkled. She palmed another ginger snap and presented it.

The puppy took it carefully from her hand, leaving nary a crumb. Or even a drop of moisture.

Strolling out from the kitchen with Oliver, Kate reached into the brown lunch bag on the bakery counter and pulled out a small parcel wrapped in wax paper. "I love the idea of eating something I didn't actually have to make first."

"Got some news that might improve your appetite, too," Peter said, grinning at Maxi.

Kate held her breath.

"Sam gets to stay in the Coral Cay jail," he announced. "At least for the time being."

"Oh, Peter!" Maxi said, kissing his cheek. "That's wonderful. How did you do it?"

"I can't take the credit. This was Doc Patel. And Annie Kim."

"How?" Maxi asked.

"Doc evaluated Sam late yesterday. And submitted his recommendation that Sam Hepplewhite needs to stay where he is. For medical reasons. And Annie let us review the pharmacy records for Sam and Ginger without a subpoena. Practically begged us to, in fact. She even helped Ben and one of the investigators from our office sort through the records most of the night, just so they'd understand what they were reading. Basically, Sam didn't have access to the drug that killed Muriel Hopkins and Stewart Lord. It's not something he or Ginger had ever taken. And it's not exactly easy to get, lemme tell you. You need a prescription, and it's pretty tightly con-trolled. Granted, that isn't much. We still have to figure out if Sam could have picked it up online or through the black market or from a less-than-scrupulous pharmacy. But this is the first thing that's broken in Sam's favor. And his lack of access to that drug—together with the medical eval—was enough to convince a judge to issue an emergency injunction. So, for now at least, he stays put."

Maxi kissed him again. "You're brilliant."

"Much as I'd like to take credit for it, it wasn't me. Well, the medical eval was. But don't tell anyone. The assistant state attorney is hopping mad. The official story is that Sam's lawyer demanded it. And that's true. Even if I might have dropped a bug in his ear. But Annie? She called us. Persistent as all get-out. Wouldn't get off the phone until someone agreed to look at what she'd discovered. No idea how she found out exactly which drug killed Lord and Hopkins. But she's Sam's pharma-cist, and she really did the legwork."

Kate smiled and polished off what was left of her sandwich, surreptitiously slipping a slice of crispy bacon to Oliver.

Maxi had never mentioned the name of the drug that had killed Muriel Hopkins and Stewart Lord. But she had written it down. Out of habit, the florist jotted down names and numbers from phone conversations—usually floral orders—in case she needed to refer to them later.

But Maxi had been in such a state after Peter's call yesterday that she'd never even realized she'd done it. Much less that Kate had pocketed that little piece of pink paper.

Chapter 45

As the skies darkened, Kate locked her bike to a nearby rack and walked through the front door of Sunny's yoga studio. Dubbed simply "The Studio," it always reminded her of Sunny herself. Clean lines, classic, and welcoming. Cream-colored plaster walls with simple molding surrounded wide-plank honeyed oak floors. Abundant skylights normally flooded the place with lots of sunlight. But today, between the early hour and the approaching storm, soft lighting did the heavy lifting. The place held the bare minimum of furniture. And the few existing pieces looked like pricey antiques. Pared down and elegant, but with a definite energy. Exuberance.

Early on a Saturday morning, just one of the studios was open. And Sunny was leading this class herself. Kate peered through the glass. She was stunned. There were more than twenty students. Some of the faces were sort of familiar—people she'd seen around town but didn't really know yet. Most were total strangers. But a few, like Bridget O'Hanlon and Rosie Armand, she actually recognized.

She was glad she'd baked an extra dozen. The pastry chef's motto: Too many is perfect; one short is disaster.

Sunny, clad in a dusty-rose leotard and matching stirrup tights, rolled gracefully up from her chocolate-colored mat, stretched, and waved from the front of the class.

Kate returned the gesture, feeling suddenly shy. She set down the trays on the large pine cabinet, already laden with butter, and jars of jam and marmalade, along with an assortment of small china plates, teacups, and silverware. On top of the hutch, someone had placed an industrial-sized warming urn. Which, judging from the scent, held an ocean of hot green tea.

"So how is it going for the big reopening?" Sunny asked, shutting the classroom door quietly behind her. "Are you girls all ready?"

"As ready as we'll ever be," Kate said. "We're just hoping people show up. It's been kind of a rough week. Especially for Sam."

"Posh! The crowd in Coral Cay loves any excuse for a party. They'll turn up. Wait until our Pirate Festival later this summer. You'll see what I mean. I just hope that old fool knows how lucky he is to have you. And he'd better be paying you well."

"Right now, honestly, I'd settle for a good turnout."

"Well, I called a few old friends of mine on the mainland. Teachers and such. Spread the word. And I know for a fact that Bridget and Andy have been telling all the tourists about it. So you might get a few from the resort crowd, too. Even better because they don't come with the baggage of knowing Sam Hepplewhite. That man's no murderer, but he can be a damned fool."

Kate smiled.

"Why don't you join us for snacks this morning? I have a student I'd love for you to meet. Glen. A photographer. He lives on the mainland, but he's a regular at my Saturday classes. Single. And very flexible," she finished with a wink.

"Next Saturday for sure," Kate promised. "But Maxi's holding down the fort right now with Peter, so I have to get back. Fingers crossed, they might actually need me."

"They will, and you'll do fine." She stopped and cocked her head, studying Kate for a split second. "A little piece of unsolicited advice? This day will go by in a blink," she said, snapping her fingers. "Stop worrying and enjoy it. Soak it in—it's a celebration. And nice choice on the bike, by the way. Best way to get around the island."

Kate had to smile as she pedaled back to the Cookie House. Nothing got past Sunny. But she definitely wasn't ready for a fix-up. Not yet.

Although she had gotten a glimpse of Glen through the window. Sunny was right. He was cute. Or "yummy," as Sunny would put it.

But the other thing Sunny mentioned kept swirling through Kate's mind. Could she just let go and enjoy? Her entire adult life it always felt like she had absolutely no margin for error. So she'd planned everything. With contingency plans, and double contingency plans, just in case. The first time she hadn't, she'd ended up on Main Street with no money, no job, and a smoking car.

But she'd survived. And thrived. And found her way.

A clap of thunder heralded a flash of lightning off in the distance. A storm was coming. And if the darkening sky was any indication, it would be a doozy.

Scary but exhilarating. Kind of like her life lately.

Kate shifted into high gear and stood on the pedals, pumping furiously to reach the bakery before the deluge started. She'd had more fun in the past few weeks than she had since she ended things with Evan. Possibly even before.

So maybe she could keep living in the moment. For one more day, at least.

Chapter 46

"It is pouring out there," Kate declared as she burst through the front door of the bakery with her bike. "Literally coming down in buckets."

"Oooh, somebody looks like a drowned rat," Maxi admonished. "I'll grab you some paper towels."

Kate looked around the empty shop. She didn't know whether to be panicked because it was already 8:05 or relieved that there was no one here to witness her impromptu wet T-shirt contest.

"I'm taking this upstairs," she said, wheeling the bike through the kitchen. "It's coming down too hard to leave it outside. Hey, where did Oliver and Peter go?"

"My guy is playing deliveryman for a couple of flower orders that have to go to the resorts this morning," Maxi said, looking Kate up and down before finally handing her the entire roll of towels. "But first he's dropping off Mr. Oliver at home with *mi mami* and the kids."

"I already miss the little guy," Kate said, wiping off

the basket first. "But you're right. We probably shouldn't have him in the bakery for the reopening. And he'll be safer at home. Especially with this storm."

"If it makes you feel better, I sent him home with a bag of ginger snaps. And if he runs out, something tells me he'll be back. That little one is very independent. And those towels are for you. That bike isn't gonna catch a cold."

"Yes, but you don't have to return me to Claire if I can't come up with the next payment. Any customers yet?"

Maxi shook her head. "I don't think we'll see any for a while. I can't even see across the street. And the balloons? Forget it. Good thing I left them at the flower shop."

Fifteen minutes later, in a fresh navy-blue T-shirt, Kate reappeared in the kitchen. "I thought that tin roof was loud from down here. Upstairs it sounds like a herd of elephants tap-dancing on the ceiling."

"There's coffee on the counter," Maxi said, lifting her mug. "It's that weak *americano* stuff you ordered from the food supplier, so it's not as good as the brew you're used to now. Hey, how did you get those jeans dry?"

"Blow-dryer. And please thank Peter for including it in the suitcase."

"He figured we'd need showers at some point, spending so much time in a hot kitchen."

"Well, I got my shower outside this morning. Even if it didn't include a bar of soap."

"How's Sunny?"

"She's great," Kate said, grabbing a mop and following the wet path from the kitchen to the front door. "She's called some friends and invited them to our reopening. So we might get a couple of people from the mainland.

Man, that woman is a living, breathing ad for yoga. Oh, and she wanted to fix me up with one of her students."

"Yeah. I was wondering when that would start. You're the cute new single girl in town. Get used to saying no a lot. Or yes. Either way, everybody's got a brother or a nephew, or a neighbor, or a cousin they'll want you to meet."

"Did that happen to you, too?"

"Not here. Peter and I didn't move here till after we married. But in Miami? Ay, I couldn't walk down the street without one of my aunties pushing a single man in front of me. It was like stepping around potholes."

"I know it sounds ungrateful, but it's too soon. I just broke off an engagement. We were planning a life together. I can't pivot that fast."

"Just say that. Or that you don't date during months that don't have an "r" in them. Or that you still love the last guy, but you can't remember where you buried him."

"That one I like. As long as we never use it within earshot of Kyle Hardy. Besides, it was her I wanted to bury, which makes zero sense. Why *is* that?"

"Because him you loved," Maxi said, brushing flour off her bakery apron. "And it was all good until she showed up. So some part of your heart says, 'Hey, it must be her fault.'"

"That is oddly accurate. I still can't believe Evan hired a P.I."

"I can't believe you got the P.I. to work for you. It's like something out of a spy movie. He's a double agent."

"I'm not sure Manny Stenkowski would ever make it as a double agent. I'm not even sure he'll cut it as a private eye. But at least I don't have a stalker. And at least he's willing to try and dig into whatever Lord was up to in Coral Cay."

"Tell him to dig fast. By the way, if I'm locked in a bakery and no one comes, does that mean I can eat all the cookies?" Maxi said, topping off her coffee.

"I think we can spare a few cookies even if we do get customers," Kate said. "My plan is to keep baking all day. I just wanted to get a head start so the place would be stocked and ready."

"Prepare for success," Maxi said happily, selecting a Toll House cookie from one basket on the counter, along with a peanut butter chocolate chip from another.

Her remark reminded Kate of what Sunny had said about savoring the moment. "Does Sam have anything around here that plays music?"

"Sure, he's got an old radio. Like a little boombox? I think it has a CD player, too, but I don't know if he has any CDs."

Kate searched the kitchen and finally found the small silver Sony crammed into one of the lower cabinets. She set it by the coffeepot, plugged it in, and started flipping stations. "Please tell me the radio signals around here are better than the cell phone signals."

"Much," Maxi said. "On a clear night, you can get Cuban music. Straight from Havana. But today we'll be lucky to get the Florida stations from the mainland. If we can even hear it over the music from our own roof."

"Yeah, it kind of sounds like a steel drum band. But it's strangely comforting."

Kate played with the buttons and finally hit a channel that wasn't half static.

"WRAB," the announcer said smoothly. "South Florida's home of classic R and B."

"Oh, this is great!" Kate said.

"I bet Francine would like it," Maxi said between bites. "You going to invite her to the party?"

Kate grinned, snagging a peanut butter chocolate

chip cookie for herself. "At this rate, I just might. You know the first thing we should buy with all our many millions? An iPod and a couple of decent speakers." She reached over and cranked up the volume as the Four Tops launched into "It's the Same Old Song."

"You mean, after we pay off that super expensive ride you bought from Claire?" Maxi teased.

"Exactly. So what are you going to buy first?"

"A decent bed for this friend I know. I can't believe you really slept on that pile of Popsicle sticks upstairs."

"It's like a hammock," Kate admitted sheepishly. "It's very comfy once you get settled. It's just a little tricky getting in and out."

"It's a death trap. Seriously, if we had *las ratas* we could put a piece of cheese in the middle and use it to capture them. But only the really slow-moving ones."

"Hey, I'm one of the really slow-moving ones. And I like that cot. It may not be resort quality, but it beats my sister's guest room."

"Which is nowhere as good as *my* guest room because she doesn't have the Star Wars sheets with matching drapes. She doesn't, does she?"

"Not in this lifetime," Kate said. "Nothing below an eight-hundred-thread count. Besides she hates that movie."

"She doesn't like Luke Skywalker? And Yoda? Who doesn't like Yoda?"

"Calls the whole franchise 'subversive.' Jeanine isn't a fan of anything that even hints at children defying their parents. She's a little tightly wound." Kate sighed. "She's also mad at me for dumping Evan. Part of the reason I haven't charged my phone?"

Maxi nodded.

"I know there's going to be, like, a dozen messages from her demanding that I make up with him. Listening to her is like taking a bath in vinegar. It doesn't change anything. It just hurts."

"Yowch! Why's it so important to her?"

"Evan is a Thorpe."

"So?"

"One of *those* Thorpes. You know, the *Mayflower*. Old money. Lots of connections."

"Yeah, I know who they are, but so what?"

"This is a horrible thing to say about my own sister. But I think she loved the idea of being related to Evan. I mean, I don't know what she pictured, exactly. It's not like his mother was going to have them over for Thanksgiving dinner. But I think Jeanine saw our wedding as opening the door to a new world. And maybe not so much for her as for the twins."

"Like country club doors and Ivy League doors?" Maxi asked.

"Exactly. Now that imaginary door's closing and she's livid."

"So let her marry him."

Kate giggled. "You know, if I ever charge that phone I might say exactly that."

"Hey, Cookie Lady! Is this place open?"

"Oh my gosh," Maxi whispered. "We have a customer!"

Kate hustled into the shop to find a band of bedraggled, half-drowned teens in bathing suits and board shorts.

"Hi, Justin. We're open, but we didn't think anybody would be out in this weather. How about some hot coffee to warm you guys up? And we've got towels if you want to dry off."

"Nah, we're good. We just needed to get off the beach until the storm blows over. I told the guys I knew exactly where we should go. Parked the boards on the porch, if that's copacetic?"

"Absolutely. So what would you like to start?"

As she said that, Maxi came through the swinging doors with a tray of steaming mugs. "Here you go. This will help you get warm. And it goes great with any kind of cookies. Not that I'd know."

"Oooh, thank you, Mrs. Más-Buchanan," said one blond girl in a black wet suit as the rest clustered around the tray.

"Thank you," another one mumbled.

"We've got lots more," Maxi said. "Just made a big pot."

"I told 'em about your trick," Justin said. "The one you did on my sister. Where you guessed her favorite cookie?"

"Yeah," said the blond girl. "But we didn't believe him. How's it even possible?"

"Kind of like standing on a board supported by nothing but a moving wave of water," Kate said. "It doesn't seem possible, when you really think about it. But with enough practice, no sweat."

Justin grinned as Kate presented him with a tray of shortbread. He grabbed four cookies with a large paw, and she set the tray on the counter so everyone could help themselves.

"And something tells me you're a Toll House girl," Kate said, retrieving another tray from behind the bakery case and placing it carefully on the counter.

"How about me?" called a teen in a blue swimsuit with a Union Jack patch.

"Oatmeal," Kate said, placing another tray on the counter. "Have them right here."

"Oh man, these are so good!" Justin said happily. "Buttery."

"And you," Kate said to a shy girl in a drenched blue Gators sweatshirt who lingered near the doorway clutching her coffee mug. "Something tells me you like peanut butter cookies." Kate set a fourth tray on the counter. "But you might also want to try these," she said, lifting out a fifth tray. "Peanut butter chocolate chip. They could become your new favorite."

"I like those a lot," Maxi admitted. "Salty and sweet."

Tentatively, the girl moved toward the counter and took one. As she nibbled the edge, her face bloomed into a smile.

"Justin, I don't know if you've had the chance to really see it, but the Cookie House looks gorgeous. You guys did a beautiful job."

"Well, if you run into my dad, I had nothing to do with it. Mom knows, but he thinks I was out chasing nugs."

Kate mimed turning an imaginary lock over her mouth. "Surfing at the beach, got it. But stop by later today, too, and you can take home some breads. You don't have to say where you got them."

"Ooh, contraband carbs! Love it!" Justin cackled.

"Is this a private party or is anyone welcome?" Ben said, banging through the door.

"How do you like your coffee?" Maxi called over the counter.

"Well, uh . . ."

"Relax, it's that weak *americano* stuff," she added.

"In that case, black. A nice big cup. It's wet out there. Blowing in right off the water. I swear it's half rain, half salt. Nasty."

Maxi appeared in the shop with a tray bearing a steaming mug and a glass pot full of coffee. She handed off the mug to Ben with a wink. "It's the biggest cup we have. But refills are free," she said, topping off everyone's cup.

"So what will you have for breakfast, Detective?" Kate asked. "We've got cookies, we've got croissants. And we've got some great yeast rolls."

"And if you pick cookies, she can tell you exactly what kind you like best," said the girl in the wet suit. "It's spooky cool."

Ben scratched his chin. "Well, I've got to admit, I've never seen that before. Give it your best shot."

Kate took a deep breath and let everything else go. In that second, she could practically taste it. A deep, rich chocolate crinkle cookie. With a light dusting of powdered sugar.

"You're in luck. We popped in a batch just before dawn. Have them in the back, freshly dusted."

She reappeared from the kitchen with a basket full of crinkle cookies.

"How did you . . . ?" Ben started.

"Observation and deduction. And more than a few years as a pastry chef."

Ben grabbed a handful and popped one in his mouth. Then he closed his eyes and smiled. "Oh man, this takes me back. To my nana's kitchen. Lady, you've got a serious talent. And I don't mean the cookie-guessing thing."

"Thank you. We're baking cookies from here on," Kate said. "I want to do some sort of a cookie contest, too, but I haven't worked out that part of it yet."

"These are great," Justin said after tasting a chocolate crinkle. "How do you get them so chocolatey?"

"Unsweetened cocoa powder. And a little less sugar. That way, you really taste the chocolate."

"These are really good," Ben said, delicately taking two more in his mitt-sized hand and dropping one right into his mouth. "At this rate, I might pitch a tent on the porch. Nice music, by the way."

"It's a party," Kate said. "And what's a celebration without music?"

"Got that right," Maxi seconded, circling through the shop with the coffee carafe. "Hey, I think the rain's letting up!"

At that moment, the door opened and more people piled into the shop.

"Hi, Andy, how're things down at the pub?" Ben asked.

"Typical Saturday. Although I think the rain slowed some of them. Place is full right now, so I've got to get back quick."

"How about some hot coffee?" Maxi asked.

"I've had so much, I'm practically floating. But Bridget thought you might need a few of those big collapsible tables. For the reopening? I've got 'em out in the SUV. And I wouldn't turn down a couple of loaves of bread. Whatever you've got. The breakfast crowd is cleaning us out this morning."

"We've got plenty of everything," said Kate. "Except the sourdough. I haven't gotten that one in the oven yet. Come on back into the kitchen and you can take your pick. Then we'll get those tables."

"I'm on it," the detective said. "Toss me the keys."

Andy pitched them overhead, and Ben snatched them out of midair. "Just save me a couple more of those crinkles," the detective said, lurching out the door.

"We can help you lug 'em in," said Justin. "Don't want anybody scratching our sweet paint job."

An hour later, the sun was shining and the porch was standing room only. Most people had spilled out onto the lawn, hot cups and cookies in hand. Someone—Kate didn't know who—had lent them an iPod and set it up out of sight on the porch.

Kate and Maxi had hung the balloon banner from the eves of the porch, and Maxi had tied bunches of balloons—in pink, white, and fuchsia—to the railing, the mailbox, and the food tables.

Amos Tully showed up with three grocery bags stuffed full of paper plates, napkins, and hot cups. "All of 'em biodegradable," he assured Kate. He left with three dozen assorted cookies and a half-dozen loaves of bread "for the shop."

Kate studied him while he was chatting with Maxi, and tucked in an extra dozen oatmeal cookies with raisins. Just for him.

Harper Duval contributed a few large tubs of pricy cheese spread and some rich Irish butter, "so the bakery could showcase its breads." Then he quietly handed Maxi a bottle of French champagne, "so you all can pop a cork later to celebrate."

Maxi had dragged over three of the industrial-sized green garbage cans she used at the shop and spaced them at regular intervals on the lawn. "Otherwise, we're gonna spend all day tomorrow picking up trash," she explained. She even tied balloons to the handles of each can, "so people notice 'em."

Halfway through the day, Peter reappeared with the kids, Esperanza, and Oliver in tow. By then, the reopening was taking on the air of a block party. A jazz quartet had set up in the grass right off the porch. Iced tea had replaced hot coffee. And the throng of tourists streaming in from the resorts was so steady it looked like a parade coming down Main Street. Parking was nonexistent.

Somewhere amidst all the ruckus, Kate managed to slip back into the kitchen. For a minute, she tried to absorb it all. The music, the happy thrum of people mixed with the smells of cinnamon, butter, yeast, and chocolate from the bakery. The bright summer sunshine filtered through the humid salt air. Maxi's green grass and flourishing flowers. Kate popped a ginger snap into her mouth and thought of Oliver.

The mischievous puppy turned out to be a one-dog ambassador—for Coral Cay and the Cookie House. Peter had fitted him out in a blue polka-dot bow tie. And everyone wanted to take selfies with him.

Luckily, the pup relished the attention. Especially when it was accompanied by a ginger snap.

Kate pulled out one of the kitchen drawers, reached her hand to the very back, and gently lifted out a folded-up crossword puzzle page. She read it slowly. Twice. Then she refolded the paper and slipped it into her slim jeans pocket.

She measured out the flour, dumped it into the blue bowl, added a bit of tap water, and—last but not least—reached for the infamous Francine. Then Kate began mixing up a batch of Sam's famous sourdough.

The reopening party—and the cleanup—lasted well into the night. While Maxi blamed the tourists, Kate recognized a lot of the faces who stayed until the bitter end.

And they were both thrilled.

"Let's pop that cork," Maxi said when they finally got home. "What kind of cookies go best with champagne?"

"Swedish butter cookies. Oooh, and my grandma's anise and almond cookies. Did you notice someone actually put out a tip jar?"

"With Sam's face on it! For his defense fund. The photo was from our last town tree-lighting party. I remember 'cause he was wearing a red flannel shirt and he was actually smiling."

"Who did it?" Kate asked.

"No idea, but there were some pretty serious checks

in there. I had Peter lock it in my office safe. I figure we can count it Monday and take it to Sam's bank."

"Wow," Kate said quietly. "And I was worried that no one would come. We did it. We really did it."

"We did. Us and the whole town. Even the *bobo* showed up."

"You're kidding," Kate said. "I didn't see him. Are you sure?"

"You were in the back. He brought a date, and they didn't stay long. But give the boy credit, he came. So, should I ask about the sourdough?"

"You wanna know what goes best with champagne? Sourdough."

"I'll pop the cork, if you slice," Maxi said.

"If it's anything like that second batch, we're gonna need more than a bread knife."

"If it's anything like the second batch, I'm gonna skip it and have another glass of bubbles."

Maxi grabbed an orange tea towel and twisted the cork until there was a gentle *pop*. Then she put the bottle on the counter and headed for the fridge.

"What now?" Kate asked as she sliced into the loaf.

"Hey, if I'm eating sourdough after midnight I want the whole experience. I'm getting some butter. So how does it look?"

Kate cut off two slices and offered one to Maxi. As the florist slathered the bread with butter, Kate sniffed hers, broke off a piece, and popped it into her mouth. She smiled.

"Ay, that must be a good sign," Maxi said. "If even you like it. Umm, this is good! Like Sam-quality good. How did you finally do it? What's the big honking secret?"

"Sam gave me his recipe," Kate said. "As much as he has a recipe. And a pep talk. And I think that last part is what I really needed."

"So tomorrow we can sell the whole load of this stuff to the pub?" Maxi asked. "*Hola, dinero!*"

"Yup. Right after I drop off the first two loaves to Gabe at the garage. That man loves a good sourdough."

Chapter 47

As the morning sky turned from pink to flame, Kate planted one foot firmly on her orange beach towel, stretched upward with all her might, and strained not to fall over.

Down the beach, she could hear the waves washing the shore as the seagulls screeched overhead.

"Relax and breathe . . . ," Sunny instructed rhythmically. "Just like the tide in front of you. In. And out. And in. And out."

"How am I s'posed to relax and stretch and breathe?" Maxi mumbled from Kate's right. "Pick one, already."

"Sunrise yoga was your idea," Kate whispered, struggling to hold the position. "You said it was calming."

"Well, yeah," Maxi countered. "'Cause if you survive, you feel like you can do anything. Plus, Sunny's outdoor classes are an excuse to hit the beach."

"And down," Sunny said. "Now, the Dead Man pose."

"Finally, one I can do," Kate said softly as everyone lay on their mats.

"Dead men don't talk," Sunny admonished with a wink. "At least, not the ones I've met."

Most of the two dozen students wore bathing suits. Including Sunny herself, who was trim and firm in a baby-blue one-piece. And while some had dutifully toted yoga mats, others—like Kate and Maxi—showed up with colorful beach towels. "Easier to clean," Maxi explained on their bumpy, predawn Jeep ride.

But the visitors from the resorts, who'd arrived en masse on a shuttle, sported matching yoga mats, headbands, and water bottles. They even carried identical navy-blue gym bags.

"It's a cult," Maxi said under her breath as the crowd disembarked from the small white van.

Kate had to admit, Maxi had been right about taking her first class on the beach. Between the exercise, the sound of the waves, and the sea air, she was so relaxed she was limp. It was all she could do not to fall asleep between poses.

But Sunny's "gentle stretching," which felt like a cross between physical therapy and Twister, was an ugly wake-up call. In New York, like here, Kate had hiked nearly everywhere. And a third-floor walk-up had been great cardio.

But flexibility, apparently, was a whole other carton of eggs.

Kate resolved to just give up and get through it. So what if her first yoga class was also her last yoga class?

Then something clicked. Literally.

As she exhaled a boatload of stress and worry, Kate felt her vertebrae shift and heard a *crack*. Then she pushed herself infinitesimally forward.

"That's it," Sunny encouraged, from off to her left. "Juu-st relax into it. Let everything go. Empty your mind. It's just you and the beach."

Kate focused on the skyline. Flame had turned golden as the sun rose slowly above the water, breaking through thin clouds. Beneath it, the Gulf was a calm deep blue.

Everything else faded. Kate could hear the rush in her ears, the waves in the background, and Sunny's melodic instructions off in the distance. The air was cool and humid. The sand was soft and welcoming. At one point, two lemon-yellow butterflies tumbled by, almost as if they were chasing each other—playing. She could smell coconuts—someone's sun tan lotion—and wild roses, growing just off the beach.

And then it was over. Kate had no idea how much time had elapsed. It was as if she'd been somewhere else. But she'd really been here—totally in the moment. It was everything else that had faded away.

"Now our class is complete," Sunny said. "Go out and have a wonderful new day—and make the most of it!"

Kate stood up and rolled her shoulders. She felt happy. Energized and calm at the same time.

"What's next?" she asked Maxi.

"Are you kidding?" her friend said as they watched their classmates run toward the surf. "This is the best part. Now we hit the water!"

Chapter 48

As she cleared the lunch dishes from Maxi's outdoor table, Kate mentally ticked off boxes in her head. The grand opening had pretty much cleaned out the shop. She wanted to spend the afternoon baking, so they'd be ready to open tomorrow morning. Plus, she'd been playing around with a new idea for a cookie recipe she wanted to try. One with coffee and chocolate—inspired by Esperanza's special brew.

Still, she was surprised when Maxi was the one who suggested stopping by Flowers Maximus.

"Just need to see about some tulips for later this week," the florist confessed. "And I want to check on the bedding plants out back. Course if you want to start by offering me a cup of coffee and some leftover cookies next door, I wouldn't object. Even if it is that weak *americano* stuff."

Twenty minutes later, Kate was standing in the upstairs doorway of the Cookie House, staring at a beautiful new bed.

With a low-slung Japanese design, the mattress appeared to float on a horizontal platform over the floor. The wood was a dark, rich mahogany color, flanked on either side with a delicate rice-paper column lamp. The headboard just tall enough to allow her to sit up and read in bed. It was topped off with soft pastel aqua sheets and a thick turquoise comforter.

"Best of all, it has two big drawers to give you extra storage," Maxi said. "In a small space you have to be super organized. I learned that watching the show about people who live in those teeny tiny houses."

"This is . . . it's absolutely . . . I can't believe . . . ," Kate started.

Maxi wrapped an arm around her friend's shoulder as Kate teared up.

"It's beautiful," Kate finally finished in a whisper.

"Yup, it looks great," Maxi said happily. "Like it was made for this room."

"You had this planned all along?" Kate asked.

"Not just me. Pretty much all of Coral Cay," Maxi said. "Rosie found it. Andre and his guys hauled it over and set it up while we were at yoga this morning. They got it at cost. And all of us chipped in to cover it. Oh, and Mitzy Allen supplied the sheets and pillows and comforter from her shop. She thought you'd like beach colors. Course I think that's just 'cuz she didn't have anything with Yoda on it."

"I can't accept this," Kate whispered as a tear trailed down her cheek.

"You're not accepting anything," Maxi said matter-of-factly. "If he was here, *mi padrino* would be paying you a salary. So you'd be biking around town buying up everything you need. But instead, no money, tons of work, aannd you're gonna sleep on that pile of pick-up sticks? Uh-uh, no good. And in this town, we take care of our own."

"I can't believe it's the same room," Kate said, her voice husky. "This beats any suite at the resort."

"Well yeah," Maxi said, giving Kate's shoulder a squeeze. "*Esto es hogar.* This is home."

Chapter 49

Later that afternoon, Kate prepped her latest cookie experiment: Thin, crisp mocha wafers. She cranked one of the small bakery ovens to 350 degrees, then resumed mixing the dough.

Technically, the Cookie House was closed—with the sign on the door to prove it. But Kate also left it unlocked for Maxi. Or anyone with a bakery emergency.

So she wasn't all that surprised to hear the front door—combined with the tinkle of a bell—alerting her to someone in the shop.

"Now you stay right there," a man's voice pleaded. "I'll be right back. Promise."

Kate came through the swinging doors just in time to see Manny Stenkowski hesitating at the front door.

"Hey, got some news. Thought I'd come out here and trade," he said, furtively glancing back at the porch.

"What's out there?" Kate said, pointing.

"Oh, I got custody of John Quincy today. I figured if I had to be out here, I'd show him the town."

Kate peeked around him, saw two intelligent almond eyes staring back, and grinned. "You guys get settled on the porch, I'll bring us some coffee. I think I might have something that he'll like, too.

"You missed our reopening yesterday," Kate said as she carried a tray through the door minutes later. "I thought for sure you'd be here with the telephoto lens."

"Hey, for what I was doing yesterday I should get combat pay. Figured the best way to get the skinny on your friend Lord might be to venture into his jungle. And let me tell you, it was brutal."

"What exactly is his jungle?" Kate asked. The man she'd seen didn't travel anywhere without bespoke suits, a stretch limo, and a uniformed driver.

"Swanky country club. The nineteenth hole, to be specific."

Kate looked puzzled.

"The bar at his favorite golf course. Private, naturally. Had to pull a few strings to get in. But luckily, I know a guy who knows a guy who stocks the vending machines. Anyway, let's just say your friend Evan paid for more than a few rounds. But it was worth it."

Kate took a ginger snap and put it in front of John Quincy. The beagle sniffed it. Then he licked it. He must have liked the taste, because it was gone in one bite. He settled himself by her feet and looked up hopefully.

She put another ginger snap in front of him. When she looked back a split second later, it was gone.

John Quincy looked up at her with innocent brown eyes. She couldn't help smiling. She let him sniff the top of her hand, then scratched behind his ear. His coat felt like warm velvet.

Manny grinned. "He's a charmer," the detective said proudly. "Anyway, it seems that for the last couple of months your friend Lord had been spreading the word that he was part of a consortium that was going to buy up Coral Cay and develop it. Starting with downtown."

"But it's already developed. Some of these buildings have been here for more than a hundred years. Including this one."

"To that guy, they were just placeholders. Until he and his buddies could build what they wanted. But lately, that all changed. He'd been telling everyone that the group put the brakes on. They'd pulled out of Coral Cay and abandoned the project."

"Why? When?"

"Little less than a month ago."

"That doesn't make sense. Lord was trying to buy the Cookie House on the day he died. Did he ever say why the group pulled out?"

"Oh yeah. That's the headline. And it really would have been a headline, if he'd lived. Still might be, for all I know," Manny said, stroking John Quincy's back and holding out a ginger snap, which promptly vanished.

"The consortium commissioned some sort of land report," the P.I. continued. "Soil and water quality. Apparently, it's standard ops before launching something that big. Then, before any final permits are issued, the government guys will follow up with a second report of their own. You know, dot the i's and cross the t's. But this was the first report. The private one. Just for the consortium. So they could decide if the deal was worth all their time and money. And downtown Coral Cay flunked big-time. Lord's been telling everybody that the whole area is sitting on a giant sinkhole."

Chapter 50

Maxi sat at the bakery's kitchen table as Kate pummeled a shiny ball of dough. Oliver was curled up snoozing at the florist's feet. The sun was sinking fast over the Gulf.

"OK, just whose face are you seeing when you punch the daylights out of that poor, helpless blob of dough? Stewart Lord or the floozy real estate *chica*?"

"If it was true, if there really was a sinkhole, why would Lord be trying to buy downtown? I mean, what can you do with land once it has a sinkhole?"

"Nada, nothing. The whole area would become unusable. You couldn't even park cars on it. It would be a money pit for real."

"But Lord was trying to buy parcels."

"At super low prices," Maxi interjected.

Kate nodded, slamming a fist into the dough. "And he was telling owners their property was going to drop in value."

"While he was telling his buddies about the sinkhole," Maxi finished. "And who were his buddies? I can't imagine anyone wanting to be friends with that jerk."

"I asked Manny the same thing. Apparently, a lot of the people from the consortium were from his club—the Emerald Coast Golf and Country Club. From what Manny says, it's gorgeous. On the mainland, right on the water. And it's a hotbed of up-and-comers. Doctors, dentists, chiropractors. People who have a good bit of extra money to invest."

"And our friend Lord just happens to have a place to invest it," Maxi said.

"And a decent track record with property," Kate said. She paused, turning the new information in her mind, like a three-dimensional jigsaw puzzle. "OK, why do you make a fire?" she said suddenly.

"Ay, is this one of Javie's riddles?"

"Close. An old joke in restaurant circles. Man runs a restaurant for years, and the place just keeps losing money. Right before he goes bankrupt, it burns down. And he puts in for the insurance. But he's a lousy arsonist, and he gets caught. So the arson inspector asks him, 'Why did you do it—why did you set the place on fire?' And the guy says, 'I had to make a fire 'cause I can't make a flood.'"

"I don't get it."

Kate grinned. "A little gallows humor from an industry where you work all hours and never know if you're going to have a job next week. I think Lord was making a sinkhole—or the rumor of a sinkhole—because it was going to get him what he wanted."

"Downtown Coral Cay!" Maxi exclaimed.

"Exactly."

"He was using the sinkhole to sink the property values," the florist breathed.

"All he had to do was start the rumor and make sure it caught fire. Not only would all the downtowners be trying to sell, but he'd get their land for cheap."

"But he wanted to build," Maxi said.

"After he's collected the land, he commissions another report. This one reveals that the first report was wrong. The land is solid. And he owns all of it. Heck, he doesn't even have to share it with his consortium buddies. I'm guessing they were just a convenient front—an excuse for him to spread the phony information."

"If any of them suspected he was cutting them out of the Coral Cay deal, they could have killed him," Maxi said.

Kate nodded. "And that crowd of doctors and dentists at his country club would have no problem getting their hands on the drug that killed him and Muriel Hopkins."

Chapter 51

Early Monday morning, as Kate walked into As Time Goes By, she was amazed by how warm and welcoming it felt.

The antique shop looked nothing like the dark, hole-in-the wall stores she'd explored in her travels. This space was large and bright—laid out like a private house. The wood had a polished glow. The fixtures gleamed. And there wasn't a speck of dust in sight. Or that sickly scent of mildew and mothballs that haunted some antique shops like a spectral presence.

Instead, she smelled furniture polish, vanilla candles, and a lingering waft of perfume. Expensive perfume.

Rosie emerged from the back room carrying a tan leather day planner in one hand and a gold pen in the other. "Hey there, Kate! So glad you stopped by."

Kate smiled. "I know this is small, by comparison," she said, holding out the large, white bakery box. "These are my grandmother's special holiday cookies. I baked a fresh batch this morning. My way of saying thank you."

"No need, but we never turn down cookies," Rosie said with a twinkle in her eye. "Especially my better half. Andre, we have a guest!"

Andre Armand stuck his head through the burgundy curtain at the back of the store. His face lit up in a broad grin. "No returns!"

"No chance!" Kate replied.

"She brought cookies. How about some coffee?" Rosie called.

"Ah, *bien*! Let me prepare a fresh pot."

"This place is beautiful," Kate said, her head on a swivel. "And it's so sunny and bright. Usually antique stores are—" she started before catching herself.

Rosie laughed. "I know, right? Like someone's dusty old attic. And that's exactly what we didn't want. I mean, I love antiques. But I don't want to spend my days working in the dark picking my way through cobwebs and doilies. And that's not the atmosphere that makes customers happy, either. We wanted it to be like visiting a friend's house—a friend with really good taste."

"That's it exactly," Kate admitted. If Evan's mother ever found this place, she'd pick them clean in less than an hour. Right down to the delicate silver candlesticks.

Andre came out of the storeroom minutes later with a French press and three exquisite porcelain cups and matching saucers balanced on a shiny silver tray.

He set the tray on a chocolate-colored ottoman between them.

Kate picked up the cup and brought it to her lips. The coffee was strong and black, enclosed in china so fragile it reminded her of an eggshell.

Andre opened the bakery box. "Oh, *magnifique*!"

"My grandmother used to serve them at Christmas," Kate said. "But Maxi says we could use a little of the holiday magic right now."

He plucked a sugar-dusted treat from the box and popped it into his mouth. "Oh, *bon! Très, très bon!*" he said happily.

Rosie nibbled on a cookie. "Oh, this is good." She quickly polished it off and reached for another.

"Anise and almond," Kate said. "As a kid, I nicknamed them pickle cookies, because they're shaped like those little cocktail pickles."

"Ha, I like that," Andre said, plucking several more from the box and putting another in front of Rosie.

"They're sweet but not too sweet," his wife said, smiling. "Luscious."

"There's a lot of butter in there," Kate said ruefully. "I think that's why my grandma pretty much only made them at the holidays. If we'd had them in the cupboard year-round, that would have been dangerous. The almonds give it a certain richness, too."

"I'm glad to have something good to associate with anise," Rosie said blissfully. "Something yummy and happy."

Andre nodded and put another cookie in his mouth, crunching contentedly.

"What do you mean?" Kate asked, retrieving a cookie from the box.

Rosie shook her head. "It was just something Muriel mentioned. Another habit of her lovely boss. He was a smoker. But he didn't want anyone to know. So he was always sucking on these anise breath mints. According to her, he positively reeked of them."

Chapter 52

After Kate flipped the sign on the bakery door to "open," she grabbed the ancient avocado phone on the wall and dialed the flower shop.

"Flowers Maximus, this is Maxi."

"Maxi, I can't leave the shop right now, but I learned something that could help us. Can you come over for your next coffee break?"

"Of course. See you soon!"

Kate stared at the phone in her hand as the line went dead. She shrugged. The florist must have had a customer.

Maxi breezed through the front door less than a minute later, with Oliver by her side. "So what's the news?"

The pup stretched his neck, put his nose high, and sniffed furiously. Then he trotted into the kitchen and stationed himself by the table. Like a guard on the alert.

"As Oliver's already deduced, I've got some cheddar biscuits cooling. How about you pour us a couple of mugs and I'll grab us a plate?"

"Don't keep a poor old flower lady in suspense. *¿Qué pasa?*"

"I think I know who broke into the bakery."

"Well, I still don't think it's Carl. Or Harp."

"Stewart Lord," Kate said.

"No!"

Kate nodded. "Think about it. The guy was always impeccably dressed—right down to the soles of his handmade shoes. And I found out from Rosie and Andre that he was a smoker who was constantly sucking some kind of anise breath mints. Muriel used to talk about the smell. And he died the next day. So we never considered him as a suspect."

"But why would he break into the bakery?"

"No idea. But I have a feeling it had something to do with his plans to buy the shop. And Coral Cay."

"Maybe he was looking for something," Maxi said. "Something he could use against Sam. To make him sell."

"I'm guessing he didn't know I was upstairs when he broke in—but he found out pretty quick. So he probably didn't have a chance to finish what he started."

"And the next day, he was gone," Maxi said. "So he couldn't try again."

"Which explains why the break-in was a one-off."

"It makes sense. But can we be one hundred percent sure?"

"No," Kate admitted, shaking her head. "Not yet. I smelled three things in the shop right after the break-in. Cigarettes, anise, and something else. Something cloying—like a sweet soap or cologne or deodorant. And so far, I can only link Stewart Lord to two of the three."

"Plus the hard shoes," Maxi added.

"Plus the hard shoes," Kate conceded.

"But we also found that Coral Cay has a lot more smokers than we thought," Maxi said, grabbing a biscuit, breaking off a piece, and slipping it to Oliver. "And we learned a few of them have hard shoes, too."

"I can't explain it, but this just makes sense. It's a sneaky move. And Lord was a total sneak. And it fits the facts we have. I mean, Harp likes anise. But not so much that we ever smelled it on him. And both he and Carl smoke, but secretly. So secretly that we never smelled cigarettes around them."

"Yeah, because their wives would kill them," Maxi said.

"Exactly. But Stewart Lord walked around exuding a cloud of the stuff. And . . ."

Kate paused. She recalled the moment Lord entered the bakery. Something about him had made her skin crawl.

"What is it?" Maxi asked.

"When Lord walked into the bakery, for some reason I just wanted to run."

"Well, yeah, he was a real *cabrón*."

"No, I mean, this was visceral. Before he ever opened his mouth. Before I knew who he was. Or why he was there."

"His smell," Maxi said simply.

Kate nodded. "I may not have realized it at the time. Not consciously. But the last time I smelled it—that mix of scents—I was afraid for my life."

"So when suddenly it's there again—thump, thump, thump—your heart beats the mambo, and you want to run away."

Kate nodded. "I want to know for sure. If it was him. And why. This could really help Sam. But how do we find out?"

"I have an idea," Maxi said, grinning. "How do you feel about a little road trip?"

Chapter 53

As they cruised over the bridge toward the Florida mainland, Maxi cranked up the radio. "Pitbull," she explained. "I love this song!"

Kate realized it would be the first time she'd left the island since she'd arrived. This time, with all the windows down and the breeze coming off the bay, they didn't even need air conditioning.

"Are you sure about this?" Kate shouted over the wind. "The plan, I mean."

"We can wait until we think of something better, or we can go with what we got," her friend said, slowing the Jeep for traffic. "I say, 'Go for it!' What's the worst that can happen?"

Kate had a mental picture. The two of them sharing a holding cell next to Sam. And Peter, on the other side of the bars, shaking his head sadly. She dismissed it and tried to focus on the bright sunshine and the blue water lapping beneath the bridge.

"You think Justin will be OK in the shop?" Kate asked finally.

"Oh yeah. He's very responsible. I let him watch the flower shop for me all the time."

"What about the flower shop? I don't want to cost you any business."

"I usually close Sundays and Mondays. Or most Mondays. But I also forwarded the phones to the bakery. That way, Justin is really watching both shops. No sweat! And he's got my cell number, if he needs us. When you run a store, you can't worry about every little thing. If you do, the stress will kill you. But first it will make you very unhappy."

Forty minutes later, they pulled into an office park just outside Bonita Springs. It was a collection of rounded mirrored buildings, some tall, others squat.

"See that one, there?" Maxi said, pointing to the tallest one in the park. "Lord Enterprises is on the top floor."

"If this doesn't work, will Peter post my bail, too?"

"Relax," Maxi said, retrieving the long gold box from the back seat. "Have a little faith in the power of flowers."

"Shouldn't we look more like delivery people?" Kate asked as they marched across the parking lot.

"I got news for you, this is what delivery people look like. I make deliveries all the time. This is exactly what I wear. Jeans and a T-shirt. Here, if it makes you feel better, you can hold this," she said, handing Kate a clipboard with a pen attached. "I deputized you. You are now officially an employee of Flowers Maximus. But don't let all that power go to your head."

Kate took a deep breath. Her heart was thumping and her limbs felt like lead.

"You know what to do, right?" Maxi asked as they passed through the front door and headed for a bank of elevators.

"After we locate Lord's office, you're going to distract his new secretary," Kate whispered. "And I'm going to slip into his office and nose around. With my actual nose."

"Don't worry, you'll be fine."

"I've never done anything like this before—what if I get caught?" Kate asked as they entered the elevator and Maxi pressed "20."

"You're not breaking in. They're inviting us. So what if we wander a little? If someone walks in, just say you got lost. This building is big and round. I bet that happens a lot."

Kate was dubious.

"OK, there's one trick you can use, but save it for if you really need it," Maxi said. "You hop from one foot to the other and say you're looking for *el baño*. And you are in a *super* hurry."

"Does that work?"

"It's better if you have a squirmy toddler by the hand, but we have to use what we've got."

When the door opened, they were facing a reception desk. Apparently, the entire floor belonged to Lord Enterprises.

But the desk was empty.

"Lunch break or layoffs?" Kate asked sotto voce.

Maxi shrugged. "C'mon," she said, fast-walking to the back.

"Where are you going?" Kate called softly as she followed.

"Lord's office. I make deliveries to places like this all the time. His office is gonna be as far from the reception desk as you can get. And he's going to have the best view. The biggest glass window."

When they got to the other end of the office, Kate saw it. Two cherrywood doors. Raised gilt letters spelled out: "Stewart Lord, Esq., Owner and Founder."

But outside the door was a secretarial gauntlet: a cluster of three desks, all of them occupied.

"Uh-oh," Kate said quietly.

"Just hand me that clipboard and get ready to do your thing," Maxi said softly under her breath.

The florist planted herself in front of the first desk in the group—directly opposite Lord's door.

"Ladies, I have a flower delivery for this office, and I'm hoping you can help me. Your boss, Mr. Lord, ordered a dozen long-stemmed red roses before he died. For one of you. The card is very personal. And it uses a pet name. The teenager who took the order over the phone? Unfortunately, the *bobo* garbled the real name. When I myself called to talk with Mr. Lord, I heard the awful news. You have my deepest condolences. But Mr. Lord has already paid for these roses. For a lady. So I must find her. And give her his beautiful gift."

The three women clustered around Maxi and the gold-foiled box, all talking at once. As they did, Kate slipped into Stewart Lord's office.

The lights were off. But one wall was glass and sunlight flooded the room. Suddenly this seemed like a really crackpot idea. Lord had been dead more than a week. Who knew how many people had been in and out of this office since then?

Kate planted her feet and tried to get her bearings. The word "ostentatious" didn't quite cover it. It was a virtual apartment. Off to one side Lord (or more likely his flunkies) had set up a conversation nook, complete with a sofa, several overstuffed chairs, a Persian rug, and a marble fireplace. Gas, she guessed.

Lord's desk and bookshelves sat atop a raised platform in front of the panoramic window, like an altar. On the other side of the room, an alcove off to her left housed a wet bar that looked more like a small kitchen. Next to that, another set of double doors.

Curious, Kate walked over and opened them slowly. The lights popped on, startling her. Motion detectors. She hoped she hadn't also triggered an alarm.

A bathroom. But calling this a bathroom was like calling Versailles a house.

Every inch of the vast room was covered in marble. Off on one end, a sunken tub. On the other, what appeared to be a walk-in steam shower. In the center, a padded adjustable shaving bench that could double as a massage table. For the egomaniac on the go.

The marble vanity held one oversized golden sink, shaped like a giant clamshell. Gold towel rings on each side offered plush, spa-like white towels. The space was set off by an enormous mirror in a baroque gold-leaf frame.

Kate opened a white door just to the left of the sink. The scent nearly smothered her. Cigarettes, anise, and that cloying cologne.

A selection of half a dozen suits hung neatly in the center. On either side, perfectly square marble cubbyholes held neatly folded dress shirts, socks, and other necessities. On the floor, several pairs of handmade shoes in black, navy, oxblood, brown, and tan—a neutral *ombré* rainbow. Which ones had he been wearing the night of the break-in?

Because there was no doubt in her mind now. Stewart Lord had been their would-be burglar. So what had he been he looking for at the Cookie House?

The top niche on the right was curious. Puzzling. It held only two items: a tall brown bottle and a silver charm bracelet. She leaned into the closet to get a better look at both. The scent was suffocating.

The glass bottle was Isla Tropical rum. Not a familiar brand. But it must be tasty because there were only a few ounces left.

Odd. She'd never pegged Lord as a rum drinker. According to Harp, the developer preferred expensive scotch. And the crystal decanter on his office bar appeared to hold just that. Was this his secret stash?

Almost instinctively, Kate reached for the bracelet. She turned it over in her hands. The silver links were solid and heavy but graceful at the same time. Most of the charms were delicate. Light and ethereal. But a few were colorful, cheap, and almost juvenile. It was definitely a woman's. And in this shrine to masculinity, gold, and opulence, it didn't fit.

She glanced at the front door again. It felt like she'd been in here for hours. Just how long could Maxi hold off the gaggle of secretaries? And while sneaking in was relatively easy, how would she walk out without being seen?

Without thinking, Kate slipped the bracelet into her pocket. She carefully closed the bathroom doors and tiptoed to the front door. She could hear Maxi, holding court outside, punctuated by exclamations from the other women.

She glanced over at Lord's desk. Dare she risk it? Surely the police would have been through it by now.

But he was the victim, not the killer. And from what she heard through the Coral Cay grapevine, Stewart Lord's company attorney threw a temper tantrum every time the investigators mentioned wanting anything even connected to company records. So maybe they hadn't.

She'd been here too long. She had to leave. Now.

Anxiously, she depressed the door lever. In millimeters, so that no one would notice it moving. Then she pulled it open in one fluid movement, pushed herself through, and swung it quietly shut behind her.

For a few seconds, Kate stood there lounging casually in front of the door, as if she'd been there the entire time, while her heart beat a syncopated rhythm in her chest.

"Ladies, once again, I am so very sorry for your loss," Maxi said. "It sounds like Mr. Lord was a very special man."

Kate fell in behind Maxi as they motored for the front office and the elevator. Luckily, the elevator car was empty. They rushed in, and Kate poked "G" twice. After an eternity, the doors finally closed.

Only then did Kate realize she'd been holding her breath.

Chapter 54

Maxi threw the Jeep into reverse as the words exploded from her mouth. "OK, so was Stewart Lord our burglar or not?"

"It was him," Kate said. "Definitely him. The office had that same awful smell."

"Good, 'cause I'd hate to think I went through all that drama for nothing. Those *chicas* think they're on a telenovela. Or one of those shows about the rich housewives who are single and don't keep house."

"Now that we know the 'who,' we have to figure out the 'why.'" Kate paused. "Do you ever remember Cookie wearing a charm bracelet?"

Maxi shook her head. "Uh-uh. She hated bracelets. She wouldn't even wear a watch most of the time. She felt like it got in the way when she was working with the dough. Why?"

Kate raised her eyebrows. The more she heard about Cookie Hepplewhite, the more surprised she was how much they had in common. Maybe it was a pastry chef thing.

"That office of Lord's is more like a small apartment," Kate said. "Maybe a crash pad. But in the little executive closet where he keeps a couple changes of clothes? I found a woman's charm bracelet."

"You think he had a girlfriend?"

"I don't know. It didn't feel like that. I mean, there weren't any other women's things. Or even a toothbrush. Just a little shelf with the bracelet and a bottle of rum."

"Maybe he was dating a lady pirate."

Kate laughed. "So what did the office girls say? Did they ever decide who gets to keep the roses?"

"The skinny blond one. She swears she and Lord were 'practically engaged.'"

"Maybe it's her bracelet," Kate said.

"What did it look like?" Maxi asked.

"Heavy silver, possibly antique."

"Nope. Blondie is definitely a gold girl. She was wearing a lot of it. And that young lady isn't gonna mix and match, lemme tell you."

"Seems to be a theme around there. You should have seen Lord's bathroom. That place was a gold dealer's dream. The stuff was everywhere. And not gold colored. Actual gold."

Maxi shook her glossy black hair. "That's just a waste of money. And how are you s'posed to clean it, huh? 'Cause at my house, when you tackle the bathrooms, you better have a Brillo pad. Or dynamite."

"Did any of them mention Muriel?" Kate asked, touching the jeans pocket where the bracelet rested.

"One of them, the older lady with the carroty hair? She misses her. But it doesn't sound like they were super close.

The *flaca* blonde? She says that Muriel had a thing for Lord."

"Well, we know that's not true," Kate said. "Pretty much the exact opposite."

"I know. I'm just telling you what she said. She says Muriel secretly gave him a present. A box of chocolates."

"The poisoned chocolates?"

"I dunno. Skinny Girl just said that Stewart Lord made a big deal about the fact that a secret admirer gave him expensive candies. And he told everyone he'd actually seen Muriel sneak in and put them on his desk. That she had a big, giant crush on him and it was embarrassing. 'Cause he wasn't interested in her at all. He said he was trying to be kind, so he just told Muriel she could have them because he didn't like chocolate."

"Oh yeah, 'cause he was always so kind. Besides, if Muriel had poisoned the chocolates, she wouldn't have eaten them. But she was Lord's assistant. So if anything had been delivered for him, she'd have probably been the one to put it on his desk."

"I know. He sounds like the playground trolls at my kids' school. They like to make up stories, too. So much drama!"

For the next few minutes, they rode in silence as Maxi battled washboard roads, stop-and-go traffic, and crazy drivers. In spite of it all, with the warm sun coming through the windshield Kate felt herself growing drowsy.

"It's too bad you didn't get a picture of that bracelet," Maxi said as they stopped at a light. "We could ask around to see if anyone recognized it."

Kate reached into her pocket, carefully extricating the bracelet. She held it aloft. "We still can."

"Oh my gosh, you didn't! But you did. OK, I totally

approve, but we can't tell Peter. He would never under-stand."

"I'm not sure I do, either," Kate confessed. "All I know is that it looked so out of place. Like it was the only thing in that room that belonged to a genuine, real person. And I couldn't just leave it there."

Chapter 55

Kate recognized relief on Justin's face as she and Maxi walked through the front door of the bakeshop.

"Hey, Cookie Lady," he said. "Man, it's been crazy since you left. We're totally sold out of sourdough. And chocolate chip cookies. And those peanut butter cookies with the chocolate chips in 'em. OK, I might have eaten a few of those myself. And Andy Levy called. He wants to put in a standing order for sourdough, along with some white and wheat for sandwiches. He also wanted to know if you could give him a dozen sourdough rolls for something new they're trying at the pub. Some kind of experiment with pot roast sandwiches. Which sounds pretty good right now. And you had three phone calls from people who want cookies for birthday parties. And one for a 'gender reveal,' whatever that is."

"It's a very new tradition that means more business for us. So, basically, awesome," Maxi said, slapping her friend on the back. "Mention that they might want balloons, too. I do really good balloons."

"Oh, Mrs. Más-Buchanan? You got a couple of messages, too. Mr. Kim wants some flowers for Mrs. Kim. One of the resorts called about flowers for a big dinner-dance. And one of your neighbors wants to know if you can make her front yard look like this place."

Maxi fished two twenties out of her purse, handing them to Justin.

"Do any of the girls you know wear charm bracelets?" Kate asked him.

"Not that I've noticed. Not on the beach, anyway."

"Silver wouldn't mix with sand and salt water," Maxi said. "Unless she just wore it for special occasions."

"Why? Do you want me to ask around?" Justin offered.

"Could you?" Kate asked. "But quietly. I don't want to get anyone in hot water." *Especially me,* she added silently.

"Sure. No sweat. I'm gonna grab some grub and some nugs. See ya!"

"What did I tell you?" Maxi said, shuffling through her messages after he left. "Not only is everything totally fine, but we have some new clients. Whoa, Delores Philpott wants me to make her yard look like the Cookie House? That woman is gonna need a dump truck full of rye seed and a few less cats."

Kate put her phone messages on the counter. How would a smart businesswoman prioritize? Return calls first, then whip up more cookies and sourdough.

As Kate sorted through the slips of paper, Maxi made another pot of coffee. Once she flipped the "on" switch, she snapped her fingers.

"Do you remember what you said when I asked you to describe the bracelet?" the florist said excitedly.

"I said it was heavy silver," Kate replied, studying the phone messages and making notes on a small pad.

"And that it looked like an antique. I bet Rosie or Andre could tell us which of the local antique stores specialize in something like that. And if they can, we might be able to learn a little more about it."

"That's brilliant!" Kate said. "If we could find out when it was made, or what country it's from, or what some of the charms mean—anything like that could help us pinpoint the owner."

"Be funny if it belonged to Mary Larde or their *mamacita*," Maxi said. "A little keepsake Roly Paulie swiped when he ran away from home."

"If that's the case, we can return it to her when she shows up to take over Lord Enterprises. I would so love to be standing there the first time she walks through that door. Can you picture the look on her face when she gets a load of that gold sink?"

"Or Blondie? That girl is toast."

"At least she got some flowers out of the deal. How much do I owe you, by the way?"

"Nada. Those flowers are a symbol of true love. And you can't put a price on true love. Although Leonard Kim will. And I'm betting it's gonna be about fifty bucks."

"At least let me pay half. And don't think I didn't see you slip cash to Justin. That's a Cookie House expense."

"Nah, it's a get-Sam-the-heck-out-of-jail expense. But I'll send you a bill. Instead of numbers, it's gonna be little pictures of cookies I wanna try. And maybe some of those sourdough rolls. Those sounded good."

"Sheesh, we missed lunch. No wonder we're so hungry. Make you a deal. If you watch the shop for ten minutes, I'll take Andy a half-dozen sandwich loaves and get us both some lunch. Anything special you want to eat?"

"Whatever he's got ready to go. I am starved."

"Two delivery-woman specials—got it," Kate said. "I

was also thinking, if we packed up my stuff after work I could move in tonight."

"Tonight, tomorrow, next week. I don't think Javie and Michael are gonna give up that tent, whatever you do. And I've kinda gotten used to having fresh cookies every morning."

"It's time," Kate said, shaking her head. "You and Peter opened your home when I had no place to go. That blows me away. And if I leave before your poor husband gets too sick of me, he might not mind if I pop up for a meal now and then. You know, as long as I bring bread. Or pizza. Plus, there's no more stalker danger. And I think we can be pretty certain the burglar's not coming back."

"Not unless he haunts the place," Maxi said.

"Oh sure," Kate replied, grimacing. "Like that won't give me nightmares."

Chapter 56

The next morning, as Kate pushed two trays of sour-dough rolls into one of the double ovens, the bell announced a customer in the shop.

"Hey, it's just me!" a familiar voice called.

"Hey, Rosie," Kate said, sticking her head over the swinging doors. "Have you got time for coffee? I just took a fresh batch of yeast rolls out of the oven."

The antique dealer giggled. "I shouldn't. I just had two at Sunny's Stretch and Starch. But what the heck."

"By the way, that bed is a dream," Kate said. "It's the best night's sleep I've had in a decade."

"Oh, I'm so glad," she said. "We kind of had to guess on the mattress. And Mrs. Allen picked out the sheets and the duvet. I love the deep green-blue. It reminds me of the ocean."

"It's perfect. I don't think I was awake for two minutes after my head hit the pillow."

She left out the part about sharing it with Oliver. By

the time she'd cleaned up the bakery kitchen and gone upstairs, she'd found the pup curled into a downy ball at the foot of the bed, fast asleep.

"I'm so glad you're settling in OK," Rosie said. "Have you heard anything else on Sam's case?"

"Nothing. The state attorney offered him a deal if he pled guilty, but he turned it down flat. Said he wasn't going to confess to something he didn't do. And you were right. He doesn't remember ever meeting Muriel Hopkins. His lawyer showed him her photo."

"I don't think she ever mentioned the bakery, either," Rosie said. "With her heart, she was pretty careful about her diet. Besides, chocolates were her weakness. And Sam doesn't sell those."

Kate set two full mugs on the table and followed up with a plate of yeast rolls, butter, and a jar of strawberry jam.

"Cream or sugar?"

"Not for me," Rosie said, putting a generous dollop of jam on her roll. "This is plenty."

"I don't know if Maxi mentioned it, but we went to Stewart Lord's office yesterday."

"No! For real? Did you learn anything interesting?"

"Other than the man was even more of a tool than we thought? But there were a couple of new wrinkles. Stewart Lord claimed that someone sent him chocolates on the day Muriel died. Anonymously. He also told several employees that he saw Muriel putting them on his desk. He claimed she sent them because she had a crush on him."

"That rat! If there was ever a man who deserved what he got, it was that pig. I don't know how she put up with him. Or why she stayed."

"If it makes you feel any better, his sister will probably

inherit everything. And this is the sister he stole from to launch his business."

"He stole from his own sister?"

"The payout on their late mother's burial policy, to be precise."

"That man was a real piece of work," Rosie said, shaking her head. "I bet the sister is tap-dancing on his grave. So were those chocolates the poisoned chocolates?"

"No idea. But unless there were a few boxes floating around, it seems likely. Can you keep a secret? I mean a serious secret?"

"Yes, and I am totally intrigued," Rosie said. "What is it?"

"The reason we went? I suspected that Lord might have been the one who broke into the bakery. Because of what you said about his breath mints. Right after the break-in, after the burglar ran out, I went into the shop. And I smelled cigarettes and anise and some heavy-duty cologne."

"Was it him?"

Kate nodded. "Not a doubt in my mind. But that's not the secret."

Rosie put jam on the second half of her roll and took a bite.

"Stewart Lord's office was like something from another age. Marble, gold, panoramic view, fireplace—and a bathroom larger than my Manhattan apartment."

Rosie nodded. "Muriel described it pretty well. How did she put it? 'How Marie Antoinette would have decorated if she'd had real money.'"

Kate grinned. "She nailed it. Anyway, while I was there, I snooped around a little."

Rosie leaned forward as she reached for another roll. "Spill."

"I found something that definitely didn't belong in Versailles by the Sea. A woman's bracelet. It looks like it might be an antique. I'd love to find out a little more about it—and maybe find the owner. If I show it to you, could you refer me to an antique dealer who specializes in, well, whatever it is?"

"Of course. Do you have a picture of it?"

"Not exactly. That's the secret part. I brought it with me."

Rosie's face lit up. "Well, it certainly doesn't belong to Lord Stewart Lord. And it's not like he's going to return it. I say this falls under a little legal code called finders keepers."

"Ben Abrams would probably disagree. Peter Buchanan, too. And sooner or later, I'm either going to have to tell them or return it to its rightful owner. Probably both."

"In the meantime," Rosie said, sitting up in her chair, "let's see this beauty."

Chapter 57

Kate gently laid a white linen handkerchief on the table in front of Rosie and slowly unfolded it. It had seemed thoughtless to keep the bracelet jammed in her pocket, so she'd stored it carefully in one of the drawers beneath her new bed.

Rosie's eyes opened wide as she reached for the bracelet. "Where exactly did you find this?"

"Stewart Lord's private office bathroom. He had a closet where he kept a half-dozen suits, shoes, that kind of stuff. This was in an upper niche alone. Except for the dregs of a bottle of rum."

"This was Muriel's," Rosie said in a hushed voice. She picked up the bracelet and laid it over one palm. "She bought it on her last trip out here. That was about two weeks before she died. What was he doing with it?"

"No idea. I don't suppose Muriel drank rum?"

"Muriel didn't drink anything. She was even careful about her coffee intake. Decaf only." Rosie shook her head. "This is weird."

"What?" Kate asked.

"This bracelet came with charms. See these?" she said, running her finger lightly over the silver form. "Also in sterling, also original to the period." She pointed to three gaudy plastic discs, each the size of a quarter. "But not these. I've never seen them before."

"I wondered about those," Kate said. "They're colorful. But they don't exactly match the style."

"Hot-pink, orange, and blue plastic charms on a fine piece of Edwardian jewelry? I'll say they don't match the style. Muriel never would have done this. She appreciated beautiful things."

"Maybe they meant something to her personally. You know, sentimental value."

"Maybe he did it," Rosie countered. "The funny thing is, that last visit? She was spitting mad at Stewart Lord. But she was happy, too."

"What do you mean?"

"She'd been pricing homes out here," Rosie recalled. "Actually shopping them, I mean. Before, it was always more of a daydream. You know how people say 'oh, someday'?"

Kate nodded. She'd done way too much of that in her own life.

"Well, this was different," Rosie continued. "She was different. Angry. At Lord anyway. But proactive and happy, too. Does that make any sense?"

Kate nodded. "More than you know."

"It was like she'd had some sort of a wake-up call. She was done idling in neutral. Muriel Hopkins was moving forward with her life."

Chapter 58

Kate was baking cookies for three different birthday parties. Luckily, two customers wanted chocolate chip. But while one woman wanted actual cookies—four dozen for a kids' party—the other wanted one giant cookie.

"Like a pizza," the woman explained. "But with 'Happy Birthday, Mike' written on it. In red icing. He likes red. He also really likes golf. Can you draw a golf course on it?"

Kate talked the woman down from an entire golf course to just the putting green with a jaunty red flag.

She grinned as she hung up the phone. Culinary school had prepared her to work in a kitchen. But dealing directly with the public? That was a whole different skill set. She needed to be part baker, part psychiatrist, and part mind reader.

In between making cookies and breads, she created a color palette of pink royal icings. Another part of the job that was truly fun. She decided on a delicate shell pink for the gender reveal.

When the phone rang, Kate grabbed it—smearing several shades of icing on the handset and her apron. "The Cookie House, this is Kate."

"I've got some news," Maxi said rapid-fire. "Not good or bad. Just news."

"Me too. I've been dying to talk, but the cookie orders are backing up. Head over before you go home. I have a little surprise. My way of saying 'thank you.'"

"I know I said I'd miss having my very own cookie elf, but you don't have to do that."

"This isn't cookies," Kate said. "It's dinner. Something I learned from a very talented Greek chef. Kreatopita. A meat pie. It's got garlic and fresh herbs and a really flaky crust. And if you ever want a midnight snack, it's just as good cold."

"OK, now that I will take. *Mi mami* is out with her friends tonight. She tells everybody they play bridge. But I know they really play poker. Sometimes, even dominoes. But don't tell her I told you. Good Cuban ladies don't play dominoes."

"However will you live down the shame?" Kate teased.

"That all depends on how much dinero she wins."

Chapter 59

When Maxi walked into the bakery kitchen, four meat pies were cooling on a rack.

"Oh, this smells delicious! But how come this one has a little hole punched in the middle? And what's with the little baby one on the end?"

"That's a single serving for Sam. And the one with the hole is for Oliver and me. No garlic or onions because they're bad for dogs. Instead, I substituted grated carrots and added extra rosemary, thyme, and basil. I made it look a little different so I wouldn't get them mixed up."

"If you want, I can take Sam his dinner on my way home. The news I mentioned? I finally counted the donations from Saturday and got the money to Sam's bank. His lawyer had to stop by and sign off so they could drop the money into Sam's account."

"I never understood that. I mean, signing off to take money out, sure," Kate said, vigorously washing her hands to remove all traces of icing. "But if any stranger wants to put a few dollars in my account, I say let them."

"Ay, but this was more than just a few dollars. Between the checks and the cash, nine thousand, six hundred, and fifty-three dollars."

"Oh my gosh! What did Sam say?" Kate asked.

"I haven't told him yet. But I think he'll be pleased. Even if he doesn't admit it. It means people believe in him"

"In a big way. That's fantastic."

"And that's not all," Maxi said, bouncing in her chair. "While we were waiting on the bank manager to get everything signed, his lawyer—Bob Gifford—told me the assistant state attorney is having trouble linking Sam to the drug that killed Muriel Hopkins and Stewart Lord. So he wants to play *Let's Make a Deal* again. If Sam pleads guilty to two counts of involuntary manslaughter, he'll recommend ten to fifteen years in prison. And this time, he's not asking for any of the details. Just sign the paper and say he did it. Bob said that Sam could be out in seven years. Or maybe even less."

"What did Sam say?" Kate asked, tensing.

"Sam said 'no way!' *Mi padrino* won't confess to something he didn't do."

"Thank goodness."

"But the assistant state attorney making another offer?" Maxi said. "That's a very good sign."

"It is. It really is. What did Bob Gifford say?"

"They still have a long way to go to clear Sam. But it's looking better."

"Wow, that is good news."

"So what's your gossip? Or am I s'posed to take my meat pies and go home?"

"The bracelet was Muriel's."

"No! Who told you that?"

"Rosie. Muriel bought it from their shop the last time she visited Coral Cay. About two weeks before she died."

"How did that slimy toad Lord get it?"

"That's the puzzle. I guess he could have found it in the office after she died. Or when they were clearing out her desk someone might have discovered it and turned it over to him. But none of that explains the rum. Oh, and there's one other weird thing. The bracelet and most of the charms are sterling silver and old. Edwardian, Rosie said. But the bright-colored plastic charms? They weren't on the bracelet when Muriel bought it. Someone added them later. And Rosie is convinced it wasn't Muriel."

"That is super strange."

"I know, right? A lot of little, nagging details that don't seem important. Like the bits of stray dough trimmed from a piecrust. So why can't I shake the feeling that they actually mean something?"

Chapter 60

The next morning, Kate padded down the stairs, opened the back door for Oliver, and plugged in Sam's coffeemaker. It was an old-fashioned model from the nineties that the baker had probably bought new. Black plastic, with a glass carafe, it made up to twelve cups at a time. And she was grateful for every single caffeinated drop.

As Oliver galloped down the stairs and slipped quietly out the door, she pulled Muriel's bracelet out of her robe pocket and placed it carefully on the kitchen table.

As the coffeemaker burbled and gurgled, she stared at the bracelet, finally picking it up and feeling its weight in her hand. She turned it, fingering each of the charms. The plastic discs were modern and cheery. But next to the antique silver they looked cheap and awkward.

Muriel purchased the bracelet. But Stewart Lord ended up with it. So which one added the new charms? And why?

Kate recalled the antique dealer's anger when she

noticed the colorful baubles. She half-expected Rosie to rip them from the bracelet on the spot.

Oliver trotted through the back door and made a quick circle of the kitchen. He disappeared into the shop and came back with his bright red Kong. The toy had been a gift from Barb Showalter, and the puppy loved it.

Kate filled her coffee cup and splashed in some cream. As she sat down, Oliver dropped the conical toy gently next to her chair and gazed up into her eyes.

Before presenting it to Oliver, Barb had revealed that the Kong wasn't just a toy. It was also a game. "A smart dog like Oliver needs mental stimulation," the bookseller had explained.

And this rubber toy concealed a secret: a little niche inside to place a dollop of peanut butter, cheese, or liverwurst. It was a puzzle, treat, and toy all in one.

Unfortunately, Oliver was good at puzzles. He located and consumed the hidden treats in no time flat. Kate suspected he felt the same way about peanut butter as she did about chocolate.

"Time for a refill?" she asked the eager pup. "Already? I'm going to put a stopwatch on you one of these days," she said softly, petting his silky head. "I think you're setting a new record."

She reached into the fridge and pulled out a jar of peanut butter. She smeared some onto a paper towel and then worked it into the hollow space in the toy. Then she offered the toy to Oliver.

"OK, this should keep that crafty brain of yours occupied for a few minutes. Seriously, I think it takes longer for me to put the peanut butter in than for you to get it out, you know that?"

Oliver dropped to the floor, rolled onto his back, and held the Kong with his two front paws, wrestling it energetically.

Too bad he couldn't solve the puzzle in front of her. The puzzle of the mismatched charm bracelet. Maybe if she smeared peanut butter on it—

Suddenly Kate snatched the bracelet off the table. She carefully turned it to the dark blue plastic charm and tried to remove it from the bracelet. When that didn't work, she grabbed a small fork from the cutlery drawer. She slid one tine gently through the charm's metal connecting loop. When she'd pried it far enough open, she lifted it gently off of the bracelet.

The charm was heavy. Heavier than she expected, considering that it was made of plastic and chrome. She flipped it in her hand. Perfectly round, slightly larger than a quarter, and about half an inch thick. Edged all the way around with a shiny chrome band.

She grabbed the top and tugged. Nothing. She put her thumb and forefinger on the front and back of the charm, squeezed hard, and gave the link on top a quick yank. It came apart in her hand.

The two parts fit together so seamlessly, they'd looked like one. The first piece was most of the charm. Two thin round plastic discs along with almost all of the chrome band. It was hollow. The second piece was smaller. Just the metal connecting link that had fastened the charm to the bracelet, the remaining bit of the chrome band, and—protruding from that—a short USB stick.

Chapter 61

Kate sat at the computer in the flower shop as Maxi hovered behind her.

"I can't believe you found these things in a piece of jewelry," Maxi said quietly. "Who do you think put them there?"

"Off the top of my head, I'd say Muriel. She bought the bracelet. And from what Rosie and Andre said, she was fed up with Lord. Apparently, the last time Muriel visited Coral Cay she'd had some sort of epiphany. I think she'd finally made a decision. I think she'd decided to expose Stewart Lord."

"Not a very safe thing to do," Maxi said, shaking her head. "But why the charm bracelet? And the secret memory sticks?"

"I could be way off base, but I believe she was compiling evidence to bring him down. Muriel had access to his business records, computer files, paperwork, contact lists, you name it. But she needed a place to stash it.

Some place handy but also hidden. And face it, who'd look twice at a middle-aged woman's charm bracelet?"

"And the fact that she bought it in Coral Cay and was using it to help save Coral Cay . . ."

"A little extra measure of justice," Kate said, smiling.

"But why would Lord keep it? He'd throw it out. Or destroy it."

"He very well might have," Kate said dejectedly. "These first two sticks are empty."

"Are you sure?" Maxi asked.

Kate nodded grimly, reaching for the third. "Here goes nothing," she said, shoving it into the slot on the back of Maxi's computer tower.

Kate tapped a few keys and the screen displayed a menu. She opened a document and scanned it. Then another. And another.

"What is it?" Maxi asked, stepping closer to the display.

"This one's not empty," Kate said softly. "Definitely not empty. Page after page of documents. All related to Lord Enterprises. And Coral Cay. Reports. Memos. Receipts. Schematics. Blueprints. Government filings. Oh boy, we are going to need some serious time to go through these. But it looks like this could be the mother lode."

"See when they were put onto the stick," Maxi prompted.

"Let . . . me . . . check. . . ." Kate's voice trailed off as she pecked a few more keys. "OK, the first one was loaded last month. The eleventh at six fourteen a.m. And the last document was downloaded on the fifteenth at nine fifty-two at night."

"Nothing since then?" Maxi asked anxiously.

"No. And Muriel died the next day. You're right—that date clinches it. These have to be hers."

"She was super cagey," Maxi said. "She did her sleuthing early in the morning or late at night—probably when no one else was at the office."

"And since she was Lord's personal secretary, it would be natural for her to be the first one in or the last one to leave. Just your typical diligent, devoted assistant."

"So how did Lord catch on?" Maxi asked.

"That," said Kate, "is exactly what I'd like to find out. And I think I know just who to call."

"Yeah, I've seen more than a few of these document dumps in my time," Manny said as his thick fingers typed away at Maxi's computer.

Sporting a red Hawaiian shirt, the P.I. had traded the cargo shorts for jeans. No hat today, Kate noticed. But he had a pair of sunglasses perched on top of his head.

"You don't want to know how many of my cases involve corporate espionage," he said. "That and divorce work keep me in dog chow."

"It's going to take forever to read them," Maxi said.

"Nah, the secret is triage. What do you want to know most?"

"Did Stewart Lord find out Muriel was on to him?" Kate asked. "And if so, how?"

"That part's a piece of cake. Or, in your case, some of those ginger cookie things. John Quincy really likes those."

"That's a deal," Kate said, smiling. "So how can you tell?"

"A lot of what your lady saved are photos. Pictures of paper documents. You start with those."

"Why?" Maxi asked.

"Two reasons," Manny said, holding up two tanned fingers. "Paper means someone wasn't putting it into the computer. Probably stuff your developer friend didn't want on the company hard drive. Two, a lot of these photos are receipts."

"Follow the money," Kate said, remembering Dr. Patel's advice.

"Yup," Manny said, typing. "Huh. This is weird."

"What is it?" Maxi asked.

"See this receipt? Syntegration Solutions?"

"Yes," Kate and Maxi said in unison.

"Spyware. Company's pretty well known in certain circles. And I've seen this program in action. Nasty stuff. Dump it on somebody's phone and it'll tell you everything but what they had for lunch. That too, probably."

"What do you mean?" Maxi asked.

"Well, basically, it's a phone bug. Records calls, copies emails. Can even track somebody in real life with GPS. And that's cheating, if you ask me. If you can't run a tail the old-fashioned way, you got no business spying on people."

Kate met Maxi's eyes and tried not to smile.

"Odd thing is, according to the receipt, your guy bought two dozen copies," he said, pointing to the monitor. "That means he can put it on twenty-four different phones. Most cases, it's a one-off. One spouse or business partner tracking the other."

"Remember our field trip?" Maxi said. "The office ladies were amazed how Lord remembered everything about everyone in the office. He knew who was quarreling with their spouse or whose kid was doing lousy at school. One time, one of his executives made an appointment for a job interview. Lord called the guy out to the reception area five minutes later and fired him."

"Lord was spying on his employees," Kate said quietly. "Probably the executives. And the executive assistants."

They both fell silent as the horror of it hit them.

"Manny, is there any way to email all of these files to someone anonymously?" Kate asked.

"Eh, I may know a little something on that subject," he said, cracking his knuckles over the keyboard. "Wouldn't do it from here, though. Too easy to trace. A library's your best bet."

"What about the video cameras at the library?" Maxi asked. "Couldn't they find you from those?"

"Nah, libraries have been underfunded for years," he said. "Half the time, those cameras don't even work. And I know a few primo locations where that's definitely the case. Don't ask me how. So if someone were to go in and fire off an email, who would be the lucky recipient?"

"Detective Ben Abrams," Kate said. "At the Coral Cay police department."

Chapter 62

It was well past the noon rush before Kate finally had time to think about lunch. She heated up some of the leftover kreatopita. Magically, the minute she opened the warm oven door Oliver trotted down the stairs.

"You have a good nap? Guess what? It's lunchtime. Way past lunchtime. But I'm betting your nose told you that. First, though, we let this cool," she said, lifting the pie protectively to a rack at the back of the counter. "Trust me on that one."

The phone rang. Reflexively, Kate grabbed it.

Oliver let out a soft whine.

"I know, I know," she said, covering the receiver. "But business is business. More puppy toys and big tubs of peanut butter."

Oliver licked his chops.

"The Cookie House, this is Kate," she announced brightly into the phone.

"Kate, it's Annie Kim. Listen, I've been poking

around, and I think I might have found something interesting."

"Have you had lunch yet?"

"No, and don't tell my moms," Annie whispered into the phone. "She'll freak."

"You're not a vegetarian, are you?"

"Not in this lifetime."

"In that case, come on over. The lunch crowd is gone, Oliver's here, and I've got a meat pie you're going to love."

"Oh man, this is good," Annie said. "Moms makes something similar. She calls hers a 'hand pie.' But the crust is different. And I really like the hamburger in this. What did you say this was?"

"Kreatopita. Or, at least, my dog-friendly version of it."

Annie smiled. "Yeah, the little guy really likes it, too."

They both looked down at Oliver, who was going to town on his own piece. His tail wagged furiously, and the paper plate in front of him was nearly clean.

"So what did you discover?" Kate asked when she could no longer contain her curiosity.

Annie swallowed, smiled, and cut off another bite with her fork. "The drug that killed Stewart Lord and Muriel Hopkins? I already told you guys and the police that Sam didn't have access to it. At least, not from what I've seen. The truth is, I can't even find anyone Sam knows who took it. And that's on the QT."

Kate nodded, devouring another morsel of pie.

"But there's a guy in Lord's office who takes it regularly. Re-upped his monthly prescription on the eleventh of last month. But he came in and bought *another* month's supply on the sixteenth."

"That was the day Muriel died," Kate said.

Annie nodded, taking another forkful of the savory

pie. "I had to call in a few favors. And, frankly, I'm not sure it's strictly 'legal,'" she said, using air quotes. "But I had his pharmacist examine his usage patterns. Regular as clockwork. The guy's been taking the stuff for years. Never 'spilled' pills or 'lost' a bottle. And trust me, as a pharmacist, you see plenty of that. But he has a routine. He usually picks up the new prescription the weekend before the old one runs out."

"Everybody runs errands on the weekend," Kate said.

"Exactly," Annie seconded, neatly helping herself to another slice of meat pie. "He takes one pill a day and should have finished his old batch on Tuesday, then started the brand-new bottle on Wednesday. Instead, he's back to the drugstore on Thursday saying he's all out of meds."

"Who is he?" Kate asked. "Or can you tell me?"

"Technically, HIPAA regs prevent me from sharing anything. But just between us, I'm calling Ben and telling him he should take a much closer look at Stewart Lord's company attorney."

Chapter 63

As the moon rose above the Gulf, Kate leaned over the counter in the kitchen of the Cookie House, carefully piping pale pink royal icing onto a tray of crispy, thin butter cookies. Her coffee sat untouched on a nearby counter.

Maxi helped herself to a second mug, stirred in two teaspoons of sugar, and added some cream. "If Muriel was nosing around the company, could Lord have killed her to shut her up?" the florist ventured.

"That makes sense. But who killed Lord? And how does the company attorney fit in?"

"OK, so maybe Lord tells the attorney Muriel's going through files. And the attorney gets nervous. And kills her. That would explain why he threw hissy fits every time Peter's office asked about company records."

"Or it could just be the lawyer being a lawyer," Kate said, deftly smoothing her work with an offset spatula. "Especially if he knows that our friend Lord was playing it fast and loose with rules and regs. Face it, anybody working for that company had the same motive for killing Muriel Hopkins. Lord Enterprises was pumping a lot of money into a lot of pockets. Muriel's digging around threatened to shut off the spigot. But why turn around and kill Lord? And how? Did anyone ever check out Lord's driver? That guy was actually on the scene at the time."

"Squeaky clean," Maxi said, watching her friend finish each cookie with a sprinkle of multicolored sugar. "Peter told me he's some little college boy making extra money over the summer. Lord leased the car from a service that also supplied the drivers. And the poor kid didn't have any links to Stewart Lord. Or Paul Larde. But he was super freaked out when his first-ever passenger died."

"Now I feel bad," Kate said, looking up. "That would have been awful."

"What if Lord killed Muriel, then the lawyer killed Lord in revenge?" Maxi said. "Because he was secretly madly in love with her."

"OK, who's been watching telenovelas again?" Kate teased as she piped royal icing onto a second tray of cookies.

"I hit the TV button and it appeared," Maxi said, grinning. "It was fate."

"Sure, someone could have killed Lord if they found out he'd murdered Muriel. But wouldn't it have been easier just to turn him in?"

"Maybe they knew it but couldn't prove it."

"Rum and a bracelet," Kate mumbled as she directed the flow of pink icing onto a cookie. "Why does a guy with no girlfriend who loves showy toys and expensive scotch stash an almost empty bottle of rum and a silver charm bracelet in his private closet?"

"They mean something to him," Maxi concluded.

"I agree. But what?"

"What if Lord found out the lawyer killed Muriel and was blackmailing him?"

"OK, that one seems plausible," Kate said as she evened the icing with her spatula. "But it still doesn't explain the rum."

"Too bad Sam's in jail. He's our rum expert."

"What brand does he drink?"

"Local stuff," Maxi said. "Isla Tropical."

"That was the brand in Lord's closet!" Kate said.

"It's popular on Coral Cay. It's really good, and around here folks support the home team."

"I didn't know there was a distillery on the island," Kate said, reaching for the shaker of coarse rainbow-colored sugar.

"There isn't," Maxi said. "It's just over the bridge on the mainland. Very small, but very cool. And the guys who run it are out here all the time, because of the resorts. I think one of them even came to the reopening Saturday."

"Any idea just how much Sam supported that particular local business?" Kate asked cautiously as she started icing a third tray.

"Not much anymore," Maxi said. "I mean, right after Cookie died, yeah. But now? He just takes a little sip now and then."

"What about the bottle under the counter?" Kate asked. "When I first landed here practically everyone in town warned me about the bottle under the counter."

"It's, like, an urban legend," Maxi explained, her hands flying as she spoke. "But you can't keep the hours Sam does if you're always drunk or hungover. That man was working himself to death. And not eating nearly enough. Or sleeping enough. But the bottle under the register? It's like his security blanket. He doesn't need it. But it makes him feel safe to know it's there."

"So where could someone buy a bottle of Isla Tropical?"

"At the distillery. Or some of the liquor stores."

"That's it? Not at the resorts or Harp's shop?"

"No way," Maxi said. "Not in Florida. It's very strict. Harp runs a wine shop. So he can sell wine and beer, but that's it. And the resorts, they sell rum in mixed drinks. Like the ones with the little umbrellas. But if you want to buy a whole bottle? It's just the liquor stores and the distillery. And the distillery can only sell, like, a certain number of bottles to the same person. So they are super careful about keeping records."

Kate gave each cookie a few strokes with the spatula and the pink icing gleamed. When she followed up with the rainbow sugar, the crystals caught the light and sparkled.

"Somehow, I think we're making this much too complicated," Kate said, stepping back from the counter to assess her work. "One thing you learn in a kitchen: Humans are simple creatures. Give them a little grilled meat, a starch with butter, and something sweet for dessert and they're happy."

"Like our boy Oliver," Maxi said.

They both glanced over at the pup, who had fallen asleep under the kitchen table. Curled up around his woolly lamb toy.

"Exactly," Kate said softly. "And I'm willing to bet this is the same deal. It's not a big, convoluted plot. It's fairly straightforward. We're just not seeing it."

"We need Harp's murder board," Maxi said.

"We need something," Kate admitted. "Wait a minute, I have an idea."

She pulled open a drawer and rifled through it until she produced a pad of yellow Post-it notes and a marker pen. She handed both to Maxi.

"We write down the points we know," Kate explained. "And we can paste them up on the refrigerator. It sort of lets you see the big picture all at once. And if you discover something's missing, you just slap up another sticky note. One of my instructors used to do this to help us analyze what went right and wrong after a kitchen session.

"Lord had a nearly empty bottle of Isla Tropical," Kate said. "And Sam drinks Isla Tropical."

"Lord had Muriel's bracelet, too," Maxi added. "Next to the rum bottle."

"Rum!" Kate exclaimed. "That was the secret ingredient in Sam's rolls. That morning, he came out front and grabbed the bottle from under the counter. When Sam saw me, he said it was just for flavoring. I thought he was embarrassed that I caught him reaching for the bottle. What if he said it because it was true?"

Maxi wrote: "Sweet rolls with rum," and slapped it onto the fridge.

Under the table, Oliver stirred, stretched, clamped down tight on his lamb toy, and rolled over. As his furry chest moved rhythmically up and down, he snored softly.

"The stuff the police confiscated and tested—was there a rum bottle on the list?" Kate asked.

"No idea. But I know who we could ask," Maxi said, walking into the shop.

As Maxi chatted on the phone with Peter about the kids' homework, Esperanza's evening plans, and—evidently—his proposal to throw a couple of burgers and some veggies on the grill, Kate forced herself to focus on the refrigerator collage. She moved a couple of the

Post-its around. Then moved one back to its original spot. Slowly, the information filtered through her brain.

Lord lied.

Lord spied.

Lord cheated.

Lord broke into the bakery.

Lord enjoyed squeezing pressure points.

So if someone at Lord Enterprises poisoned Muriel Hopkins, Stewart Lord himself was the simplest solution.

Then he took Muriel's bracelet. Maxi was right. Since he didn't destroy it, he must not have known about the memory sticks. It was a memento.

She stared at one note: "Lord had Sam's brand of rum."

She grabbed the thick, black marker off the counter and crossed through two words. Now it read: "Lord had Sam's rum."

Another memento. From a would-be murder. Only this time, something went awry.

But how could Lord have stolen Sam's rum during the break-in when the bottle had been under the register the very next morning?

Kate sighed, turned her back on the fridge, and returned to her cookies.

Oliver moaned softly and scrambled to his feet. Woolly lamb, now slightly moist, was still clasped firmly in his mouth.

"Did you have a bad dream?" she asked, stroking his silky flank as he cocked his head and studied her with bright black eyes. "It's OK now. You're here. You're safe. And your friend Peter's talking about grilling up some burgers for dinner. I know you like those."

"It's official, I'm hosting a barbecue," Maxi said,

coming through the swinging doors. "*Mi mami* is inviting some of her card shark ladies, and Javie has a friend from school. Not Jessica-the-biter, thank goodness. And Delores Philpott wants to come over and talk more about the grand plans for her yard."

Oliver dropped his toy in front of Kate. When she reached for it, he grabbed it and danced away.

Then he dumped it just shy of her lap. Playfully, she extended her hand slowly toward the lamb. At the last second, the puppy snatched it back and raced around the table.

"One of Oliver's favorite games," Maxi explained as she poured more coffee. "Speaking of which, you are both expected to attend my *muy elegante* gathering this evening. White gloves only, *por favor*. And we make the little one wear his bow tie again."

"Only if I can contribute something. How about some fresh egg rolls for the burgers?"

"Yes, but you still have to wear an evening gown. And change the subject when Delores asks about her yard."

"OK, but I'm just warning you—my good tiara's at the cleaners."

Oliver dropped the lamb under the table and gamboled to the back door, whining urgently.

"Looks like that's my cue," Kate said, opening the back door and watching the pup race into the yard.

"Oh, and Peter says there was no rum on the list. And he checked twice. What does that mean?" Maxi asked.

"I don't know," Kate said, craning her neck to keep Oliver in sight. "I had a theory, but it doesn't work. The bakery was robbed late Wednesday night. Early Thursday morning, if you want to get technical. And Lord died later that same day. I was thinking that the rum bottle in Lord's office was Sam's. That Lord had stolen it during the robbery."

"Why?"

"The poison came from someone in Lord's office. And if he had his people bugged, he'd have known what prescriptions everyone was taking. He'd have also known that last month Muriel had just started downloading files and copying sensitive documents. I think he stole his lawyer's meds, poisoned the chocolates, and gave them to her. Probably told her that they'd been gifted to him, but he didn't want them."

"Why tell everyone else she was the secret admirer?"

"He was a bully," Kate said as she scrubbed up at the sink. "He wanted to embarrass her. Make her look foolish. And it's not like she'd be able to contradict him. Besides, if it ever came out she was poisoned . . ."

"It would look like someone was trying to kill him," Maxi said slowly. "Because if the box had been delivered, Muriel would have been the one to place them on his desk."

"Right, he'd simply admit he was mistaken about the identity of his admirer. And the police would be off looking for someone with a grudge against Lord."

"A very long list," Maxi said. "But what about the bracelet and the rum?"

"As horrible as it sounds, I think he took the bracelet as a trophy. You were right. He had no idea that three of those charms were memory sticks."

"And the rum?" Maxi asked.

"I think he was planning somehow to kill Sam," Kate said. "With what was left of the heart medicine. To speed up the timetable on his Coral Cay project. I think that's what the break-in was about. At first, I thought that he'd also taken Sam's rum bottle as another memento."

"That rat!"

"But that part of the theory doesn't make sense," Kate said, shaking her head. "Because the bottle was there the next morning. Sam used it to flavor those cinnamon buns."

Kate grabbed the handle of her coffee cup with three fingers, tossing back a long slug of cold brew. And dropped it on the counter when the coffee scalded her mouth.

"What's wrong?" Maxi asked.

"My coffee's been sitting here for hours," Kate said, reaching for a towel. "I thought it would be ice cold by now."

"That was your old cup. I swapped it with a fresh one, while you were opening the door for our friend Oliver. You've been working all evening. You deserve hot coffee in a clean cup. And a nice hamburger dinner. Trust me, you don't want to turn into Sam."

"It's not the same cup," Kate said slowly. "You switched it."

"*Sí.* That other thing was getting a scum on top. It was gross, as *mi niños* say."

Kate's face lit up. "Maxi, you are brilliant. That's it."

"Well, of course. Now, why am I brilliant? Besides my love of excellent coffee?"

"I think you solved it. First thing tomorrow, I need to see a man about some rum."

Chapter 64

The next morning, after making her delivery for Sunny's yoga class, Kate found herself standing in the back of In Vino Veritas, sharing a cup of New Orleans–style coffee with Harper Duval.

"Well, that's a very peculiar question," he drawled.

"I know, right?" Kate said. "But it could be the key to freeing Sam. And proving who really killed Muriel Hopkins and Stewart Lord. So is it even possible? Either part?"

"Well, I don't rightly know," Harp admitted. "Maybe. But I do know who to ask. And he'll take my calls. Do you have a time frame? When this might have happened?"

"I don't," Kate said. "My best guess is sometime between the first of the month and the day before Lord died. But for some reason, I think it'll be during the last few days of that window. Monday, Tuesday, or Wednesday. He's not exactly a delayed-gratification kind of guy."

Harp topped off her coffee cup. "Would it be asking

you to betray your tender secrets to tell me exactly how this figures into our friend Sam's little situation?"

"Honestly, it probably doesn't. It's just a notion. And, for Sam's sake, I want to explore every angle."

"I get it, you don't want to tell ol' Harp," he said lightly.

"If I find out I'm wrong, I'd just as soon go down in flames alone," Kate said.

Harp smiled warmly. "That, my dear, will most assuredly never happen."

Luckily, the bakery was crowded all morning. Tourists clamored for cookies by the dozen. Locals were relieved that their favorite breads—especially Sam's prized sourdough—were back on the shelves.

Amos Tully even let it slip that a certain uptight patrol officer had purchased a half dozen of the bakery's peanut butter cookies from his shop. Along with a pint of milk. Strictly for detection purposes, the policeman had hurriedly assured the shop owner.

But no matter how busy it was, Kate still found time to watch the clock. And today the hands were crawling around the dial.

Maxi came through the door with a big smile on her face.

"How was the delivery for the gender reveal?" Kate asked anxiously. "Did they like the cookies?"

"Loved them—total success," the florist said. "Everybody really liked the color, too. The grandmother said she was afraid they'd look like that bright stomach goo— but your cookies were pretty and delicate, like something from a fine restaurant. I told her, 'Hey, lady, we don't live in the sticks. My best friend is a fancy New York pastry chef who graduated from the best cooking school in the whole country.' No, really, I just said, 'Thank you.' One of the resort's event planners was there. And I could tell she was super impressed. So I think you might get more business out of it, too. Oh, and here's your check."

"Won't even cover the light bill," Kate said, slipping it into the register. "But it sure feels good."

"Any word from you-know-who yet?"

"Nada," Kate said. "But I've got my fingers crossed."

"I've got my whole body crossed. You know how hard it is to make deliveries like that?"

Kate jumped when the phone rang.

She and Maxi exchanged glances. Kate took a deep breath and reached for the avocado-green phone.

"The Cookie House, this is Kate." She could feel her heart pounding.

"Yes, those were mine," she said. "Kate McGuire. . . . Ah, nice to meet you, too! It was the CIA actually, how did you know? Pastry arts. All over Manhattan. High-end hotels and restaurants."

Kate went silent, cradling the phone, as Maxi mouthed a one-word question: "Who?"

Kate shrugged.

"Well, that is interesting. . . . No, that's very fair. I'll definitely consider it. How about I get back to you later this week? . . . Wonderful—thank you!"

"So who was that—another cookie order?"

"Not exactly," Kate said. "It was the events coordinator from the resort where you made the delivery this morning. They want to hire me."

Chapter 65

As Kate pulled the standing rack out of the oven, a wave of heat rolled out and blanketed the kitchen with the smell of fresh sourdough.

For once, the phone had gone silent. And she was secretly glad. As long as she didn't know anything for certain, there was hope.

Oddly, when she first hit town all she wanted was a job. Any job. A position at one of the resorts? That would have been a home run. Her dream. But if she'd gotten it right away, she might never have seen downtown Coral Cay. Or met the people she now counted as close friends. Now that she had, the stakes were higher. And she wanted more than just a gig with a steady paycheck.

Kate heard the familiar bell tinkle, followed by the muffled sound of Oliver's paw pads scampering across the shop floor.

"OK, you seem to know where you're going," a man's baritone pronounced, with more than a trace of humor. "So just lead the way."

Kate walked into the shop to find Oliver sitting up at attention in front of the bakery case, a tall, good-looking man beside him. If she didn't know better, she could have sworn the pup had a mischievous smile on his face.

Clad in jeans and a white dress shirt, his gray eyes crinkled warmly when he glimpsed Kate.

"Hi, I know this little fella's probably not supposed to be in here," he said, smoothing an unruly lock of dark hair. "But I'm trying to find his home. And he just marched right in like he owned the place. You wouldn't happen to know where he lives, by any chance?"

"It's kind of a long story. I'm Kate McGuire, by the way," she said, extending her hand across the counter.

Simultaneously, the phrase *chocolate chip cookies* popped into her head. She could almost taste them.

"Jack Scanlon. Honestly, I don't make a habit of following strange dogs. I'm a vet."

"So you're chasing after new clients?" she said lightly.

"Pretty much," he said wryly. "In town looking for a house, actually. I'm moving here next month to open up a practice. On the island. Saw this little guy down the block, but he didn't seem to be with anybody. And he obviously belongs to someone. So I trailed him and ended up here." He shrugged.

"Jack, meet Oliver. He's sort of the town dog, and he has free run of the place. But he's current on all his shots, and this is his clubhouse. Just don't tell the health department."

"Scout's honor," he said, raising a hand. "So, do you own this place? The Cookie House?"

"Running it temporarily for a friend. I just moved here myself from Manhattan. I'm a pastry chef."

"Really? I'm here from Denver."

"Sick of the snow?"

"Big-time. It's great if you ski. Which I do. But the

rest of the time winter's a bear. Loved the idea of warm weather. And being near the beach. So when I heard this place needed a vet, it seemed like a good fit."

"In that case, Dr. Scanlon, welcome to Coral Cay."

Just as Jack Scanlon left—with a dozen chocolate chip cookies fresh from the oven—the phone rang. Automatically, Kate reached for it without thinking. "The Cookie House, this is Kate."

"It turns out it wasn't a peculiar question so much as a very perceptive one," Harp said.

"Really? What did you learn?" Kate asked, her heart hammering.

"Your friend Sam puts all his bottles on a credit card. The same card he uses for everything, by the way. Kind of a no-no. A business card would give him much more flexibility with better benefits, but I digress. He bought his last bottle of Isla Tropical at Causeway Liquors on the fourth of last month. And because this is a micro-batch product and they are insanely—and quite rightly— proud of it, there is a unique batch and bottle number. I have both."

"That's fantastic! I'm almost afraid to ask about the other guy, but . . ."

"Also a very astute query. Someone matching the description of your gentleman friend purchased a lone bottle of Isla Tropical on the same night as the break-in. Paid cash."

"Cash," Kate said dejectedly. "I should have known."

"Ah, but all is not lost. This particular store owner is very security conscious. Has a bank of hidden cameras. Digital. And your friend is on them. From several angles. He's really not terribly photogenic."

"Are you sure?"

"That's what took me so long, dear lady. I had to wait

for the owner to tab through it, find the relevant sections, and email them to me. Along with the receipt. Which gives us the batch and bottle number for *his* bottle. I promised the gent a rather good vintage of champagne for his legwork. Would you like me to send you the email?"

"Harp, this is wonderful!" Kate said. "Thank you. Email it to Maxi. There's no computer here, and I still haven't charged my cell. But she has a computer at the flower shop."

"Oh, that's right," Harp said. "I keep forgetting. Sam's bakery is the technological black hole of Coral Cay. An avocado-green push-button phone? We really must drag that man into the modern age one of these days."

"Wait, Sam bought his bottle early last *month*? That means he had it for nearly two months."

"It does," Harp said. "Seems our friend has slowed his drinking practically to a stop. He could have gone to some other establishment, of course. And the police could check his card records to be certain. But one thing about Sam, he is a creature of habit. Causeway is the closest liquor store to Coral Cay. And the proprietor, one Frank G. Cooke, knows him on sight. It seems that three years ago our baker friend was purchasing regularly and in rather alarming quantities. But that's no longer the case. Picks up a bottle now and then, plus a couple of lottery tickets. Tells Frank he doesn't know what he'd buy if he won—because he already lives in paradise."

Chapter 66

Ben Abrams relaxed in one of the flower shop's over-stuffed chairs. In his massive right hand, he cradled a hot mug of coffee from the carafe that Kate had smuggled over from the Cookie House. A platter stacked high with tea sandwiches had been placed on the low table in front of him like an offering.

Oliver stationed himself next to the table, eyeing the plate with interest.

"Don't even think about it, buddy," the detective warned him.

Undaunted, Oliver took two steps closer to Ben's chair and put his snout on the detective's knee, looking up into his eyes.

Ben scratched the plush, soft hair on the top of the puppy's head. Then slipped him a sandwich.

"Besides putting a dent in your food bill, does anybody want to tell me what I'm doing here?" the detective asked.

"It's kind of a long story," Kate started.

"There's a pot of coffee and plate full of little sandwiches," he said, shrugging. "If you keep 'em coming, we'll call this my dinner break."

"We know who killed Muriel Hopkins and Stewart Lord," Maxi said, bouncing in her chair.

"Knowing it's one thing," Ben said, reaching for a cheese and pickle sandwich. "Proving it's another."

"That's why it's such a long story," Kate said. "It comes with proof. Lots of proof."

Ben finished off the morsel in two bites, took a slug of coffee, and looked over at the shop's computer. "You two wouldn't know anything about a document dump I received on our friend Stewart Lord, would you? Big ZIP file? Anonymous sender?"

"What's a ZIP file?" Maxi asked innocently.

"Buried poor Kyle Hardy in a mountain of paper. Take the kid ten years to claw his way out. Found a few interesting bits, though. Not that I can share them with you. Since you don't know anything about it, that is."

Kate and Maxi exchanged a nervous look.

"OK," he said, reaching for another sandwich. "You've piqued my curiosity. Shoot."

"The whole thing starts a little over a month ago," Kate began. "Muriel Hopkins loved Coral Cay. She visited a lot. And she planned to retire here."

Ben nodded. Oliver looked up at him expectantly.

"As you already know, Muriel worked directly for Stewart Lord," Kate continued. "She handled a lot of paperwork at Lord Enterprises. She knew Lord was planning to redevelop Coral Cay. She'd watched him in action. She knew that he would lie, cheat, and steal to put his plan in motion. He'd push out the residents and business owners, buy their land for a song, and expand the resort area. Condos. Hotels. Golf courses. Airport for the jet-setters. But the living, breathing Coral Cay? The working small town? Gone. Wiped off the map."

"And Muriel had fallen in love with Coral Cay," Maxi said. "It was her happy place."

Ben reached for two more sandwiches. Thick slices of ham spilled out of one, while the second appeared to be a smoky cheese with mayonnaise. He held out the ham sandwich to Oliver, who took it gently from his hand.

"With you so far," the detective said.

"So Muriel decided she was going to derail his plans," Kate said. "From the inside. She searched out reports and records. Proof of what Lord was doing. And the lies he was spreading."

"He told everyone that Coral Cay was sitting on a giant sinkhole," Maxi added.

"Is it?" Ben asked, sitting forward suddenly.

"No, that was just a story he wanted to put out there," Kate said, smiling slightly. "And I'm betting there might also be a little something about it in that mountain of paperwork Kyle's shoveling through."

"So how does this circle back to two murders? Not that I mind, as long as you have plenty of these," he said, waving a sandwich in the air as Oliver followed it with his eyes.

Ben broke off half and slipped it to the puppy.

"She was bugged," Maxi said. "Muriel."

"What Muriel didn't know was that Stewart Lord had installed surveillance software on his employees' phones," Kate said. "His executives and executive assistants, from what we've been able to learn. The stuff reads emails, listens in on calls, and tracks you in real life."

"There something in the paper pile about all of that, too?" Ben asked.

Kate shrugged. "Or you could just have your tech guys look at a few of his employees' cell phones."

"So Lord knew that Muriel was on to him," Ben said evenly.

"No, he learned that she was actively working *against* him," Kate countered. "To keep him from getting the one thing he wanted most. And he reacted like a toddler when you take away his favorite toy. Pure rage."

"And you know this how?"

"Muriel and Lord were poisoned with the same drug. A heart medication. Lord was keeping tabs on his workers. He knew who had which medical conditions, and what they took for them. He wanted to get rid of Muriel. And he needed something that wouldn't trace back to him."

Ben went quiet. He looked from Kate to Maxi and back again, then nodded.

"I'd be willing to bet you a dozen cookies that someone in Lord's office lost a full bottle of that medicine shortly before Muriel Hopkins died," Kate said. "And I'd go double or nothing that the employee in question kept those meds at the office."

Ben stopped eating, mid-bite. He looked at her hard. "You're guessing."

"About that part, yes. But it would be easy for you to prove. Or disprove."

"The medicine bottle was in a briefcase, as a matter of fact," Ben said. "But the guy always kept the briefcase open on a table when he was at the office. So what happened next?"

"Stewart Lord put the drug into candy—a little box of chocolates," Kate said. "It had to be chocolate because that was Muriel's one weakness—the only indulgence she allowed herself that wasn't on her diet. The box had to be small—just a couple of pieces—because he had to make sure she ate all of it herself."

"Because if she shared it and a couple people got sick and no one died, his plan might be discovered," Maxi added.

"He knew that Muriel was going in early and staying late digging through files," Kate continued. "So he showed up early and gave her the chocolates. He claimed someone had delivered them for him. Probably told her to throw them out. I'm guessing by the time her co-workers arrived, she'd already eaten them. There were only a few pieces. And a couple of hours later, she was dead."

"And everyone thought it was her heart," Maxi said. "Even her doctor."

"So Stewart Lord's first murder is a success," Kate said. "His enemy is gone. His Coral Cay development project is back on track. And no one is any the wiser. I'm guessing by this time the man was just about insufferable."

"Not the word most folks used, but in the same general ballpark," Ben said with a wry smile.

"No wonder," Kate said. "He'd always been an egomaniac. Then he discovered he could literally get away with murder. There was absolutely nothing to hold him in check."

"Why do I get the feeling there's a 'but' coming?" Ben said as Oliver stretched out sphinxlike at his feet.

Kate smiled. "A few weeks went by and, despite Lord's best efforts, he can't get a toehold in Coral Cay. But he's convinced that if he can snag just one piece of downtown property, they'll all topple."

"Like dominoes," Maxi said, grinning. "Don't ask."

"He has two likely candidates. Sam Hepplewhite and Harper Duval. Sam's been barely breaking even for a long time. And Harp, well, he's looking at getting rid of his shop for personal reasons."

"Yeah, I heard about Caroline," Ben said. "Damn shame."

"But Harp's torn about selling. And Lord has seriously underestimated Sam's tenacity. And his love for the Cookie House."

"*Mi padrino* is tough. Like, Cuban tough."

"Well, Stewart Lord is not a patient person," Kate said. "And he sets his sights on the bakery. He knows Sam is a proud man who also has a lot of business debts. And medical debts from Cookie. And Lord enjoys a little coercion and shame. That's in his wheelhouse. He probably figures he can goad Sam into selling. Failing that, he might be able to disrupt business just enough that the bakery goes under. Call in a few favors. Get suppliers to cut off credit. See if he can convince a lender friend to call in a loan or raise the rates. If the bakery went into foreclosure, Lord could pick it up for pennies on the dollar. And a land transaction in downtown Coral Cay means he can get some traction with the phony sinkhole story. A few merchants hear the gossip and want to sell. Nervous bankers hesitate to underwrite the loans. And Lord comes in with his patented combination of lowball offers and ready cash and buys up everything he can get."

"And as the town started losing businesses and business leaders, the downtown district would get weaker," says Maxi. "Some people leave town, so businesses fail. Then more people move and more businesses fail."

"He was creating the perfect storm," Ben said.

"He was," Kate agreed. "But he needed one piece of property to kick it all off."

"The first domino," Maxi added. "The Cookie House."

"Stewart Lord broke into the bakery early on that Thursday morning. He picked the lock. Not much of a challenge. He'd been a low-rent criminal back in his native London, all those years ago."

"How would breaking into the bakery help him buy the bakery?" Ben asked.

"Because he was going to kill the owner," Kate said.

"But Sam wasn't there in the middle of the night," Ben argued. "Sam was at home in bed. Asleep."

Kate nodded. "But Sam's rum was there. Everybody knew he kept a bottle under the counter. Lord alluded to it when he swept into the bakery that last morning. So he definitely knew about it."

"So Lord broke in and dumped the drugs into Sam's rum?" Ben asked.

"No," Kate said. "As a former street thug, Lord didn't want to hang around any longer than necessary. He came prepared. He had his own bottle of rum, purchased earlier that night. Probably dumped out most of it. He wrote off Sam as a drunk. And if a drunk finds a little less in his bottle, he'll just assume he drank it. No problem. Lord doctored the remaining rum with that heart drug. Then he broke in and switched the bottles."

"Wait," Ben said, holding up a burly palm. "Can you prove that?"

"We can," Kate said evenly. "Sam's rum of choice is Isla Tropical. They number every batch and bottle. Sam bought his bottle at Causeway Liquors early last month. It's on his credit card. And I have a copy of his receipt, which has the batch and bottle number. Stewart Lord bought a bottle of the same rum the evening of the break-in. At a liquor store about forty miles north of here. I'll give you his receipt, too. Lord paid cash. But I have security footage of the sale. The clincher is that after Lord switched the bottles, he kept Sam's. Like a trophy. It's in Lord's personal bathroom at his office. If you check the bottle number, you'll find it matches the one on Sam's receipt."

"What happened to Lord's bottle?" Ben asked.

"We'll have to ask Sam. I'm guessing he used what was left and threw the empty bottle out with the trash."

"The recycling goes out back," Maxi said. "They come Thursday afternoons."

"So it was already long gone when we showed up with crime techs the next day," said Ben, shaking his head.

"If you can track down that bottle, you'll find it matches the number on Lord's receipt," Kate said matter-of-factly. "It should also have traces of the drug that killed Muriel Hopkins and Stewart Lord. And, if we're really lucky, you might get a couple of Lord's fingerprints, too."

"Wait a minute, if Sam drank the poisoned rum, why isn't he dead?" Ben asked, exasperated. "And what the blazes happened to Stewart Lord?"

"For a guy eating free sandwiches, he's awful cranky," Maxi said to Kate.

"We're getting to that," Kate said, smiling. "The next morning, Lord stops by the Cookie House to survey his handiwork. Much to his surprise, Sam is perfectly fine. Working in the kitchen. Just like normal. So Lord decides to prime the pump. Make a scene, embarrass Sam. Get him to reach for the bottle."

"But that didn't work?" Ben ventured.

Kate shook her head. "By the time Stewart Lord came through the door, Sam had been on his feet baking for ten hours. He was exhausted. He wasn't up to sparring. He gave Lord a half-dozen cinnamon buns just to make him go away. Rolls that Sam had made for himself. His own special recipe."

"Sam was planning to eat them on the beach," Maxi said. "Like a picnic."

"Just one thing Stewart Lord didn't know," Kate said.

"What's that?" Ben asked, sitting up straight.

"The secret ingredient in those cinnamon buns? It was rum."

Chapter 67

Kate sat the pitcher of lemonade in the refrigerator as Maxi and Peter came through the front door.

"Peter helped me string up the balloons, and they look fantastic!" Maxi said proudly.

"Not bad, if I do say so myself," he agreed. "This place looks a lot like it did for the reopening. Minus the hordes of people."

"We wanted something small and classy," Maxi said. "Sam's not a big fan of crowds. Some cookies and lemonade in the kitchen, then a nice, hot home-cooked meal."

"From whose home?" Peter teased.

"Bridget's place—and she's going to be cooking your dinner, if you're not careful," Maxi warned, giving him a playful swat on the shoulder.

"Apparently, her Irish stew sandwiches are Sam's new favorite," Kate explained. "Although I wouldn't repeat that to Esperanza. Bridget said she'd bring over dinner as soon as she saw Ben's car."

"We left the front door open but flipped the 'closed' sign," Peter said. "So no more customers today."

Kate shook her head. "I don't know how Sam will feel about closing two hours early."

"It's our last official act as managers of the Cookie House," Maxi said. "I say we go for it. But I still can't believe it took a whole week to get him out. Even after we knew the who and the how."

"Hey, only TV detectives can solve a crime in an hour," Peter said, shaking his head. "Real-world forensic tests take real time. And if Kyle Hardy hadn't literally stumbled onto that rum bottle at the recycling center, we wouldn't even have been able to do that."

"Yeah, I guess I'm gonna have to stop calling the *bobo* a *bobo*," Maxi said.

"I'm just glad the bottle was still there," Kate said. "Especially after all this time."

"I never doubted it," Maxi said. "I was a chaperone when Michael's class went to the center last year. I always thought recycling meant it went into some big machine and boom! New stuff. Uh-uh. First they stash it for a while, like squirrels. Then they process it."

"Well, that delay turned out to be a win for the good guys," Peter said. "Not only did the bottle contain a residue of rum and that drug, but it also had a big juicy thumbprint from one Mr. Paul Larde, aka Stewart Lord."

"Carl dug through his scrap metal drawer and found the hardware he'd removed from the back door of the bakery after the robbery," Kate said. "Ben's team lifted a couple of Lord's fingerprints from that, too."

"Which the *bobo* would have found weeks ago, if he'd bothered to look," Maxi fumed.

"Hey, it's a new day," Peter said, pulling Maxi to him and kissing the tip of her nose. "Time to let *bobos* be bygones."

Chapter 68

"So, are you gonna take the resort job?" Maxi asked, wiping down the kitchen counters, as Kate scrubbed out the sink.

"Well, Sam's going to want his kitchen back, and it means I can stay on Coral Cay, so yeah. The manager said they'll even put me up for a few weeks until I can find an apartment."

She looked around the bakery. "But I am so going to miss this place. And my kitchen hours will be pretty brutal. At least, to start. I'm going to hate not being able to pop over all the time."

"Admit it, it's my coffee you're really going to miss."

"Of course. And that coconut cream."

"When do you start?" Maxi asked.

"Ten days," Kate said, pausing. "Until then, I figure I can give Sam a hand and get the bakery fully stocked. If he lets me bake. And you have to help me convince him to keep going with the cookies."

"Convince him? That man makes a mule look easygoing. But I have a little something that might help."

She dried her hands, walked over to the table, grabbed a notebook, and pulled out a sheet of printer paper with a colorful bar chart. She held it up in front of Kate.

"What's this?" Kate asked.

"I used our access to the bakery to organize Sam's books. This shows how the business was doing before you showed up. And this," she said, pointing, "is the two weeks following the big reopening. While you were selling cookies and doing special orders."

"Oh my gosh, Maxi, this is great!"

"Yup. A guy like Sam needs to see the facts in black and white. Or blue, green, and red, thanks to my snazzy printer. Javie's teacher calls them visual aids. And now that Sam's had a nice little rest and put on a few pounds, he might just see the sense in doing something that actually makes his business grow."

"Well, I've got a visual aid of my own," Kate confessed, rinsing her hands and quickly drying them. "I'll show you, but you've got to promise to give me your honest opinion. If it's bad, I need to know. I'm so tired at this point, I can't tell."

"Hey, I can be super mean. Like those judges on that singing show."

Kate carefully lifted a tall cardboard box up and off the counter and stepped back to give Maxi a better view of what was underneath.

"Oh my gosh," the florist said, clasping her hands under her chin. "That's us! That's the Cookie House! Made out of cookies. How did you do that? It's wonderful!"

Kate grinned.

Maxi shook her head in astonishment. "You even got

the little window boxes. With the new little bushes. And the color. Perfect. How? When?"

Kate sighed. "It took a while. And I didn't get much sleep the last two nights. But I wanted to surprise Sam. And I wanted to show him what this place could be again. Bread is important. It'll keep you alive. But people have milestones. They need to gather, to celebrate. A wedding cake, a birthday cake, a special cookie. It feeds the soul. We need that stuff, too. It's the difference between surviving and living."

"Is this . . . ?" Maxi asked, pointing.

"Oliver. It didn't seem finished somehow, and I couldn't figure out what was missing. Then it hit me. Or, rather, looked up into my face."

"It's so real. It looks just like him. Fluffy."

"Well, to be fair, I used the real thing for a model. The little guy is very patient."

"You even got my flowers out front," Maxi marveled.

Kate nodded. "Want to hear something weird? I know I've only been here a few weeks, but this place feels like home. Not just Coral Cay, but here. The Cookie House. Don't tell Sam, but I am really going to miss it."

"Maybe he'll let you rent the upstairs room," Maxi said.

"I was kind of hoping he might. But I think the resort would frown on that. I just found out they want me to sign something promising not to do any commercial baking on the side. So if they discovered I was living over the bakery where I used to work . . ."

"Now that's just selfish. What if *mi niños* want some of those really good camp-out cookies?"

"Gifts for friends and family are fine. They even said I could contribute to charity bake sales. But that's about it."

"Ay, that's nice of them to *let* you. Especially since it's your time and talent."

"Does Oliver ever visit the resort area?" Kate asked suddenly.

"Where Oliver goes is a real mystery," Maxi said. "That puppy has a life of his own. But I've never seen him over there. And I'm not sure it would be a good place for him, either. They're super strict about rules and stuff. And he's kind of a free spirit. Why?"

Kate felt herself tearing up. It was stupid, but she'd come to think of Oliver as "hers." Or was it that she was "his"?

Maxi studied her friend, then handed her a paper towel.

"So rent a place in town that's Oliver friendly. I'll help you find something this weekend. In your spare time. When Sam doesn't have you chained to the oven."

Kate dabbed her eyes. "Really? That would be great. That way, maybe we can still make time to meet for coffee. Or lunch. And we can both keep an eye on Sam. And what's going on around town."

"And you could take more classes at Sunny's," Maxi said. "You gotta take care of yourself, too. Otherwise, you're gonna end up just like you-know-who."

They both heard the shop bell and looked up. Kate quickly lowered the box over the house. "That can't be him yet. We're not ready!"

"We've got decorations and food. We've got a house made of cookies. We're ready. And the bakery looks great. Sam's gonna think he's in the wrong place."

"Hello, ladies, brought a few nibbles for the man of the hour."

"Harp," Kate said. "Come on in."

"This is a cocktail party in a bag," he said, setting the canvas sack on the kitchen table. "A little sparkling cider, strictly nonalcoholic. Along with some savory butter crackers. And a generous chunk of this gorgeous soft cheese from Belgium. Just got my hands on it. Wonderful stuff!"

"Oooh, this is nice," Maxi said, setting the items on the table. "Thank you!"

"Is he here yet?" Amos Tully called from the doorway.

"Not yet," Kate said. "Ben's bringing him. Apparently, they have some papers to sign first."

"Don't see what's taking so long," the grocer complained. "The man's innocent. You open the cell door and let him walk out. It's that simple."

"It certainly should be," Peter said, clapping him on the back. "In the meantime, can I get you a glass of lemonade?"

"Wouldn't say no," Amos replied. "Figured you might need a few supplies for this shindig. Got paper cups and plates. And a pound of that coffee Sam likes. And a few cans of tuna fish and deviled ham. Sam likes his canned meats."

Maxi slid an eye over to Kate, who tried not to giggle.

"Sam will love this," the florist said, hefting the brown paper bag. "Let me put these in the pantry."

"Hi there, are we too late?" a familiar woman's voice called from the shop.

"Rosie!" Kate answered. "We're back here. In the kitchen."

Rosie and Andre bustled through the swinging doors.

"We know it is like you say, 'coals to Newcastle,' but we wanted to drop off something sweet," Andre said.

"Pralines," Rosie said. "A little 'welcome home' gift for Sam."

"Oh, these look delicious," Kate said.

"They should be," Rosie said with a grin. "They're the real deal straight from New Orleans. A little candy shop right off Bourbon Street."

"You're in plenty of time," Peter said, checking his watch. "They're not here yet, but it should be any minute."

"You do know that if you leave that front door un-locked, anyone could just wander in," Sunny called as she breezed into the kitchen. "Brought a little turkey casserole. Something Sam can heat up for later," she said, depositing a covered baking dish onto the crowded table.

"Pretty soon we're gonna need a bigger kitchen," Maxi whispered to Kate. "So who's that big blond guy behind Sunny?"

"Pothole," Kate said quietly. "Definitely a pothole."

"Hmmm," Maxi said, surveying him. "Nice pothole."

"Hey, are we too late? Is Sam back yet?"

"C'mon back, Gabe!" Maxi called. "We're all in the kitchen."

"Hey, it's a party!" he said cheerfully, hefting a basketball-sized object wrapped in foil.

"We weren't quite sure what to bring," Claire added. "So we decided on a ham. It's one of those spiral-slice ones. Sam should be able to get a few meals out of it."

"Already brought him ham," Amos sniffed. "And mine won't go bad."

"By the way, Carl and Minette were coming up the walkway behind us," Gabe said to Peter. "Looked like she had a pie. Doc said he'll stop in, if he finishes early. And I saw Barb Showalter and Mrs. Kim heading this way with gift bags."

"You didn't see Ben's car, did you?" Peter asked.

The mechanic shook his head.

"Guess who's here?" Minette called.

"The fire marshal?" Maxi whispered to Kate. "Because this kitchen is seriously crammed."

"Oh my," Minette said as she and Carl walked into the kitchen. "Are we the last to arrive?"

"If they're not, we're gonna have to move this party to the lawn," Maxi said to Kate.

"Actually, that's not a bad idea," Kate said. "Guys, if we all reconvene on the front porch, we can greet Sam as soon as he gets out of the car. And Maxi and I will set up drinks and a nosh on the counter in the bakeshop. That way, everyone can circulate."

"Right this way," Peter said, holding open one of the swinging doors. "And I'll bring out a tray of cold lemonade and some cookies to get everyone started."

"Don't have to ask me twice," Gabe said happily, stepping back to let Claire go first.

"Kitchen's too stuffy," Amos said. "Could do with a nip of fresh air."

Twenty minutes and several drop-in visitors later, the porch resembled a cocktail party. Guests mixed and mingled, snacking on imported cheese, chipped ham, crackers, and yeast rolls. Kate put out a couple of plates of cookies, too, in case anyone had a sweet tooth.

"So how many people did you actually invite?" Kate asked Maxi as they retreated to the kitchen to mix up another batch of lemonade.

"You, me, Peter, and Bridget," she said, grinning. "Welcome to small-town life. No big secrets. No small parties."

"He's coming!" Peter called over the shop door. "They're pulling up now!"

Kate grabbed the pitcher, and they hustled out the front door. Oliver, who'd been napping on one of the benches, sat up at attention.

Ben's car pulled up to the curb and stopped. Then, nothing. No doors opened.

"That's weird," Maxi said softly to Kate.

Ben and Sam appeared to be talking. Sam wiped his face with his sleeve. Then Kate saw Ben take off his Ray-Bans and hand them to the baker.

A minute later, Ben got out, lurched around to the passenger's side, and opened the front door. Sam, decked out in sunglasses, a sea-green Hawaiian shirt, and jeans, climbed out of the car. He said something to Ben, who grinned. The detective pointed to the house.

Sam gave a little wave.

Everyone on the porch broke into loud, long applause.

Sam looked at Ben, who nodded. The baker shook his head, squared his shoulders, and marched up the walkway, Ben at his side.

At the bottom of the steps, the crowd gave way and Peter jogged forward, handing Sam a glass of lemonade.

"Everybody just wanted to say 'welcome back,'" Peter said.

Up close Kate realized how much healthier Sam looked. He'd filled out. Gone was the gaunt, haunted look. Even his cheeks were pink. Or maybe he was blushing.

"Place looks different," the baker said, looking around. "Better."

"So do you!" one of the teenagers shouted from the back of the porch. "Dope shades!"

Sam raised his glass. He took a sip and cleared his throat. And wiped his cheek.

"Not one for fancy words," the baker said haltingly. "Thank you. All of you. Took something pretty bad to realize I have it pretty good. Won't forget again."

"To Sam," Peter said, raising his glass in return. "Welcome back!"

"Welcome back!" the crowd repeated.

"Now come on," Peter said, pulling the baker up the steps. "We've got all kinds of food."

"Yeah," Maxi said, "you must be starving."

Sam nodded, smiling slightly. "I could eat."

Chapter 69

When Kate tripped down the stairs at 4:15 the next morning, Sam was sitting at the kitchen table drinking coffee and reading the paper.

"Morning," he said, raising his mug. "Fresh pot."

"I could use some of that."

"Heard about your offer," Sam said as he turned a page and folded the paper. "One of the resorts?"

"Yeah, they finally tried some of my stuff," Kate said, filling a cup. "They want to put me on the special events team."

"Imagine that's good money," he said.

"Not bad. And they're promising raises and bonuses, if they like my work. Lot of hours, though. So you guys won't see me around town as much."

Sam nodded.

"I made something I wanted to show you," Kate said. "A gift. To say 'thank you.'"

She walked over to the counter, carefully lifted the cardboard box, revealing the gingerbread house.

Sam stared at it, transfixed. He walked toward it. A foot from the counter, he bent over—tilting his head as if he was searching for something. Slowly, he reached out an index finger and gently touched a window. The window with the red ginger flower.

His face lit up in a smile. "Wonderful."

"Cookies make people happy," Kate said. "They make me happy when I bake them. And when I see other people enjoy them. People need that. People in Coral Cay need that."

"Saw Maxi's chart," Sam admitted.

"This isn't about the chart. Or profits and losses. People want to celebrate the good moments. Sometimes that's sharing chocolate cookies on the beach with your little ones. Sometimes it's singing around a birthday cake. Or a birthday cookie. Which, believe it or not, are bizarrely popular."

Sam smiled and held up his hands. "Sold."

"Really?"

"Time to think recently," he said, studying the house. "Realized some things. Love this place. Love baking. But can't spend all my days here."

He stopped and looked down at the floor.

"Need a business partner," he started. "Junior partner. New ideas. But no crazy notions. Someone with a good head. Can't offer much. You've seen the books."

"So basically, you're asking me to give up a generous salary and benefits in exchange for fifty percent of a failing business?" Kate summarized.

"Forty percent."

"Forty-nine percent," she countered. "Plus, I get the room upstairs and you help me hide Oliver when the health inspector comes."

"Deal," he said.

The baker looked longingly at the house. "Put this in the shop? For advertising?"

"We could," Kate said tentatively. "Or we could eat it."

Sam shook his head. "Lot of work there. That gingerbread?"

"Your favorite."

"Just a small taste," he said. "Mailbox looks good."

"Break off a big piece," Kate said happily. "They're cookies. We can bake lots more."

Acknowledgments

A heartfelt thank you to the wonderful team at St. Martin's Press.

Especially my editor, Alexandra Sehulster, who has championed this book and the Cookie House from the very start. For you, a tall glass of cold lemonade, a batch of warm cookies, and a very grateful "thank you!"

Also a big thank you to editorial assistant Mara Delgado Sánchez, for her endless patience and kindness.

Many thanks to eagle-eyed copy editor, Barbara Wild, for keeping the plot grounded in reality. And for keeping Maxi in the right car!

A big bouquet to Kayla Janas and Holly Rice in the St. Martin's publicity department. You guys are champs!

And huge thanks to Lesley Worrell, who designed the cover, and Mary Ann Lasher, who did the terrific cover illustration. It's great to see Oliver running around and causing a little mischief!

Last—and definitely not least—thank you to the world's best agent, Erin Niumata of Folio Literary Agency: You've been my friend and sounding board every step of the way.

Read on for a sample from the next exciting Cookie House mystery, *Sugar & Vice*— out soon from St. Martin's Paperbacks!

As schooner-sized white clouds sailed high across the turquoise South Florida sky, Kate McGuire tugged at her green gardening gloves. Despite what the label proclaimed, one size definitely did not fit all.

"So what happens if I ditch the gloves?" she asked, pausing as her best friend rhythmically shoveled wet sand.

"Nothing super horrible," replied Maxi Más-Buchanan, sinking her shovel into the soft ground with a "thunk." "Just keep 'em away from Mr. Oliver. Thanks to him, my last three pairs are buried all over Coral Cay. One at a time. The least that puppy could do is bury them in pairs. That way, if anyone ever finds them, they can maybe use them."

Kate had to admit, the two of them had accomplished a lot in one afternoon. Two of the three raised beds were prepped and ready to go. One more and they could call it a day.

Oliver, in his wisdom, already had. Passed out under

a shady tree, she could hear his soft snuffling sounds above the bird calls on the breeze.

Maxi looked over her shoulder and grinned. "Some work ethic," the florist said. "Our best digger has up and quit. On the bright side, you get a promotion."

"Aye aye, captain," Kate said, giving a mock salute. "So what's going into this one?

"Oh, it's gonna be tasty. I'm putting in those juicy, old-fashioned tomatoes and little baby lettuces. And we're gonna surround the whole thing with hot peppers. *Muy picante.* 'Cause they keep the bugs away. That one over there," she said pointing at a completed bed, "will be herbs. Basil, dill, oregano and chives to start. And peppermint—oooh, it'll smell so good. And that other one's gonna be filled with edible flowers. Not too shabby, huh? If these do well, I'll sell what I grow. Like a side business. Maxi's Kitchen Garden. All organic. I've talked to a couple of your chef buddies at the resorts, and they're super excited."

"I can see why," Kate said, tucking a stray lock of caramel-colored hair under her navy ball cap. "An organic, small-batch garden? Nobody's doing anything like that anywhere near Coral Cay. You'll clean up."

"But first, we dig up the yard and get super dirty. Poor Oliver's going to need another bath," she said, brushing a smudge of wet sand off her cheek. "Me too, for that matter."

"How about we take a cue from Oliver and stop for a rest?" Kate suggested. "I've got a pitcher of lemonade in the fridge at the Cookie House."

"Right now, I'd settle for cold water out of the sink. Or the hose."

Fifteen minutes later, with frosty glasses in their hands, Kate and Maxi relaxed in lawn chairs, surveying their handiwork.

As they chatted, Oliver scrambled back to the area they'd excavated for the last raised bed.

"OK, so we've removed two-and-a-half feet of sandy top soil. Now what?" Kate asked, eyeing the neat rectangular trench on the left side of the yard.

"Just like last time. We'll fill it up with my super secret planting soil mix. Then we drag out the frame for the raised bed, tack it down, and fill that up to the top with more planting mix. Then we're done. And I'll put in the plants over the next few days."

Oliver circled the pit several times, then he hopped in and scratched the soil with his front paws, yelping. He put his head down, digging furiously. All they could see was sand flying past his fuzzy oatmeal-colored rump.

"What's he doing?" Kate asked.

"Probably digging up one of the gloves he buried. Or one of his other treasures. Oliver's got stuff buried all over town," Maxi said with a rueful smile.

They watched as the poodle-mix pup paddled furiously with his front paws for several minutes. Then he sat back on his haunches and howled.

Maxi sat forward, alarmed. "He's never done that before," she said, setting her glass on the ground.

"Maybe the little guy hurt himself," Kate said, as they both hurried over to the half-grown pup.

As they neared, Oliver began digging again, his oversized paws clawing frantically at the sand.

"Oliver? Come here, baby," Kate called softly. "Come up here."

When he jumped out of the pit and trotted over, Kate stroked his soft curly coat, and scratched him lovingly behind one ear. "Now, let me see those paws of yours," she said, gently examining each one in turn. "Nope, you're fine. Everything looks good," she called over her shoulder to Maxi.

"I don't think so," Maxi said softly.

"What do you mean?" Kate said, turning to see her friend's face pale. Maxi silently pointed down. To the hole where Oliver had just been digging.

And that's when Kate spotted it. In the sandy soil. Scraps of an ancient leather boot. Long and brackish brown. In tatters. Kate could barely make out what had probably been a wide cuff at the top. And a big silver buckle, blackened with age, at the bottom. It reminded Kate of something out of *Treasure Island.* Or the *Discovery* channel. Exposed at the top of the boot, yellowed with time, was a barely visible swath of bone.

"What? Who?" Kate gasped.

Maxi took a giant step back and crossed herself. "It's him," she whispered. It's really him. It has to be."

"Who? Who is it?"

"Gentleman George Bly. The pirate king. I thought it was just a story," she said in a hushed voice, shaking her head. "Something to tell *mi niños* at bedtime. But it's real."

Kate stood and took a step closer to her friend. Oliver followed suit. The three of them stared down into the pit.

"I admit that boot looks old," Kate said. "But what makes you think it's him?"

"It's all part of the legend," Maxi said quietly. "Gentleman George, he pretty much founded Coral Cay. He and his men. They're the reason we have our Pirate Festival every year. Well, them and to celebrate the end of tourist season. His crew used to raid the Spanish treasure ships sailing to and from Florida and the Caribbean. This island was their home base. He was smart, and he was sneaky. He bested the Spanish king every single time and swiped their loot. But he had a code. A sense of honor. And he was only stealing what had already been stolen in the first place. But one time—

the last time—they were attacked by a galleon. A big war ship. He was wounded, his ship was nearly sunk. But Gentleman George? He still had a few tricks up his sleeve. And he got his ship and crew to safety. Back to Coral Cay."

"What happened after that?" Kate asked, never taking her eyes off the boot buckle.

"No one really knows," Maxi said. "Local legend has it once he and his men reached the harbor, they burned the ship to cover their tracks. And shortly after that, he died. Supposedly, his men laid him out in his very best clothes and even shined up the silver buckles on his boots. And, as a gesture of respect and gratitude, they buried him in a secret spot on the island with his share of the treasure—a fortune in gold and jewels. And the site has never been found."

"And you think . . ." Kate started.

"I think our friend Oliver has discovered the last resting place of Gentleman George Bly, pirate king of Coral Cay."